MW00627373

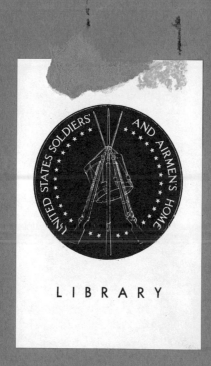

ICARUS

By Peter Way

Dirty Tricks
Icarus

ICARUS

Peter Way

Coward, McCann & Geoghegan
NEW YORK

First American Edition 1980

Library of Congress Cataloging in Publication Data

Way, Peter.
  Icarus : a novel.

I. Title.
PZ4.W357Ic 1980   [PR6073.A93]   823'.9'14   79-25792
ISBN 0-698-11030-7

Printed in the United States of America

This must my comfort be,
That sun that warms you
here shall shine on me.

William Shakespeare

F

PART ONE

PART ONE

1

It seemed very warm. Or perhaps he was sweating for other reasons. It was certainly very quiet, except for the cicadas. They were singing and you could believe they were happy.

Michael French stopped moving. Ahead of him was a snake. *It* was moving, all right. It was an extraordinary sight: the thing had looped itself so many times through the branches of eucalyptus that one could not see where it began or finished. But it was *all* moving. Sections of snake were travelling in different directions from each other, all at the same speed. It was most strange, no beginning and no end. It was very green. Just before he caught where the head was he saw an odd, unmoving object on the ground, as if someone had sliced a honeycomb with a razor. The snake had been shedding a skin.

Much faster than the rest of its body was the snake's tongue. He saw that now. Almost pulsating, so fast was it dabbing in and out towards him. He stepped back quickly.

Then there were other footsteps. He did not turn around. He went on watching the snake. One of the cicadas was sitting on a twig, gazing with the stupid intentness of all insects. The snake raised its head, a tiny one for such a large body, and looked at the cicada. Michael French turned around.

The girl was facing him.

It was unbelievable. She was not like the pictures he had seen. Or rather, the pictures were proven to be the ghost of the beauty that now stood before him. Michael French was a man who always looked at a woman's eyes first.

He could not see her eyes.

She did not move. She seemed to be posing. Her face was shadowed in a greenish light. But it was *her*. There was no doubt. He could not tell if she was looking at him or not. But it was enough to see the way her dark, cropped hair seemed to hold those beautiful eyes as if she were in her own embrace. She raised her chin bravely, just as in the pictures.

She was smaller than he had imagined. You can't tell that from photographs. That was all that was necessary; she was strong and small. Very pale, he thought. All wrapped up in her fox fur coat.

She walked away.

Michael French did not follow. That was the arrangement. That was all for now, they had said.

Fifty yards away, outside the gorilla's glass cage, two men were studying one of London Zoo's most popular exhibits. One of the men was shivering in the bleak morning of a London winter.

"They've gone. Come on."

But the other, an older man, seemed to like watching the big ape.

"A rendezvous in London Zoo," said the first. "I tell you. I'm a Londoner. Do you know how *corny* that idea is?"

"You are *not* a Londoner. And 'corny' is not a popular slang word. However, the old songs are often the best ones." The voice was guttural.

"Like a girl and a boy."

"Exactly. Like a girl and a boy."

The man watching the ape lifted a hand, stretched all five fingers towards the giant gorilla, and held his hand there.

From folds of muscle and fur the showpiece seemed to concentrate its attention.

"Well, I grant you," said the younger man, "rendezvous in the reptile house *is* probably new. What was all that chirruping?"

"Breakfasts waiting to be eaten."

"You know something, Viktor? You're macabre."

The gorilla hauled himself off the floor and approached the glass.

"Do you think this is going to work?" asked the younger man.

The gorilla was close against the bulletproof glass. For years he had been watching the human race cavort in front of him, making faces. Most of the faces were the same. Most of them were grinning. The gorilla never grinned unless he was angry. The person in front of the glass now was not grinning. Several yards of space and metal fence and bulletproof glass lay between them. He raised a huge forelimb, with its surprisingly small and purple-pinkish finger pads flat against the glass, and to the other man it looked like a salute.

"If you really like this sort of thing," said the man who had been shivering, "we can go and watch them throw meat at the lions. Come *on*, Viktor. We have hooked our fish, now let's rope him in."

Viktor sighed. "*Wind* him in, Asimov. You *wind* in a fish. And we do it carefully, very gently. Because he is the biggest one we are ever going to catch."

2

Professor Michael French had awakened early for this rendezvous. The story was that he had an important meeting in London. It was necessary to catch the 7:17 from Cambridge. He began getting up at 6:00 A.M. when the grandfather clock in the nook beneath the old smoked beams had begun to whirr its way towards striking. Beside him, Mary French groaned and turned away into her pillow and pretended sleep. He lifted himself out of bed and felt very quietly for his shoes.

It was a question of tiptoeing past the children's bedroom because once they woke up they started fighting. Most days began with what he had been told was called "sibling rivalry." Michael French was an only child. He didn't understand sibling rivalry.

Outside the cottage, ten miles from the university city of Cambridge, he knew the ground was hard frozen. It was mid-February. In the cottage garden, cabbage stalks stood like sentinels, rotten with cold.

Michael French pushed the cat off the Aga cooker and wondered if the hotplate would warm some coffee. Mary had just abolished the electric kettle, along with the TV. The cooker seemed cold to him.

The floor, as usual, was covered from end to end with shattered toys. He had never, he realised, actually seen his children *play* with their toys; they fought over them, tore them apart and discarded them. Fragments of at least twenty jigsaws competed for floor space with limbless naked dolls and broken plastic remnants from now unrecognisable originals. While waiting for the milk to warm he looked gloomily at the kitchen floor. He picked up a cardboard box. It had been stamped on. It had contained something called a Poly-Bilda, "designed tough for hours of creative play." Mary said that tearing things apart was the child's first step to understanding how the world was put together.

He dipped his finger into the milk. It had hit blood temperature, and plainly had no plans to improve on its performance. The larder was out of Weetabix again and Michael could not face Mary's stone-ground bread this side of the dawn.

He breakfasted on lukewarm milk. There *had* to be a moral in it somewhere, he decided: the man who had just been nominated for a Nobel Prize for solving the problem of how to keep a temperature of 100 million degrees centigrade under control couldn't boil a cup of coffee.

He stepped out the kitchen door into the black ice of an East Anglian morning. Cambridgeshire had winters of marrow-chilling ferocity. He wasn't going to take the car. Mary had said "take the car" but he had said he could get the first bus. Over his head a light clicked on and threw a square of yellow across the paralysed garden. It was the kids' bedroom. They started almost immediately.

"You're a pooh pooh."

"You're a *shitty* pooh-pooh."

"You're a shitty *knickers* pooh-pooh."

He began running down the dark lane.

Running was good. While he was doing it, he had worked out, he could stay a few inches ahead of the nightmare. The awful thing in his head was definitely dislodged. It still stuck to you like a shadow, of course, and when you stopped it

climbed back into your skull. But running was certainly
better than walking.

Running this morning was better than sleeping, too. Until
recently, sleeping had been OK, when he finally got there.
Even for a few seconds after waking up it was OK. He
opened his eyes and there was a normal world being looked at
by a normal human being. But the Thing had been waiting
for him to wake up and as soon as his eyes were properly
open, it pounced.

The bus was waiting. God knows what time in the small
hours it began its scavenging and circuitous tour of the tiny
villages. It was always scrupulously punctual and the customers for their part never missed it either. It sat on the village
green like a pallid slug, the legend SMITH'S OF BUN-
TINGFORD emblazoned on its ass. In gold. On the destination board it said TOURING.

It was no tour. The blue-overall brigade was inside and
smoking dark-brown hand-rolled cigarettes as slim as they
were pungent. East Anglia had always, except for its com-
muters, been a poor enough place.

Michael nodded briefly to Braithwaite, the only other
representative of the middle classes, who only took the bus
when their licenses were removed. Braithwaite's was a bad
case. A kid had been killed. Since then, they said, he drank
more than ever.

Michael looked out the window the whole way. He didn't
want to talk with Braithwaite. If he could help it, he didn't
talk with any of the village nowadays. He was too busy with
the thing in his head. He wondered if Braithwaite woke up to
the same kind of nausea of fear and guilt and anxiety. After
all, Michael French hadn't actually killed anyone. Though
even that could happen now.

In Regent's Park, well away from the zoo, Viktor Karpov
and Joe Asimov caught up with him as he was trying to light a
cigarette. Viktor expertly raised a platinum lighter against the
wind for him.

"Well, Michael. You came. You came, you saw, you conquered."

It was going to be easy, Viktor saw. French was twitching like a rabbit. A lot of research had been done on Michael French, who now looked at the two of them with loathing. That was good too. That was normal. They were already being seen as a sordid irrelevance to Michael's dream, just as the psychologists had said. Say nothing, they had advised Viktor. Let him do it.

Michael French's reply surprised Viktor.

"When do I see her again?"

That was direct. That was very good.

"Well, now you know she is real. When do you *want* to see her again?"

"I want to see her."

Viktor made a polite gesture of admiration.

"We have a hotel room booked for Mr. and Mrs. Quist. At the Hilton."

"I'd rather choose the room."

"If you wish. But what are you thinking of? The Hilton is neutral, Professor French. There are no two-way mirrors and hidden tape recorders in the Hilton if that is what you are afraid of. In any case, we are certainly not interested in blackmail—forgive me if I am too blunt."

"What *are* you interested in?"

"Proving to you that a better life is possible, Mr. French. For someone as talented as yourself, there should be rewards."

Michael French did not seem to be able to look at them. Viktor waited, then gave him the small card with the hotel room number and a time on it. Then walked away.

3

It is time to begin at the beginning. As the worst nightmares do, this one had come out of a cloudless sky. The date was Thursday, August 16, 1983. The place was East Anglia. True, the seeds of the horror had been sown in the spring. But today was their harvest.

In the bright summer morning, Michael was in the driver's seat, steering his Honda expertly through the narrow streets of Cambridge. His passenger was still wondering exactly where he was going and why. Jim Henderson had known French for nearly twenty years, true. Since they were students at Cambridge together. But they hadn't been close recently. Not since French had got famous and married that godawful woman who this morning hadn't even offered Henderson a cup of coffee after a hard drive from London.

Jim Henderson was a crime reporter on the *Sunday Times*. He had been nonplussed when the paper's science correspondent told him to go and cover the Icarus Project. "Me?" Henderson had said. "You can put everything I know about nuclear science on the sharp end of a pin. Why me?"

"Because you're the one he wants to talk to. Your old friend, I hear. Why the hell didn't you tell me that before?"

"Sure, he's a friend. But I wouldn't know where to start talking to him about the stuff he does."

"On his front doorstep," said the science correspondent, "fast as you can. Look, Jim, no one's been allowed near ICARUS. No one. Cosmetic handouts apart. We've been trying for two years. Now the guy is going to give you a guided tour. *And*, we think, there's a good reason."

"What *is* ICARUS, anyway?"

"You mean that?" asked the scientist. "It's a fusion reactor. Will be anyway, next year. Laser-induced fusion, Jim. *Iodine* laser."

"Thanks," said Henderson. "Well that's OK then. Iodine, you said. Not Dettol or TCP?"

"Just *try*, Jim. Seriously. I'll lend you some background. If French is right, this is bigger than North Sea Oil. Fusion's the last big hot potato. You must know that. How do you know this man and you don't know he's one of the best scientists we've got?"

"He probably doesn't know I'm one of the best crime reporters we've got," said Henderson. "It was a long time ago. We were two young lads up for an Open Scholarship. I think I stopped him jumping in the Cam. We both thought we'd fucked up our big chance in life."

"I never knew you went to Cambridge."

"Yes, well. Some of us get famous, some of us don't." But he was genuinely puzzled why Michael should have asked him to do the job. Perhaps, like Jim Henderson, Michael still felt one's first friends were the best ones, though life took you apart.

Five miles out of Cambridge on the day of the interview, Henderson was still floundering. It didn't seem to be for old times' sake that French had asked him here. Reminiscences about the old days had fallen one by one like stones into a pond. French had certainly changed in the last few years, Henderson thought. Michael couldn't be more than forty, but was beginning to go grey. And he seemed to have every muscle tightened up like a violin string. Maybe that was the cost of being in the big league. Or maybe just the penalty of having married a woman like Mary French.

Henderson was never going to be big league. It was nice when one's friends made it, though. The brief trip with Michael through the corridors of the Cavendish (Extension) laboratories had convinced him Michael was doing well: people came scurrying up as if he were Dr. Christiaan Barnard doing a ward round.

"I warn you," said Henderson, "you have to start at the beginning. What exactly are you *doing* in this place we are going to?"

French smiled briefly. They took a bend in the road and the sun was pouring through the windscreen. Henderson reached up and pulled down the shade.

"*That,*" said French crisply, pointing at the golden fire in the sky, "That's what we're doing."

Henderson was really going to try to understand it. He hadn't much hope he would, but he was being paid to try.

"The sun?" he said.

For a few hundred yards Michael drove without replying. The roads were straight, easy now, across a wide land turning gold towards harvest.

"OK," said Michael. "I'll start at the beginning. Every second, that little G-1 Type Dwarf star up there loses four point two million tons in weight. That is the price of making sunshine."

Henderson grabbed his pad and started scribbling.

"Four point two million tons lost each second. It must be getting smaller, then," he suggested.

French smiled again, and Henderson was glad to see he relaxed a bit, too.

"Not so you'd notice. It's been doing it the last six thousand million years and there are another ten to go."

"Should see us out then," said Henderson, writing.

"You want any more amazing figures?"

"Yes. Sure. Always helps. Just as long as I get the number of zeros right. You'll have to check this before it's printed."

"It's not going to get printed," said Michael.

"What?"

"I'll tell you later. That's why you're here. OK. The sun does it with straight hydrogen. Down here we use an isotope—"

"What do you mean, this isn't going to get printed?"

French stopped the car. They were on a long road in the middle of nowhere and nowhere. Larks were singing. French looked straight ahead.

"I was going to save it," he said. "It's not my fault, Jim, believe me. Not that part of it. I'm going to give you the biggest story you've ever got. We all wanted you to come. I want to tell it to you. But you mustn't print it. You won't be allowed to. If you think that's a waste of a day, we can drive straight back now."

Henderson looked at him. It occurred to him Michael French was a man on the edge of a breakdown. He said gently: "You go on talking, Mike."

After a moment Michael French started driving again. They passed a sign saying CARDINGTON—ten miles. "So," said Michael. "We only get a bit of sunlight. But that's still four million horsepower worth every square mile. And that's what makes us tick. You know this, I'm sure. Coal, oil, natural gas, logs in the fire—it's all bottled sunlight, really. It's where we get the whole energy package from."

"Except hydroelectric power," said Henderson. He was glad Michael was talking again and he was trying to sound intelligent.

"*Including* hydroelectric power. It's the sun that pulls the water up to the mountaintop in the first place."

"Including hydroelectric power," wrote Henderson, who vowed to keep quiet. Michael was obviously used to lecturing. Henderson was happy he went on talking.

"We're nearly there," said Michael. "So. What is sunlight? It's what happens when you bang two atoms of hydrogen together hard enough. What you get is one new nucleus, helium, about seventeen million electron volts of energy.

And that's what is supposed to be going on at Cardington."

"Forgive me if I'm wrong," said Henderson. "Isn't that what they do in an H Bomb? And what do you mean, *supposed* to be going on?"

This time Michael French laughed. "Absolutely," he said. "ICARUS is a slow H Bomb. There it is."

Ahead of them, shimmering in the wide green fields, was a huge structure. Like an aircraft hangar, but bigger. Bigger than a cathedral.

"That's where ICARUS lives," said Michael.

The huge grey hangar began to fill the horizon, the closer they got. Henderson was impressed. "And that's all yours? You haven't done too badly, old son. I remember when we used to drink at the Mill—"

"Yes," said Michael. "You know what that building is? You should write this down too, Henderson. It's where they used to keep the R101. It's still the biggest hangar in Europe. Which is funny when you think of it. The old airships used hydrogen too. With great success, too."

Henderson noted the bitterness. "So why are *you* here?" he asked, studying the sinister hulk ahead.

"Because it's big, near Cambridge, and no one's ever needed it since."

"No. I meant, what are *you* trying to fly?"

Now the Honda was at the perimeter fence, waiting for the guard to let them through the red and white striped pole. "ICARUS," said Michael. "The end of the energy crisis. The fuel is thirty-five billion tons of heavy water, lying out there at sea. Every teaspoonful can release more energy than a gallon of petrol. No fallout. No mess. No risk. That's the idea, anyway."

Henderson was again looking at the huge building ahead of him. Even in the sunlight it looked ominous.

He could now see it was ancient. The airships must have been colossal, and all those years ago, too. He was beginning to feel edgy.

"Why did you call it ICARUS?" he asked, as the Honda

halted at the black slice of the hangar's door. He had to shout; their ears were ringing with a strange humming from the building.

"What?" said Michael, the door half open.

"ICARUS!" shouted Henderson. "The name. Wasn't he the guy who flew too close to the sun?"

He got out of the car and faced Michael French over its roof. There was a small wind blowing in the air eddies created by the huge hangar in whose shadow they stood. Michael French's greying hair above his lean, leathery face flurried above another smile. His third this trip. But colder than ever.

"ICARUS stands for the First Cardington Torus. As it happens. Come and see. Of course, this is just the engineering model."

The noise inside the hangar was a steady whine of generators. Henderson knew what a generator looked like. The rest of the equipment bewildered him totally.

The impression was one of gigantic untidiness. Eventually Henderson began untangling his confusion, visually at least. In the middle was a huge structure, sort of round and doughnut shaped.

Michael was talking with two men at a console twenty yards from the doughnut. "What did we get?" he asked.

"Last night, fifty-six million degrees."

"We may as well go out with a bang," said Michael.

Henderson looked at the doughnut. "Did you say fifty-six *million* degrees?" Maybe he hadn't read the background notes right. "Isn't that *hotter* than the sun?"

"Much," said Michael.

"Then why," risked Henderson, "doesn't it melt? Or am I being stupid?"

"No," said Michael. "That's the name of the game. Fusion doesn't happen until the hydrogen atoms are travelling fast enough to hit each other hard enough. The hotter they are, the faster they go. On Earth that means one hundred million degrees." He gestured to the doughnut. "That's the Torus. Inside there we can get it that hot."

"But it doesn't melt."

"That's the idea. You see, the gas—when it's that hot it's called plasma—doesn't touch the sides. That thing is a magnetic bottle. You have a colossal magnetic field that pinches the plasma into a stream."

By the end of the afternoon Henderson was reeling. French had doggedly taken him through the whole thing, and at the end of it, Henderson was damned sure C. P. Snow had been right in saying there were two cultures—the scientists and the rest of us. When they finally got back to French's office at the Cavendish Extension, Henderson was grateful for a large scotch.

"So tell me what's eating you up," said Henderson. "ICARUS is the biggest thing since the wheel. What's wrong with you all?"

"You gathered something's wrong. That's interesting."

"Oh come on, Michael. Those guys looked sick as dogs. So do you. All that dark stuff about going out with a bang."

Michael seemed to be screwing himself up to it. Or maybe he was just trying to tear the fingers off his left hand.

"It's safe with me," said Henderson. "If you say I can't print it, I won't print it."

"It's not that. You won't get a chance. Tomorrow they are going to slap a security sticker on the whole subject of laser fusion. We're going to be strictly government property. That's one reason I got you here. Some of us hoped we could tell the story before the lid came down. We left it until it was too late."

"I suppose the real hardware is pretty secret already."

"Not at all. Fusion research has always been wide open. We go and watch the TOKOMAK at the Kurchatov Institute in Moscow; they come here. There's never been any military significance like with fission. That's not why they're shutting us up."

"Why then?"

"We knew it's the way they would do it. Next week, the week after, they are going to shut ICARUS down. Finish it. Sell the bits for scrap. What you saw today was a gang of doomed men."

Suddenly Henderson realised why the day seemed familiar. It was like the day the chairman of a bank had shown him all around the brand-new headquarters building, then started weeping at his desk and told him the whole place was bankrupt.

"But *why?*" Henderson asked. "If you're just on the edge of getting there?"

Michael shrugged. "Politics. The European Community is running a thing called JET. The Joint European Torus. No lasers. It's going to cost a mint. They want to put all their eggs in one basket. We've seen this coming for months. Six, precisely."

"Where's this land you, personally, I mean?"

"Oh, I'm all right. I've won *my* reputation. Out there at Cardington they're just turning my brilliant stuff into nuts and bolts. The only thing now is that no one is going to know if I was right or wrong, are they? Exactly what happens when you start hitting frozen deuterium pellets with twelve damned great lasers. That's the funny part of it."

"Doesn't sound hilarious to me. You must be very disappointed." But the bitterness and tension in the man still puzzled him.

"You want to hear the funny part?" said Michael, quietly.

"Yes?"

"Six months ago I knew the project was doomed. Five months ago I discovered something else. In this very office. Checking a small bit of the original theory. You know what I found? I discovered I was wrong. The whole way through. There was a basic error in the computer print-out way back at the start of the game. And no one had picked it up. What I found out was that if anyone built ICARUS and started it up for real, the thing would simply blow up."

Henderson finally understood. "So what did you do?"

"You know what an honourable scientist does, don't you? Commit public hara-kiri. Publish an emendation in the *British Journal of Nuclear Science,* in my case. Start looking for a job in a technical college. Think about it, Jim. I have one hundred and twenty people earning their bread on my project. A project that is going to be closed down anyway. What would have happened if I'd announced that I'd got it all wrong? Every single one of them would have blamed me for the shutdown. They'd never believe the truth—that it was doomed anyway. They'd never *get* the truth either. The government would have seized the opportunity with both hands. I wasn't just being selfish, Jim. Those people on ICARUS have got wives and kids, mortgages. As it is, they'll be phased out into new jobs. It won't rub off on their reputations. Go on. Tell me, Jim. What would *you* have done?"

"Maybe you should talk to a priest. You seem in a bad way."

"Maybe. Certainly for a scientist, it's the cardinal sin."

"You didn't fake anything up on purpose."

"No. But that's what it would look like, as it happens. It really looks as though someone has tampered with the figures to give a good result. There are damned few people in the world who could know. Those that read my research never guessed it. It looks like a crime."

"Maybe—" began Henderson when the door crashed open.

A wild-haired young man said, "Sorry, Mike. I have to see you—"

"Not now. Fifteen minutes. There are doors in this country, Keegan."

As it shut again Michael said, "Australian. One of my hundred and twenty. Good example. He'd have to go back to Brisbane with ICARUS like a dead duck around his neck if

I'd told the truth. As it is, they'll be glad to get him. Because one day, I promise you, laser fusion will work. I know it. Maybe he'll do it."

It struck Henderson that Michael French had spent a good number of wee hours finding excuses for himself.

"Believe me," said Michael, "when it's all over I'll publish that 'critical emendation.' Two years from now. It will be all water under the bridge by then. Just to put the record straight."

"Listen, Mike. Are you sure it *wasn't* a crime?"

"Go on."

"If it looked so good, and even you hadn't picked it up ... I don't know what's involved. Could someone have tampered with your figures, screwed it up on purpose?"

"Thanks," said Michael. He poured another scotch. "I wanted to hear you say it. I didn't dare. I don't dare say it to myself. Otherwise I'll start imagining people are following me in cars. Yes, it has occurred to me someone has done this thing to me. Systematically taken the day's computer work and done it again. It's wrong. It's a terrifying thought, but it can't be true."

"Where is this computer?"

"Texas."

"*Texas?*"

"That's right."

"You go to and from Texas to do your sums?"

"Of course not. You dial a telephone number. Ring it up. Bounces off a satellite. It's called time-sharing."

"Jesus Christ," said Henderson. "So why couldn't someone be listening in?"

"It's not a question of listening in. There's a theoretical possibility of someone who knew my access code getting through after me and revising the day's input. But there are two good reasons it couldn't be true."

"Tell me."

"One: whoever was doing that had to be brighter than me, in this very special field. And I'd have to know who he was

already, if he were that good. Two: and this is the big one.
This kind of thing just doesn't happen in fusion research, I
told you. There have never been any secrets. Sometimes I
tell my friends in Russia things we've done before I tell the
guy in the next laboratory."

"One," said Henderson. "I'm a crime specialist right? You
may well know the guy. You may just not believe he could do
such a thing. Two. 'There have never been any secrets.' But
you just told me that from tomorrow the whole *thing* is
secret."

"Only to keep our mouths shut. Believe me, Jim. I'd like
to think otherwise. But this is something I screwed up
myself. Fortunately I may get away with it."

"Don't be too sure," said Henderson, getting up.
"Michael. I've got to go. And that young man needs to see
you. You know where I am. You think about it. You have, I
know. Just think of any names, anybody, that you wonder in
your worst nightmares could have done this to your research."

Michael looked up at him gratefully.

"I haven't tried to," he admitted. "Mary always says I'm
paranoid. I've really been too frightened to try."

"Take the risk," said Jim. He was glad he had never made
it into the big league. He had a good wife and job to go back
to. He felt sorry for this man. "You tell me and I'll check it
out. Believe me. I'm good at it."

"You'd really do that?"

"I told you."

"Why? You can't publish anything?"

"You tell me."

There was a polite knock at the door.

"OK," said Michael quickly. "If you have time. I'd like to
know about something called the Science Service. They sent
someone up here. It's part of the Civil Service, a kind of
advisory unit. I was puzzled when they worked us over,
because normally they just check out security-risk cases. And
the man who runs it is strange. Really strange."

The knock came again.

"OK," said Henderson quietly. "Be in touch."

At the door wasn't the young Australian. It was a woman in her fifties with a vacuum cleaner.

"Go *away!*" Henderson heard Michael shout. "For God's sake, I've told you this office is clean enough!"

Henderson stepped into the sunlight. Mid-August, early evening. He blinked in the golden glare. *You poor bastard,* he thought.

Alone, Michael French reached for his locked drawer. He stabbed the small key unerringly into the slot, slid the drawer out, then reached, with the same deftness, for the envelope buried beneath a square of black paper. He laid it on the desk then, very gently, slid out its content.

The photograph had arrived at the laboratories last Thursday, marked "private and confidential," in a brown manila envelope sealed with Sellotape, the address typed on a good electric typewriter. Now he opened that first brown envelope again, felt inside and remembered how at first he had expected to find more than the single card. He slid it out. The first time he had opened it carefully, planning to use the envelope again. He was conservation-conscious like that, thanks to Mary.

The photograph inside was glossy, black and white. At first sight he had assumed it was another advertising shot; there was a girl's face on the front. He turned it over. On the back, in the middle and in small writing, were the words, "I love you, Michael. Do not show me to anyone. Next week . . ."

Once again, he read it twice, then turned the picture over. She was looking straight at him. It was a real photo, not just a print. She was standing in a flower garden, maybe lilacs, and holding her small hands in front of her just so, as if a child, maybe hers, had fallen over between her and the camera. Except she was looking at the camera.

He held the picture away from him, being farsighted. What an extraordinary thing! He turned it over again. The writing was in a purple felt tip. It was very neat and careful, like a child's.

The funny thing was the shock of recognition. As if he

knew her, somewhere, long ago. That was obviously impossible. Could she be a past student? He was damned sure the row of faces in a Thursday morning seminar never included anyone as beautiful as this. She was as beautiful as any woman he had ever dreamt of. And he had been dreaming a long time.

This time Keegan knocked. With his feet maybe, but at least he was making an effort. French had just enough time to slip the photograph away before the young Australian charged in.

"You heard the news?" demanded Keegan. "You seen John Cox yet? Isn't that the most fantastic thing?"

"News?"

Keegan seemed to be waving a fist at him. Sunlight poured into the office behind him. "We've *got* it!" yelled Keegan. "It's not us they're closing down. It's JET. They're pulling out of JET! Five o'clock today. Crainfield rang you. Spoke to John. They've blown it, down there. Decided they can't meet the Lawson Criteria. Not now or never. We're home and dry, boss. The whole thing's in our lap. They're going to give us so much money we don't even have to count it."

He saw Michael and was looking at him like a creature from another planet. "Sorry," said Keegan. "Bit carried away."

"Are you sure about this?"

"You know John Cox; he's got all the contacts. He's sure. Sir, why don't we just go down to the Mill and get loaded with the rest of the boys? They took right off. I thought someone should stay and tell you, sir."

"Yes," said Michael. "That was kind of you."

It seemed to Keegan maybe the news hadn't sunk in. "We're going to build ICARUS, Professor French. John says we've even got a countdown target to Fusion on the model."

"Thanks," said Michael. "Thank you very much indeed."

Suddenly he knew he was going to be sick. His brain felt as if something were trying to squash it inside his skull. He could feel sweat spring out of every pore in his body. This time, he knew, it was for real. The *real* nightmare. The one in which, when you woke up, you had only dreamt you had woken—the monster was still there and getting closer.

"Keegan," he said. "I need to be alone for a bit. Maybe I'll join you later."

"Sure. Oh—letter for you. Came by hand, I guess."

He passed Michael a brown manila envelope.

By the time Michael got to the Mill, the party had moved on. He wasn't sorry. He was still numb. It would have showed. He'd have to learn how to behave naturally, as if nothing were wrong. Until he worked out what to do. For now, the thing was to fake it one moment at a time.

It was one of the most golden evenings yet. Greene King Bitter was one of the good beers. He sat outside, watching the punts loading and discharging their happy inmates. The river slid down here dramatically from its upper to lower level, through a weir. He had never forgotten how, on his first visit to Cambridge, he had seriously thought of jumping in just here. It had been at the time of the Open Scholarships, for Michael French the chance of a lifetime. He had been convinced he would fail. He hadn't, then. Maybe there was still time to jump.

He sipped the amber beer and watched the girls walking across the bridge. He wondered if the girl in the picture *could* be just a student who had seen him, fallen in love. God knows they did strange things. But beautiful girls didn't fall in love with Michael French, to his knowledge.

Take that one, for example. Michael followed her with his whole gaze. She was cut sharp as a jewel, obviously foreign, maybe Swiss, probably from one of the language schools. Her hair shone like coal. He couldn't see her eyes, but he guessed they were bright and carefree.

At the iron table behind him a middle-aged tourist raised his camera and took a shot towards the bridge. Then went back to writing, maybe postcards.

French reached into his jacket pocket, took out the envelope and opened it. It was a heart-stopper. She was closer now. It was just her face. She was smiling at him, a smile of such tenderness. She was very young. She had cut her hair. As she smiled, her eyebrows were slightly raised, as if she were sharing a secret joke with him.

This time, it said on the reverse, "Michael, I am lonely, too."

It was like having a co-conspirator. Like being no longer entirely alone. How had she *known* he was lonely? Well, most people are lonely. He finished his beer. It was time to go home. Time to start behaving very carefully indeed.

When he got home, he couldn't tell Mary the good news at once. Something really serious had happened.

The children were sated with summer holiday by now; that morning they'd complained of terminal boredom. "Why don't you go and play in the garden?" Michael had said.

"What at? There's nothing to *do* in the garden."

As a child, Michael French had played for hours in the garden, alone, digging pits for people to fall in, covering them with grass and twigs to hide them. That sort of game. He explained this to the children in great detail.

Now Mary had fallen straight into a two-foot cavity. When he got back this evening, he could hear the kids, still wailing in the background. "You're so *stupid*, Michael."

"Well, it was only a game, Mary."

"With sharpened bamboo spikes in the bottom of it?"

He left it until the next morning to tell her the good news. He made a little celebration of it and brought her breakfast in bed.

Mary said, "Breakfast in bed? What's this, then? Are you having an affair?"

"What on earth do you mean?"

"It's one of the signs. Tender loving care."

"That's a pretty cynical thing to say."

"*Nicholas!* No. Do you hear me? NO! You will not jump on the bed like a mad thing. How many times . . . What were you saying about shutting down ICARUS?"

"They're not going to. They're giving us the money to finish it."

"I suppose that means you'll be working even later."

"Oh, I don't know," he said. He looked out the bedroom window at the jungly garden. It was another great day. When the phone rang again it was John Cox, head of nuclear engineering, asking if French had seen the paper and telling French how he'd spent the night fixing up a great calendar which would be a countdown to Fusion Day.

It occurred to Michael French he could just walk out the door now and start walking, preferably southwards, for about twenty years.

When he got to the office the calendar was already up on the door. It was neatly done and it said: ICARUS day—100. *Bloody childish*, he thought. Immediately after he entered his office he could see another brown manila envelope on his desk. No stamp. Who in hell was bringing them? Between it and him was John Cox, waving a copy of *The Times*. "Have you read this yet?" He flapped his pink hand at the page. Michael took it. The item was headed: "Euro-Fusion Project on the Rocks." Michael felt his gut go cold.

"This is it, boyo," said John. "This is the glory road."

John Cox had a most peculiar set of verbal mannerisms.

"Aren't you pleased? I mean, I know it's tough on them. But this is where we take off. The ministry are sending a team up this afternoon. With money in their pockets."

"John," said Michael. "We don't want to go off at half cock. I'd like you to make a proper presentation. With costs. I think we ought to do that very thoroughly." It was necessary to make an effort to sound enthusiastic.

"Great," said John Cox. "Can I tell the gang? I *knew* you would be scheming something. You're a secretive bugger,

Michael. By the way, why don't you and Mary and the kids come round to dinner? Quiet celebration. The children can have a great time on the river."

"That would be lovely." Except, he thought, that if there was anyone his kids disliked more than each other it was the John Cox brood.

It wasn't until midmorning that he was able to be alone. He tore the envelope open. And sat down, shaking.

She was naked. Somehow he had been expecting it. She was curled up on a chair, an old comfortable-looking chair in a big white room, maybe an attic. Sunlight blazed from a dormer window. She was looking at him without smiling. Seriously. It was in no way a pornographic picture; he had feared that. She was too special. It was the kind of picture a lover might have taken. She was alone in this big attic room and her lover had just come in. There were lots of things in the room—pictures, furniture—he would be able to—

"What *have* you got there?"

He jumped. Mary never came to the laboratories. He had been lost in the picture. He gazed at her in disbelief.

She was standing squarely on the other side of the desk. Solid, tweedy, bare legged. The summer had baked her cheeks to biscuit red. It looked like a permanent flush of anger.

"Dirty postcards, Michael? Show me."

"It's nothing. Just an advertising gimmick."

"Show me. So this is what you do all day."

He tossed the picture down, casually as he could, but out of her reach. She mustn't pick it up. She mustn't turn it over. God knows what was on the other side this time.

"What are you doing here?" he said.

"*That's* friendly. I *told* you. Shopping. You never listen. I thought you might have time for coffee."

"Right," he said, jumping up. "Let's do that. Are you going to the market?"

But she had picked up the picture.

"Dirty old men," she said. "Oh yes. Soft focus, sunlight bouncing off the tits." Mary had amateur photography on her hobby list. She specialised in the church spires of East Anglia. "I don't know why you all fall for it. Like a lot of little schoolboys. What are they selling?"

"Selling?"

"You said it was an advertising shot."

"Computer software," he said.

"That figures. God. *Software* is the word. All junked out with furniture and fittings." She was looking at the picture, touring a secret room. He felt violently angry; she had no right there.

She turned the picture over and his heart hammered in his ribs. Then she threw it down.

"All right," she said. "Let's go."

There was nothing on the back at all. Almost as if she had known.

He had almost got Mary out of the office when his private phone rang. "I'm sorry," he said, and turned back to answer it. Mary French sighed.

The voice said, simply, "Do you want to meet her?"

He knew exactly what it was about. In his imaginings he had thought there would be a phone call. But he had dreamt *she* would ring up. He knew what her voice would sound like. The man's voice, guttural and suggestive, angered him.

"What *is* this?" French said crisply.

They hung up on him.

"Come *on*, Michael! I thought it was only at home you went round in a daze."

4

The civil servants were due at 2:30 that afternoon. They arrived at 2:40. There were four of them on the other side of the table. The department's conference room had been hastily dusted for the visit.

"So, we're going to give you a further fifty million pounds to start with, Professor French. Do you think that's enough?"

At his side, John Cox nudged him with his knee. Michael glanced down. John was jerking a pink thumb up and down in a gesture of encouragement.

"I don't understand," said Michael. "This money's coming from the General Defence Fund? There's no military connection."

"We appreciate that. But this is the way we want it done. And I have to make one thing plain. The Euro-fusion project has failed. Quite frankly, we are not going to start again and carry a lot of European deadwood. This one's ours. You can build a fusion reactor for *Britain*. After all, this *is* the country that started the industrial revolution. It's up to you. You know what it means. That's why we are going to muzzle you. I'm afraid there will be no more comradely chats with the Russians. We are going to have to check you all out very thoroughly and you will have to sign the book. I wanted to be quite plain about that."

They all nodded. Michael French felt the sweat break out. *Take it calmly. It can't be true.*

"We're going to have a lot of bloody bureaucrats on our back, are we?" asked Derek Sewell. You could count on Sewell to sour the occasion. He bared his brown teeth in a smile and flicked a glance round the table for support.

"I take it this means we can buy the Japanese lasers," said John Cox.

Michael looked at his team. Except for the computer man, Sewell, they were as excited as kids being told of the school treat.

"Of course, gentlemen. Get whatever you want. And when did you last hear a man from the ministry say *that?*" said the civil servant in the chair. "We can give Britain a lead in the energy race that will put us back on top of the heap. I can assure you, we are quite ready to sign over to this department anything up to three years' revenue from North Sea oil. It is an investment. The only logical and sensible investment. I want you people to feel that you can come in out of the cold. We don't want nuclear fission reactors. *No one* wants fission reactors. That's obvious. We want *fusion*. Limitless power. *Safe* power."

Michael French said very little as the waves of euphoria eddied around the room. A late buffet lunch had been brought in. Michael chewed his way through it, doing his best. He didn't hear the elderly civil servant, the one who had said nothing so far, the first time he started whispering to him. "I'm sorry?" asked Michael, starting.

"I said do you have an hour free? After this? I'd like a word."

"Of course," he said. "Any time." He looked down warily at a small man whose eyes were fragmented into layered discs by pebble spectacles. On the top of his bald, tortoise's head were no more than six black hairs.

They slipped out together. The civil servant had his own car, a Humber 1100.

"I don't know if you caught my name. I'm John Benson. Science Service."

"Yes." It was as he feared. They were starting.
"You seem worried. Do you mind if we take a drive?"

Benson drove like a schoolmistress. They went carefully, mostly in the middle of the road, and parked by the water meadows. Kids were plunging into the brown river.

"Do you see any problems?" Benson asked. "It's a huge thing to throw at you. I know that."

"There are bound to be problems," said Michael, "turning figures into hardware. There are always problems."

Benson lowered his window. Near at hand, on the Cam, a clatter of duck wings took off like gunfire.

"What about personal problems?" said Benson. "I have to ask. You'll be carrying a big responsibility. I know you do already. If there's anything we can do to help—I mean, if there were any problems. Like money even. We don't want you to have anything on your mind except ICARUS. That's all part of the service."

"I've no personal problems," said Michael.

"Lucky man. And you've no objection to signing the Act? And your wife? We've got our own formula. I'd like you to get it over with. And I'd like you to have a word with one of my colleagues. Just a formality. He should be meeting us here. Sorry about that. But it's my last. I'm retiring. Can't say I'm sorry. Did you ever meet Mr. Clough?"

It occurred to Michael this could be a gambit. "Let me give you a tip," said Benson. "Don't think you're being vetted in any way, Professor French. One can so easily start rumours. I've seen it happen. Just sign the papers and forget it. If I were you, I'd stay as clear as you can of the Science Service."

Michael took the papers from Benson's fat hand. Mary was not going to like any of this, he could tell at a glance. There was a long and personal questionnaire. He could just hear her: "Why should I tell them if I've ever been a member of the Communist Party? Why should I answer all this stuff? I'm not just an appendage."

"Ah," said Benson. "Here's my young friend now."

He was one of the proper Englishmen, the young man who suddenly materialised. Very sharp, very confident, very relaxed. "Patterson," he said, offering a hand. Michael took it warily. The three men began to stroll past the screaming, happy children.

"You know about us, I believe," said Patterson. "We lent you one of our people earlier on. I expect you guessed."

"Yes," said Michael. "You're spy-catchers."

Patterson laughed. "Well, it happens, you know. It's called Brain Steal. Now that you're going secret we have to warn you. We're sorry to have to make such a fuss about it, and it may never happen. But you see, Britain is terribly good up here." He tapped his golden head. "We actually produce more Nobel Prize-winners per head than anyone else. We're poor as churchmice as you all know, but a lot of you are making up stuff that a lot of these other chaps can actually afford to build. That's the temptation. Believe me, whatever your favourite tipple is, do be wary."

Michael thought: *At his age, I was a frightened working-class lad.*

"We *are* watching you," said the young man. "I know that sounds terribly unpleasant, but it really is for all our good. If you do put a foot wrong we will probably know. And believe me, this is not meant to frighten you. The day you find a Russian agent hulking out of the fog and pressing pound notes in your hand—well, that's not the way they do it, but never mind. Don't think we will come around and throw you in the dungeon forever after. In fact, I'd like to say we trust you. You are quite welcome to lead the buggers on, if it does happen. Then come to us.

"Think of us as a counselling service. On your side. We have a telephone number. I'd like you to take it down. Put it in your book."

"Thank you," said Michael French. *They know*, he thought. *They know.*

"We all have our hangups," said Patterson. "Believe me, there are no new tricks in the book. Some of us like women, some of us like men, some of us like money. They use these things. Remember that what they are after is getting something for free. You may feel that scientific information ought to be free; that is a respectable point of view. But two thirds of Research and Development in this country is on Defence Contracts and we think the paymaster calls the tune."

"OK," said Michael. "I get the picture."

"Good," said Patterson. "Tell me. The rest of your team. How do you think they're placed? Do you mind if we go through them? John Cox, to start with. In your own mind, do you see any reason why he could be a security risk?"

Dinner with the Coxes was postponed to 9:30. They lived in a bright, new, functional tract of town houses in Trumpington. Theirs was very different from the Frenches' house which, happy or not, had collected the souvenirs and rummage of family life—old lawnmowers, family antiques, children's paintings. The Coxes lived as if in an hotel suite, always ready to take off for guest appearances at universities across the world. The Cox children were pallid and weedy. Michael had said it was because they were cut flowers; kids needed roots.

Mary had replied, "Nonsense. How can you talk such nonsense? They have a very rich, varied international life. You would just bury yourself in moss, we all know that."

By the time Michael arrived to dinner, he was still shaking from the afternoon.

Over dinner, Mary launched into Rupert Brooke. It was for nearby Grantchester that he'd written about the clock standing at ten to three, is there honey still for tea. "Men are such sentimentalists," Mary said. "Such childlike ideas about the world."

Michael French decided, early, to get drunk. The Coxes splashed wine about with total abandon. Good wine too, but never uncorked or treated properly. Annie Cox poured him another glass, right to the last drip of the bottle. When he drank it, sediment grated on his teeth.

"Rupert Brooke *did* die for his country. Can't be all bad," said Michael.

"Died of food poisoning in Greece," said Mary. "Just another phoney."

Annie Cox frowned. She was wary of Mary French.

"Like Michael. Have you seen his collection of dirty postcards, John?" Mary asked. She helped herself to more wine.

"Michael?" said John with exaggerated surprise.

"I tell you no lie. I came into his office. This morning. And he was drooling over a naked lady."

"Oh go *on*," said Annie Cox.

John raised an eyebrow at Michael. The women were having their little joke. John winked at him. The men were on the same side. "Naked ladies are a very good idea," said John Cox. "You should see my new secretary."

"More soup, Mary?" Annie asked.

"Lovely. I bet you *have*, too," said Mary, looking at John. Annie Cox clattered the soup ladle against her plate.

It occurred to Michael French that dinners in the Cambridge ghetto were like picnics in a minefield.

It was the time to try out marital rows in the safety of numbers. When you could gamble no one was listening.

"I love my naked lady," said Michael. He really was quite drunk. "I have a total passion for her. Do you know I get a picture of her every week? She loves me. She sends me wonderful pictures and on the back she says, 'I love you.'"

"More soup, Michael?"

The evening ended late. John had engaged Michael in a grandiose, freewheeling discussion of the auspicious future. He had put an arm on Michael's shoulder and said, "You are, actually, Michael—and I am being quite serious—you are one of the most brilliant men we have. This country have—has. Now, you know *me*. I can work anywhere I choose. Not brilliant. But pretty good. You know why we stay with you and the department? Because we *trust* you, Michael. All of us. Ladies—brandy. A toast. I give you the man who put the sun in a bottle."

On the drive back, Mary said, "Why were you so unpleasant?"

"Unpleasant? I wasn't unpleasant."

"You're so hostile. You just sit there looking sour."

"I was making a lot of conservation—conversation."

"Don't drive so *fast.*"

The lanes were dark tunnels, hedgerows flicking the car
like whips.

When they got near the house they could hear the phone
ringing and ringing. Doubtless the babysitter was zonked out
in front of the late-night movie. Michael stabbed at the
keyhole twice and got inside.

It was the same voice. The same question. On an impulse,
he shouted, *"No.* Leave me alone!"

"Really? Let's see how you feel six months from now,
Professor."

And already, as the voice clicked out, Michael French felt
a surge of anger, desire, and regret.

5

"Professor French, this is a new kind of nuclear reactor, a
thermonuclear reactor. What happens if something goes
wrong?"

It was the press conference the next Thursday. The
reporters leant forward. Michael stood up. He glanced at
Henderson in the front row and felt glad he was there. Then

addressed the questioner, apparently an American. "There is no possibility of a fusion reactor running out of control," he said. "It is physically impossible."

"The reactor is completely safe?" the questioner pursued. "There is no possibility of *anything?*"

Michael hesitated. "Well," he said, "we are dealing with very high temperatures, obviously. But compared with the problems of handling plutonium in a fission reactor, there's no major risk factor."

"No radiation risks?"

"Not compared with plutonium. We have to handle tritium, that's all. It isn't the healthiest stuff in the world, but we have a half-life of only twelve years to worry about, not millions."

"Can you tell us why the Joint European Torus has been scrapped? And why didn't ICARUS get government backing in the first place?"

"Because some of us thought JET would work, and some of us were wrong," said John Cox from his chair. There was a ripple of polite amusement. John Cox stood up, and Michael gladly sat. "Can I say a word about JET?" said Cox. "We all feel very sad for the scientists and technologists from all over Europe who put so much effort into it. Unfortunately there's an inflexible set of rules in this game. They're called the Lawson Criteria. Basically, you have to use a colossal amount of energy to get a fusion reaction going. Obviously there's no point in doing it unless you get *more* energy out as a result. JET just failed to meet the criteria."

The correspondent of the *Daily Telegraph* stood up. "As I understand it, there are a number of people at JET who aren't convinced of this. They feel that given more time they'd have got there. Isn't it true that there is a good deal of resentment in the scientific community that you have scooped the table, so to speak?"

"Well," said John Cox, "put it this way. If ICARUS *didn't* work, I can see my good friend Professor Cranfield at Culham coming after me with his cricket bat."

"Dick Brendan, *Daily Mail.* Why the sudden secrecy on

fusion research? Is this to do with the fact you are using lasers to accelerate the deuterium-tritium reaction? Does it have to do with the military significance of new technology on the laser front? As I understood it, fusion research has traditionally been wide open to international debate."

Benson of the Science Service took this one. "There is nothing mysterious about this. There *has* been a good deal of unhelpful speculation in the press in the last few days. That is partly why we called this press conference. Open scientific debate on topics in the field of pure theory has always been customary. When you move from theory and hand over to the engineers, which is what we are now doing, then it becomes a question of straight economic common sense. *We* are building ICARUS. Our friends in Russia respect that. We are creating a technology that quite simply is very expensive. And we want to see a return on our money. We want to put *Britain* ahead. We want to protect that technology with patents in the usual way if necessary."

The man from the Communist *Morning Star* said: "Isn't that a highly cynical attitude? Haven't you learnt nine tenths of what you know from the work going on in the Russian TOKAMAK research? If fusion power is the answer to the world's energy crisis, shouldn't it be freely shared?"

"I respect the speaker's idealistic viewpoint," said Benson drily. "Of course, if our Russian friends were interested in sharing the development costs we would be happy to know. Any more questions?"

Jim Henderson stood up. He said, "I understand that the security on ICARUS is maintained by a department called the Science Service. I also understand that the Science Service is particularly concerned, as a rule, with matters of scientific espionage and questions relating to defectors. Can you comment on that?"

"I didn't catch your name," said Benson bleakly.

"Henderson, *Sunday Times.*"

"Well, Mr. Henderson, I can assure you that the Science Service is purely an advisory body."

"Set up in 1941," added Henderson.

"That may be. There is nothing sinister in this. Any *further* questions?"

It was not until dusk that Henderson and Michael could meet. They walked through the emerald-green quadrangle of their old college. It was near on twenty years since they had first trod the cobbles here. A bat, now as then, suddenly knifed the air within a whisper of their heads.

"I'm not sure you should have sprung that one on Benson," said Michael.

"I wanted to see his reaction," said Henderson. "Does the name Aloysius Clough mean anything to you?"

"No. Yes, Benson mentioned it."

"He runs it. The Science Service. Always has. And you're right. They *are* a curious bunch. What about the name Niels Bohr?"

"Bohr? Of course. One of the giants of atomic research during the war. Nobel Prize-winner. He was pulled out of Norway just in time. There was a damned good chance he could have served Hitler up with the first atom bomb otherwise."

"Right," said Henderson. "If Clough had had his way, he'd have blown Niels Bohr to fragments to stop that happening. I haven't found out much, Michael. But enough to make it interesting. You and I are going to have dinner together, Michael. And we are going to have a good long talk. I think you're hiding something from me."

"It's no good," said Michael. "I'm grateful, but it's no *good*. Whatever is going on, I can't stand any more of it. Tomorrow I'm going to resign. I'm going to tell them the whole damned thing. I can't just sit here and watch that bloody thing being built."

Henderson stopped walking and took his arm. "Oh no you're not, old son. Because if you do, you'll be playing right into their crooked little hands."

Across the darkening lilac sky, the noise of bells for
Evensong at some college chapel bruised gently against the
late roses on the walls of their old college. *What a long time
ago*, Michael thought, *since we were young here.* He nodded at
two young men who passed, recognising him as a famous
scientist. Twenty years ago Henderson used to write poetry,
he remembered.

"What have you found out?" Michael asked. "What did
you find out—about them?"

"I can't tell you," said Henderson.

They had stopped at the porter's lodge. The tourists had
gone; the undergraduates were away. The cool stone arch,
smoky gold, darkened as the first breeze of the evening
fluttered through.

"What do you mean, you can't tell me?"

"I can't tell you, Michael. And that should show you I'm
serious. I've got contacts —you know that—in my business.
This one was the best. Even *he* is frightened of them. And of
Clough, the guy who runs it. You've got to hang on,
Michael."

"You can trust me," said Michael. "Who are they? What
are they up to?" They stepped into the High Street, the last
flurry of homeward traffic.

"Should I trust you, Michael? *Have* you told me everything?"

"What do you mean?"

"Are you *sure* no one has tried to make contact? Is there
anything you haven't told me?"

Michael was tempted. It would be good to explain. About
the girl, the pictures.

"No," he said.

For a while they walked together in silence.

"Well, if they do, if anyone does," said Henderson, "you
tell me. Or when you're ready. Meanwhile, hang on. Will you
do that? Even if it takes months. Someone is after you,
Michael. That I promise you. And I'm your friend."

"OK," said Michael. "I'll wait." He hoped he could.

6

The weather had broken up at the end of August. It had rained right through to winter. Then it froze. Usually by February one could hope for some warmth. Not this time.

There were still two hours before it was time to go to the Hilton. Michael French had put the card in his hip pocket and he felt for it every now and again. He shivered. Room 220. At any rate, it would be good to be warm again.

He had lunch at an Indian restaurant on Old Compton Street he hadn't been to in years. He had taken Mary there when they were courting. Michael had never been unfaithful in his life; he had no intention of beginning now. That wasn't what it was about. He was no fool.

When they had telephoned again he had just said *yes*. It had been a long time, waiting for that telephone call. A whole, long, wet autumn and half a winter. They had given him the time and place in the Zoo. They said nothing was to be said. They said they would meet him in the Rose Garden.

Even now it was all part of a stratagem. But even now, the girl in the picture seemed, somehow, outside all of it. God knows who was doing what to her. She had to be part of a sordid scheme. But she was real, whatever they had done to make her do what she had done. Nothing could corrupt the look in her eyes gazing at his, in the picture. She was real. He *knew* she was real.

He stepped out of the frigid waste of Park Lane and confronted the hotel reception. "I want the key to 220 please."

They looked. It wasn't there. The girl explained, "Perhaps Mrs. Quist is already back." It took him a moment to remember his new name.

The lift stopped at the second floor. The corridor was cool and quiet. Michael began checking the numbers, then went back and started the other way. It was all golden, air conditioned, quiet. Midafternoon; the tourists were out foraging for goodies.

The door of 220 was just a fraction ajar. There was no need to do anything but push it. He did.

Then he walked inside. Well, what did he expect? The attic in the picture? There was nothing here except the well-groomed anonymity of a Hilton hotel room. Very clean, very nothing. Washed out by every new day's sun and the hotel staff.

God knows what fornication took place the night before. You bought a new space, cleaned each morning, innocent as the sunrise. Who could bear to think of who else has slept in a hotel bed before you?

His head was racing. Maybe there *was* a risk of heart attack for forty-year-olds. The window let onto the park. A line of trees was hanging in the air, like fretwork. It was only two in the afternoon, but the dark was gathering.

She wasn't here. No one was here.

He began wandering about. Picking things up, putting things down. She *had* to be here.

They had laid it out for him like a trail for a dog. There was a little pink toothbrush in the bathroom. There was a bottle of Arpège. There was a nightdress, silky and creamy, like the top of a Normandy milk churn. He picked it up and ran his face against it. The *bastards*. The cruel bastards. He opened all the drawers in the cabinet by the double bed. Nothing.

He got himself together. OK. That was it. If there were any more pictures he would tear them up. He laid the nightdress down on the bed and squashed his hair flat against his head. He would just leave. Now. He turned. They weren't going to mess him around like this.

She was standing just inside the door.

She just came into the room. She closed the door behind her. He had been there first, so it was no longer just *her* room. He watched her shut the door.

It was she. They were on neutral ground, just two human beings. He had it in his head to say nothing. There could be tape recorders. It would be silent, like the pictures of her.

Oh, she was so beautiful. He had been ready for deception. Well, not really; he knew she was not some kind of prostitute. She was the picture girl. She took off her white fox coat and dropped it to the floor. The huge, dark eyes were like those in the second picture, tender and surprised. She raised her arms as if in greeting. It was a greeting. It was for him. He took a step forward, unbelieving, stiff.

She put her arms around him, then raised a hand to stroke his neck. He shuddered with the joy of it. Then he burst into tears.

"Don't," she said. "Don't." Her voice was foreign, familiar, beautiful.

Six floors above, Viktor and Joe were sipping Dubonnet with white rum and lemon. The Hilton rooftop bar gave a big view of wintry Hyde Park.

"Any operation that trusts a woman—" said Joe. He made a fart noise. Viktor just sipped his cool glass. "Daft idea," said Joe. "And that's not an old-fashioned word. Daft as they come."

Viktor was not attending. A fly sat on the table before them. With a flick of his hand the fly lay dead. Neatly, Viktor picked it up by one wing and dropped it into Joe's drink. Joe looked at the black omen.

"Don't forget who is paying," said Viktor. "All right? Now we'll go down and take doggy's new bone away from him again."

"After you, Dr. Pavlov," said Joe.

"Quick," she said. "We must escape them. Now. We have got to find a way. Trust me." She took his hand by one finger, tugged him.

His head raced. He was thinking they told her to say all this, too. It would be clever, a sugar coating on the bait. But his heart was pounding.

"Kiss me," she said. Their lips approached. It was a young girl's kiss, as if it were strange to her. Her lips trembled, then opened. He put a hand behind her head and held her to him and now he could feel her heart beating.

They found out your particular tipple and worked on it. For some people it was money, for some it was sex. They've got you sized up. A pathetic, emotionally starved scientist, aged forty. Looking for someone who understands him. Hold your stupid head in their little hands. You are a bloody fool, Michael. They've found your weakness and now they're working on it. Later she'll have a big laugh with that man with the platinum lighter. Tell him how he wept like a baby.

"Please," she said. "I *will* love you. I will love you. Quickly now. Come."

At the last moment she snatched up the fox coat. They raced for the stairs, ran giddily down the fire exit. They got to the foyer, through a swinging door, then to the street. The taxis were queuing. By the time they had caught one he saw Viktor and his companion sliding through the doors after them.

"Harrods," said Michael urgently to the cabdriver. Maybe

they'd lose them at Hyde Park Corner. Certainly in Harrods.

He took her hand again once they got there, urging her into the throng of shoppers, then led her through the colourful maze of the foodhalls. In the fish department the dead fish were beautifully laid out, like flowers. The lobsters were so fresh they were still alive. Michael watched one of them blow bubbles and wave a pincer feebly at him. His heart jumped and he pulled her away.

"Listen," he said, "they're here. Who *are* they? How do we lose them?"

"I don't know."

Was she pretending to be so frightened? "All right—take my hand and we'll walk. When I tell you, we'll run."

She stretched out her hand, palm down.

It wouldn't be easy. Maybe they had dressed her up in the white fur just as a marker. They sauntered into the extravagant reaches of Patisserie, then slowly ascended the escalators to the third floor.

Looking down, he saw Viktor and his friend trying to walk unobtrusively up the stairway below them.

There was too little cover. He led her through the piano department. There must have been twenty grand pianos open and grinning, showing their teeth. A sad sack of a sales assistant was sitting at a big Yamaha and suddenly, as they passed, broke into the original score of "Pictures at an Exhibition," turning the stale air into diamonds. Viktor and his friend were pacing them at twenty yards, too close for the dash he had planned. He knew she would run if told to. He knew that now. It was tremendous to know, but he couldn't risk her being punished. He moved his hand to hold the small bones of her wrist between his finger and thumb. He could feel a quick pulse.

From pianos he turned into Harrods' zoo. Poodles the size of dusters were slithering about the floor on exercise. One of them squatted at the girl's feet and let out a tiny pool of urine. Viktor and Co. sidled in behind them.

"Can I help you, sir?" the matronly young assistant asked.

"Yes," Michael said. "I want to buy a snake. Have you got snakes?"

"What particular kind of snake?"

"A mature snake."

They had snakes. They had most people's special fancies in the pet world. The story was you could order an elephant through Harrods and they'd deliver it. Viktor was busy with the poodles. You could imagine he and his friend were two old gays looking for a new dog.

They had a very beautiful snake. It was six feet long and glossy as a new handbag. The assistant was surprised to hear him say he wanted to hold it. But he explained, "I want a snake I can handle." He seemed to know what he was doing.

In fact, Michael French had never touched a snake in his life. It wasn't anything he had particularly thought about. The snake was dry and heavy. The odd thing was feeling it breathing, up and down all those ribs, the way the weight of it seemed to flow from one hand to the other.

He walked straight up to Viktor and hung the snake round his neck like a scarf, double. "It's for my friend," said Michael French. Then pulled the snake tight.

They didn't stop running until they were in Hyde Park. They were like kids out of school. She could hardly run for laughing. Viktor had done a kind of hoppity jump when the snake went mad, and then had hit his head on an aquarium and half the water had slopped out and the other man had slipped and fallen over in it.

She ran well, like a child; her feet seemed to touch the ground more from recognition of the conventions than from necessity. She had stripped off the big white fur and flew it like a flag behind her. Michael kept pace with her until suddenly she stopped, turned to him and wrapped her arms round his head.

"Michael, Michael," she said, as if tasting the name.

They stood on the edge of the Serpentine Lake. It was frozen up. The ducks were waddling about on it in great surprise. He shook his head like a dog shaking off water. There was so much brilliance in the air. Absolutely none of it all could be true. The running, this time, had left the nightmares behind, along with Viktor and Mary and the ICARUS project. Very suddenly, soberly, Michael realised that nothing, *nothing* mattered a fragment against the delight of standing here with her on the edge of a frozen pond. Whatever happened.

"I don't even know your name," he said.

"Kyra," she said. *"Kyra."* She smiled, nodded, as if she were trying to teach him to speak.

"Kyra," he said.

Then Viktor jammed a gun into his ribs. Nobody shook Viktor off. That's why he was in the job.

7

The walk back to the Russian Embassy in Kensington Gardens was leisurely. It had started snowing. There were only a few protestors grouped around the gates of the "London Kremlin," and the big wet flakes of snow were rubbing out their slogans. They were protesting the latest dissident's plight. It was strange how the Cold War had come back like a season after waiting its turn.

The two men had walked like good friends. The girl had gone away with Joe. In the Round Pond, a tiny steamship was bouncing off the ice edges its creators had smashed for it. It looked miserable in its cage.

"Don't make a run for it, will you?" said Viktor politely. "The gun is silenced. And a lot of people just drop dead with heart attacks. It's surprising how few people come to help them, too."

"You wouldn't dare," said Michael. Viktor paused fractionally. "OK, OK," Michael said quickly.

The embassy was very sombre indeed, and baking hot. A flat-footed woman was pushing a trolley around with a big urn on it. Father Lenin was taking up most of the wall space in the foyer. Viktor took Michael a long way into the heart of the building. Very quickly, past a lot of closed doors. At the end of the corridor of royal-blue carpet he knocked at the last door of all

A green light came on above it. Michael was sweating. Had the girl known they would catch up with them? She must have. Inside the room was very little except a huge table and two chairs, on one of which was perched the tiny figure of a man he immediately recognised.

"Michael. Come in. Sit down. Thank you, Viktor."

"There were problems," said Viktor. "You will have to apologise to him."

Professor Yukhim Yeremenko nodded vaguely and waved him away.

As the door closed behind him, Michael said. "Why didn't you just telephone me?"

It was ridiculous. He counted Yukhim Yeremenko almost as a friend. On his last visit to Moscow he had stayed at his dacha. In the small world of fusion research, Yeremenko was the granddaddy of them all.

"Well, these things happen," said Yeremenko. "Neither of us is free anymore. I suppose we all knew it had to come. As soon as we get close to practical solutions, our masters begin to get greedy. But your behaviour is really very shocking, Michael."

"Look," said Michael. "Why have your people gone to all this trouble?"

"We want you to work for us. Why not? You and I know energy research is essential. We *must* do it together!"

"Go to Russia? Live in Russia?" He was astounded.

"Some people say it's a good place to live. In the right company."

Michael shook his head. "But you already know everything about my work. What do you need *me* for? It's all in there." He gestured at the file of his published research neatly stacked in front of the scientist's folded hands.

"But it isn't, is it?" said Yeremenko. "You know and I know that your double Torus wouldn't work for more than a thousandth of a second. Shocking behaviour, Michael. I cannot think of a single instance in the history of science when pure research has been deliberately falsified in order to mislead fellow scientists."

"Deliberately?"

"Of course. You mean you didn't know?" The old man's eyes were alert.

"I didn't know," said Michael.

"Ah," said Yeremenko. "Then that makes things even more difficult. You see, Michael, I had rather thought that behind all this peculiar mathematics you did have the right answers up your sleeve. Do you mean the Cambridge ICARUS is being built exactly on the lines of your figures here?"

"I'm not supposed to discuss it," said Michael.

Yeremenko shrugged. "You didn't falsify this material yourself?"

"Why do you keep using the word 'falsify'? If there are errors in it, they can be mistakes."

The Russian shook his head. "That I can prove to you," he said. "This did not happen by accident. It must be rather unpleasant watching a disaster being built, if that is what is happening at Cardington. I would say, despite your happy family life, that your professional future looks rather dim in Britain."

"I can tell you," said Michael. "Those figures are the only ones we've got. You can make what you like of that. And leave me alone. I mean, if I've no secrets for sale, you won't be trying to buy my soul anymore."

The Russian hesitated. "I'm afraid it won't be so simple," he said. "I have already written a complete refutation of your theory. It only remains to be sent to the Moscow State University *Review of the Physical Sciences* and your career will be in ruins. Meanwhile, my offer remains. Come and live in Russia. With the girl. We will make you rich. We can deposit a very large sum of money in a Swiss bank for you. You will not be a prisoner."

"Why, if the research is all wrong?"

"Because I think there is a way we can put it right. You and I together. It needs us both. As in the old days. And remember, Michael, if what you say is true, someone in this country is cynical enough to tamper with your work—to set you up high just in order to throw you down."

"It couldn't possibly have happened like that. Why would they do that?"

"Perhaps, Michael, in the hope that you would do exactly what I am now proposing to you. That you would come to Russia. After all, now that fusion research is a classified secret again, your people must have realised we would start trying to recruit. I think they imagine that they can send you to us like a disease carrier. That it will set us back years looking up the wrong garden path. If you doubt me, why not go along to your Science Service people and tell them the Russians are interested in making you an offer? I wonder how hard they will try to stop you going."

The two men were silent for a whole minute. "You seem to have aged, Michael. You seem to be unhappy."

"I want to leave now," said Michael.

"Of course," said the old scientist politely. He stood up and pressed the green light button for Viktor. While they waited, Yeremenko said, "You wouldn't have to live in Moscow. We are moving to the shores of the Black Sea. After all, why should we have to find our heavy water in the Baltic?

The Black Sea is a most beautiful part of the world. Very sunny. Think of it as freedom, Michael. A new life. A new start. How many of us wouldn't welcome such an opportunity?"

Viktor followed him out. In the corridor, as Michael nervously lit a cigarette, the platinum lighter was immediately on hand again. He accompanied Michael all the way to the front door. "No hard feelings," said Viktor. "You must think of us as your friends." At the heavy mahogany door they paused. Viktor waited, with just the hint of a smile. *He has eyes like a reptile's,* thought Michael. He knew perfectly well that Viktor was enjoying it.

"Ah yes," said Viktor, as if he had nearly forgotten. "You will be wanting this." From his top pocket where he kept his lighter he pulled another of his little white cards and held it out to Michael, far enough away so that Michael had to reach for it. He felt humiliated, like a kid being teased for sweets.

"Next week," said Viktor. "But we hope you will be in touch before then. All you have to do is ring us and say, 'I want to come home.' Please don't do that unless you mean it, of course."

Michael did not look at the card. He strode angrily out into Kensington Palace Gardens. The snow was beginning to settle; the light was beginning to go. He walked all the way to Notting Hill Gate station before looking at the card. It seemed to be warm in his hand. There was nothing on it but the address: 21a Moreton Terrace Mews, London SW1. And the date: February 20, noon.

He could crumple it and throw it away. He would do that. But what good would that do? He had already memorised the card.

Michael's absence from Cambridge had been noted.

"He's *where?*" demanded John Cox at breakfast. "*London?* He can't be. For Christ's sake. We're meeting contractors on site at ten."

"That's what Mary said. She just phoned. Two eggs, dear?"

It was February 14. Valentine's Day. John Cox heaped a thick overcoat over his shoulders and faced the cold alone. Something was definitely up with Michael French. As he drove to the airship hangar—and it *would* be bloody freezing—an interesting scenario ran a loop through his head. Maybe French was cracking up already. A lot of them did. The ones who were good on theory, but couldn't handle the real-time.

The hangar was no joke on a day like this, that was for sure. By 9:45 the crowd was all around the mobile canteen provided by the Ministry of Defence. It was a good move, that one, thought John Cox. The new project masters were a thoughtful bunch.

Warming himself with a mug of coffee, Cox walked back to the ICARUS. There was no doubt about it, a hell of a lot had been achieved. Sixty days to go and she would run. Above him the roof was so high it was invisible in the morning's fog. The contractors were queuing up for him. He ran an appreciative eye over the most remarkable of them all—the ice maiden, he called her.

Hilary Reynolds, managing director of Freeze Ltd., wore her red hair falling free above a bottle-green suit. Mid-thirties, tough as they come, she was a very beautiful young woman. "I'm the one at the other end of the thermometer," she had said at their first meeting. Her company managed the lowest temperature mankind had yet reached, down to minus 249 degrees centigrade at the last count. Freeze Ltd. was installing the heat transfer system that would tame the colossal furnace in ICARUS's heart.

John Cox decided two things in short order. One, to take Hilary Reynolds to lunch. Two, to call on the Frenches tonight and suggest Michael take a vacation.

In the train back to Cambridge, Michael decided to break his rule and take a drink at the buffet car. Normally he avoided the 5:30 swill in the buffet car out of King's Cross. There was always a gang of cronies elbowing and honking their way home: people who met only in this moving frame, the limbo between work and home. Today he joined them like a wishful conspirator. Today it made sense to him, what they were doing. The gang of drinkers had come out of the cold of the city and in an hour's time would disperse into the cold of the countryside. They could be intimate without obligations beyond the price of a drink. There were men, mostly, and a few career women, who got more sexual badinage than the share they would expect or tolerate in other contexts. It was a mobile world of its own, the buffet car. A small comet, going from unknown origins to unknown destinations. A one-way trip every night. And as it went, it cleaved through the rows of suburban houses whose little yellow-lit kitchen windows winked past.

Michael asked for a double scotch. The barman held up two tiny bottles and poured them with a contemptuous flourish. It was ludicrously expensive. He took the plastic beaker to the window and watched the suburbs flit by.

When the train slowed he could even see people in the kitchens. They had no need to draw the curtains to be private against the passing train. Why, you could stand naked in the window of a house backing onto a railway line and a thousand people. It wouldn't matter: the passengers did not stop, did not know where you were, who you were.

"Sign of a rich man, planning the summer hols in February," said the voice in his ear.

Michael looked up into the glowing red face of Braithwaite, the village disaster.

"Didn't know you tippled here," said Braithwaite. "Get you another." The train flicked through Hatfield station with a clatter of crossed lines that drowned his protest. "Sun, sea, and sex," said Braithwaite, returning with four more small bottles of scotch. "Except I always find the last one's always double booked. May I?"

With a fat hand he swivelled the brochure that Michael had been studying. Michael had picked it up on the way back from Notting Hill. A flush of annoyance burnt his cheeks as Braithwaite put his red thumbs on it.

"Very nice," said Braithwaite. "You *are* branching out."

Michael looked at the upside-down picture on which Braithwaite's veined eyes were stuck. It was a girl in a black bikini splashing water over herself.

"The Black Sea," read Braithwaite. "Where all the world is blue."

"Give me that," said Michael. He pulled the glossy page away from the wretched man.

Braithwaite seemed nonplussed. "All right, old man. All right."

For the rest of the journey, Michael put on his best imitation of good nature. He made a joke about snatching the Balkan Holidays Travel brochure. But he could see that Braithwaite was wary and embarrassed.

When Michael reached home and shut the kitchen door behind him—he always came in around the back not to track mud on the hall carpet—the house seemed strangely quiet. So he was surprised to find Mary and John Cox sitting on each side of the token log fire that Mary lit in the evening to make the central heating less obvious.

Obviously they had been talking and heard his finger on the latch and stopped.

"Well, here's the great man," said John Cox. He did not get out of his chair, Michael's chair.

A half-empty bottle of sherry stood between the two of them, Michael noticed. He smiled and raised both hands to John Cox, shaking them in the air. Michael had a small library of gestures that he had copied from people, either real or seen on TV, which expressed conviviality and good intentions.

"Darling," said Mary French. "You missed the big day. You didn't tell me."

"Big day?" said Michael.

"Now shut up, Mary," said John Cox. "The Old Man knows best."

"Would you like a drink?" asked Mary.

"Thank you. That would be very nice," said Michael.

It was not like coming home. It was like stepping into a dim hotel.

"Went off very well," said John Cox, raising his glass again.

"Why did you go to London?" asked Mary.

"Jolly good," said Michael. "Jolly good. I'm glad it went well."

There was a pause. Mary French looked at her husband carefully. "You *did* know today was the Contractor's View?" she said, accusing Michael, who gave her a big, big smile.

"Darling, I told you so. Last week." He had, and she hadn't cared a damn.

"Mary. Pour your husband a drink and give him his slippers warm from the fire. *Anyway*, Michael. It went well. *Very* interesting. A lot of them are still scared shitless though, despite the new money."

Michael thought, *Why is John Cox sitting in my chair?*

"Why did you go to London?" asked Mary, her big red cheeks aglow.

Michael took the drink and leant back.

"Don't," said Mary.

The narrow wooden chair creaked. But he leant back again. He could feel the four-times-folded brochure on the Black Sea in his pocket against his chest.

"Oh come *on*, Michael. You keep telling the kids not to do it."

But he leant back again, tipping the chair on its back legs. "Went off OK, did it, John?" said Michael, looking at the black beams.

John Cox smiled at Mary. "Terrific. That bird in Cryophysics. Ice maiden. Brrrr! Glad you weren't there."

A child was shouting upstairs.

"They want you to kiss them goodnight," said Mary flatly.

He ignored it, closed his eyes. They didn't want him to kiss them goodnight. They just wanted to prolong the day.

"Oh well, I'll go," said Mary, giving a "that's what it's like" look to Cox.

She left. "What's the matter, old chap?" asked John Cox.

Michael French shut his eyes tighter.

"You OK?"

Michael could hear the other man shift his bum in his chair. *His* chair.

"Look," said John quietly. "Is something wrong? You should have been there, Michael, if you don't mind my saying so. Bit odd, you know. But nothing to worry about. If you're feeling under the weather, I know how it goes. I can cope. I was wondering, in fact, if you'd like a holiday. Can't have you cracking up."

I bet you can, thought Michael.

"Do you want to take a few days off?" asked John. "I mean, if you do, go ahead."

Michael tipped his chair back on four feet. "No thank you, John. It's fine. Thank you. Had to go to Imperial College." It didn't sound convincing.

"Actually, Michael, while Mary's out of the room. Actually, Mary wonders if you're up to something. *You* know."

Michael opened his eyes wide. "I don't. What?"

They could both hear her coming back, down the black wood stairs. Menacing the children to sleep.

"A woman, Michael. Take it from a friend. Mary—"

Mary came in. It was John Cox she smiled at.

As he had expected, the trouble started immediately after they had changed Baby Jane's sheets and gotten in bed. Every night, between twelve and one as a rule, Baby Jane came stomping in, wafting a smell of warm urine, and just stood there. Tonight was Michael's turn. But Jane wanted *Mummy* to do it. "Mummy, Mummy, Mummy!" she bawled, bouncing up and down on her heels.

"Look, why don't you?" Michael begged.

"Because it's not fair," said Mary. "It's your turn."

"I'll gladly do some other chore."

"That's not the point. It's not a chore. It's being a *parent*."

"You know she'll just go on until she wakes Nicholas."

Mary turned angrily to the wall.

He got out of bed and the child followed him in, still bawling.

"Come on, lass. Don't wake up Nicholas." He tried to pat her head.

"No, no, no," she yelled.

Nicholas woke up, roaring.

Afterwards, he waited for Mary to start. She timed it for precisely the moment when he was beginning to dip into the first level of oblivion.

"*Michael*," she said.

Maybe he could pretend to be asleep. He breathed regularly. She would be lying on her back, staring at the black ceiling.

"That photograph you were looking at when I called on your office. Remember? Was that really just an advertisement?"

"Hmmm?"

"If you've got some other woman, I want to know. You've been behaving so—peculiarly."

"Mary, I have not got some other woman. It's time to sleep."

She was silent a minute or so. *Can one really begin life again? How beautiful she was when she ran through the park, like a dancer. Suppose it was John Cox who tampered with the figures. No. He's not bright enough.*

"John Cox thinks you have been behaving strangely, too. It's ever since we got back from holiday."

"John Cox is an expert on 'other women.' I'm not."

"It's different with him. It's just a joke."

Maybe she would stop. *Why not go along to your Science Service people and tell them the Russians are interested in making you an offer? I wonder how hard they will try to stop you going.*

"If you don't like it here, you can piss off," said Mary.

Sometimes in their rows she said things like that, just the
same words she used to say when they were first together and
had rows, before there were children and the sheer weight of
marriage had begun to settle on them.

If she would once, just once, show some tenderness, curl
up to him now.

He turned to her and tried to put an arm under her neck.
She lifted her head stiffly to let him. Then he brought his
other arm up and rested it on her stomach. Her stomach was
quite hard. He moved his hand down her stomach over the
nightdress.

"I've got my period," she said.

"I know."

"Good night."

She turned away. Downstairs the grandfather clock was
lurching from tick to tock. It cleared its throat for the striking
of 2.00 A.M. *Kvu, Kvu.* When he slept, he dreamt they were
swimming together, in deep clear waters that showed their
shadows on the golden sand below.

8

The din of traffic belting up and down the High Street in
Cambridge was shut off when John Cox snapped the sash
window in the conference room down. It was the next

morning. Sunny, 10:00 A.M. The monthly project meeting. A kind of free-for-all that Michael had instituted to sort out problems with everyone present. Usually there was no agenda, no motions proposed and seconded, nothing like that. Just a frank debate between colleagues. Michael favoured a democratic approach.

Today was going to be different. Michael looked around the table. If Henderson and Yeremenko were right, one of these twelve men had done the next thing to murder—you *could* call it professional murder. One of them had deliberately falsified the read-outs to wreck the project and his own personal career.

As they talked, Michael watched them with new eyes. George Latimer was groaning on about the problems of getting sufficient kilowatts onto the Cardington site. It couldn't be George Latimer. He was peripheral. Michael hardly knew him. On the other hand, he had access to central filing. Young Peter May: he was concerned about stockpiling enough solidified deuterium-tritium pellets by the year's end. He grinned at Michael amiably, pushing his mop of yellow hair out of his eyes. Michael smiled back. Peter was his favourite student a few years back. It was impossible it could be Peter. Wasn't it?

Michael found it difficult to concentrate. John Cox? One could imagine Cox wanted Michael's job. Paul Crockford? Sheila Cook? What could anyone possibly hope to gain?

They broke for coffee at 11:00. It was a convention that Michael, in the middle of the table, poured the coffee. In the old days, when he had been driving the team hard, it somehow showed a human touch, restored balance. John Cox, on his right, leant across him to pass the cups down.

What about Derek Sewell? Derek Sewell was an unknown quantity. He had been with them a year, but he was now on the payroll of the Department of Science, direct. Now that the department was funding ICARUS, they wanted their own man aboard. No one was very fond of Sewell, a squat and hairy Welsh Nationalist in his mid-thirties, partly because Sewell's job was to write reports on ICARUS to his masters once a quarter. Michael realised that Sewell, at least in theory, had had access to every aspect of the project. Maybe it would be educational to check out just what computer time had been run from the laboratories last summer. And who ran it. Because whoever had altered the data would have needed to put quite a few hours on the job.

Sewell caught his eye. If they had anything in common it was the disgusting habit of dunking their ginger nut biscuits into their coffee. They were both doing it now. Sewell smiled and winked.

While Cox launched into a report on the way the laser trials were going, Michael worked out his options. He had come here this morning somehow hoping for a sign—at one point in the drive in, he had even gone back to imagining he could just tell them, straight out, that the whole project was rubbish.

But he was damned if he would. He was damned if he'd finish his career and give the bloody saboteurs, whoever they were, the whole thing on a plate. Because that's what would happen. He had done a lot of thinking during the night, with only the lopsided grandfather clock and Mary's snores for company. He guessed Yeremenko meant what he said when he'd promised they could still get the sums right between them. He had begun to guess, around 3:00 A.M., that the sums *had* been right, before the sabotage started. And that whoever had done the damage also knew precisely how to put it right. If Michael simply told them now, this late in the game, the project was headed for ruin, he would without doubt be got rid of. Millions of pounds had gone into the sink already. It would cost millions more to put it right. The British like to have a scapegoat for their disasters. It soothes the taxpayer. With him out of the way, and behind their blessed screen of security, they *would* put it right. Whoever had sabotaged the first job would re-emerge with the right answer. Nothing would be published, nothing revealed. But they would use his data, the stuff they had fouled up, to straighten the thing out.

OK. If he said nothing, what would happen? If Yeremenko carried out his threat, the sky would come down the day the *Soviet Review* published its refutation. And he would be fired. Then the scenario would run as above. Except the cover would be blown.

If Yeremenko didn't carry out his threat, then what? That was a tricky one. The nature of the game was that they could get right up to the day they pressed the button to start the fusion reactor before the disaster would be revealed. But unless the wreckers were simply out for destruction they weren't likely to let that happen. Were they? Too much money would have been spent.

Around 4:00 that morning it had occurred to Michael that accidents could happen. People could get run over, have large objects dropped on their heads. He had seriously tried getting to sleep then.

But the third option followed him into his dreams. The impossible one: to take the Russian offer and go . . .

"Don't you agree, Michael?"

He woke up from his brooding with a jump. "I'm sorry?"

John Cox looked quizzical. "I was *saying,* I think our friends in security may know less than we do about some of the dangers. If we cut our heavy water orders from the usual source and go on buying tritium from the Norwegians—well, the Russians could easily put two and two together. They keep a good eye on Norway."

Michael concentrated. "I don't think we should try to do the security people's job for them. We should be busy enough simply doing our own job. Anyway, I still find it distasteful thinking of ways to dodge the Russians. They've been our colleagues up till now. Most of us have had good relations with them."

But he knew that wasn't the way the others saw it. They relished the new hush-hush; it made them bigger people. That and the fact they were now running their dreams, *his* dreams, for real. That meant money, glory, security. They were dealing in power now, not the drawing board. And power corrupts.

9

On the morning of February 20 he went to see her.

He knew he was taking a risk, even if he didn't know what risk it was. Viktor had said, "We hope to hear from you before then." And Michael had stayed silent. He was risking that they wanted him badly enough to let him see the girl again; that was all he needed.

He took the Victoria Line to Pimlico. Certainly one of London's most secretive corners. Behind every London railway terminus lurks a network of small streets, small hotels. Around Euston, the Irish gateway, they still tend to names like Shamrock and Killarney. In Pimlico, whose white-pillared porticos stand low above the Thames on ancient osier beds, the people are conscious of Europe, and the days of the Golden Arrow boat train.

Moreton Terrace Mews opened off a narrow street between two hotels named Napoleon and Capri. Printed notices declaiming VACANCIES hung from each front door.

He was trembling. Shuddering. It wasn't fear, it was sheer sexual apprehension. The mews was cobbled, very narrow.

Gentrification had reached a lot of Pimlico but not this cul-de-sac. Steel mesh burglar guards shielded the small windows of No. 21a. He hesitated. There was still time to turn around, leave, not get further entangled.

He rang the bell. The man washing the old Ford Zodiac car at the other end of the mews watched him impassively; otherwise the mews was empty. Maybe a curtain twitched in the house next door? Maybe the girl wasn't there. Another of Viktor's bloody jokes. *It's just the sort of house where a man would have a mistress,* he thought. *Well, she isn't my mistress. Yet. No, she won't be, ever. She's not even here.*

Then she opened the door. Obviously she had been taking a shower. Her hair was wet, dripping cool water on his hands as he took her head in them. He loved holding her head, so small, so finely boned. Jesus! She wore only a white towelling robe, loosely knotted. So loosely that as she raised her arms to embrace him the knot dissolved and it was her small naked body he pressed against.

"They let you come," she said. "They let you *come.* I was so afraid."

She was warm from the bath. She smelt good. He held her very close, began patting her dry. They were laughing. "Yes, I'm here," he laughed. It was a secret. *Their* secret. He held her away from him. Her body was very beautiful. But funny as well—such a tiny waist and such wide hips; a delicious joke. He saw her pubic hair was pale blonde. That was a shock on a woman with such dark hair.

"Yes?" she asked. "Yes?" She was scanning his eyes, anxiously.

He didn't know what to say. They were still standing in the narrow hall. She refastened her robe, stretched out her hand, and led him into the house. There were really only two rooms, unless that door wasn't a cupboard door. Plus a tiny kitchen in which two coffee cups stood on the table. A packet of unopened Benson and Hedges cigarettes. Fresh coffee on the stove, which smelt good. All the furniture was new, just unpacked sort of new. He wondered if Viktor had set the whole thing up just for him. Anything was believable. On the single bed was a blue and gold rug, maybe Turkish. He realised she was nervous. He stood awkwardly in her little room, the one with the bed in it.

"The coffee smells good," he said.

She seemed grateful. "Yes," she said. "You would like coffee."

For three minutes he watched her make the coffee. As he took the cup he said, "When's Viktor going to pop up?"

"It's all right," she said. "This time no one will come." She blushed.

"Well," he said. "Tell me. Are they making you do this? What did you mean when you said—"

She raised her hand urgently, signalled him to be quiet.

The bastards. The place was bugged. "—when you said you would love me," he finished. He had been going to say, "when you said we must try to escape."

"I will love you," she said simply. "Are you going to do what they want?"

"They want me to go to Russia. Do you know who I *am?*"

She nodded. "They showed me photographs of you, too." She smiled.

"But you couldn't have fallen in love with *them*," he laughed.

"You have good eyes. You looked sad. If you go to Russia we could be very happy. We would live on the Black Sea. It is very beautiful there. Of course there are very many tourists . . ."

"Yes," he said. She was doing a fine job for the hidden microphone. "Look, why don't you finish your shower?"

They went to the bathroom. She seemed uncertain what was required of her. Slipped out of the robe entirely and waited. Nude. He turned on the shower.

"We can talk here," he said. "The microphone can't pick us up while the water's running."

"Are you sure?" She looked frightened.

"I'm sure. Don't get cold."

"Do you want to make love to me?"

Not with Viktor listening in, was the answer to that. "We've got to talk," he said. "You want to get away from them, don't you?"

She nodded. But she said, "You mustn't tell them. I don't know what they would do to me. Will you go to Russia?"

"Not if I can help it. What did they do to you to get you into this?"

She shivered. He cuddled her. She spoke very softly into his ear, sometimes raising her head to look at him, with a quick movement like a bird's.

"It doesn't matter," she said. "One day I will tell you. I had to do it. But I thought, maybe *he,* the man they are going to send me to—maybe he will want to escape, too. Maybe we can do it together. When I saw your eyes I knew I was right. We *will* love each other. We will fly away from them all. Like birds. Once I am in England, he will help me. But we will have to be very careful. They are terrible people."

"Yes," he said. "I promise you." He did not rightly know what he was promising. But holding this naked stranger was stirring up something deeper than he had ever felt. It looked as if Viktor had been too clever. He really had managed to find two fish who were going to slip through the net. Together. What was he *doing* making promises to this stranger? He took her by the shoulders. Shook her. "Is this true?" he demanded. "Did they tell you to say all this?"

She was wide-eyed. "No," she said. "No." She shrank back into his arms. "Oh good," she whispered. "That *is* good."

He was shaking again. His hand ran down her spine and he cupped each buttock in turn, lifting it. She moved against him, with him.

Jumbles of poetry raced into his head. "My New Found Land." He had never slept with another woman since his marriage. He could never see how people managed the guilt, the fears. Let alone all the complications. It had never been his style. And he had been too busy. But it was all being drowned out now. She was pressing against him, shivering. The water was running to drown out everything. He wanted to make love with her, simple, urgent, here.

He said, "Get dressed. We'll go out. We'll go out and work out what to do. We must *talk*. It's too important."

"I love you," she said, meaning it. *"Please."* She ran her small hands inside his shirt, loosened his belt, slipped her hands down over his loins. *"Please.* Mi–kay–el."

He took her wrists, raised her hands. Pinned them against the wall behind her. It was the only way to stop himself, both of them. "Listen. It's too important. We've got to get it straight. Before they stop us, we have to work out what to do." He turned the shower off. Viktor wouldn't believe a longer bath than this. Down the stairs from the living room a clock chimed 11:00. She listened, as if afraid, counting the notes.

"You have to go now," she said deliberately, "and buy a bottle of wine."

"What?"

"That's what they said," she whispered. "I have to tell you to go and get a bottle of wine. For lunch. You go and come back. Then we have lunch. Really." She laughed. "And I have made lunch. You'll see."

He nodded, wary. "OK. I'll go and get a bottle of wine. Where?"

She stepped into the hall. She said for the benefit of Viktor, "There is an off-licence just around the corner. Perhaps a white wine would be a good idea."

"That *is* a good idea," replied Michael, playing the game. "I always think white wine is best at lunchtime."

The BBC's World Service English for Foreigners couldn't have sounded more convincing.

"I will give you a front door key," she said. "Then you can let yourself in."

"Thank you very much, darling."

"I *do* love you," she said.

"I love you too." He winked at her. Took the key. Let himself out.

Quite jauntily, he set off down the mews. The Ford
Zodiac washer was still hosing away. No one else. Maybe
Viktor was behind one of the chimney pots. French felt
newly alive, very happy. It could have been a warm day; he
was glowing. He felt years younger. He really would do it
after lunch. Despite all the good reasons against it. She was
just too beautiful: there was surely a level above which no
one could reasonably be expected to resist. They would share
a bottle of Gewürztraminer, and eat her lunch, and that
would be that. No doubt. He was going to carry her onto that
Turkish rug and spread those surprisingly well-muscled little
legs apart. They would make love. And he would get her out
of this; that was for sure. Rainbows never struck twice. This
was the golden crock.

In this jumble of thought he walked straight past the off-
licence, then back-threaded his way past a launderette, a
newsagent, a pub. Moreton Street was beginning to wake for
its lunchtime. Stale vapours wafted from the Moreton Arms
pub and the first tune on the juke box for this day was

Don't tell me,
I'm a going.
I'm a going,
Anyway.
Don't tell me,
I'm not staying.
I'm not staying,
Anyway.

A pup Alsacian, the kind British pub owners love, spilled
over the doorstep of the Moreton Arms and jumped on him.
Michael bent to pat him, knock him over, romp. He knew
about dogs. It was quite a village unto itself, this little street.
He could really get fond of it. He supposed that is what men
with mistresses do: they find some little corner of town and
make it all their own. Somewhere it could all begin again,
where everything is fresh and new; the lovers could chat
about their neighbours as if it were the real world.

He found the off-licence. It was full of plastic vine leaves. "I want a bottle of white wine. Gewürztraminer if you have it."

They had it; they had a bottle in the fridge. That was good. They seemed happy people, as if this bottle of wine really mattered. They wrapped it up in brown paper. He felt the cool of the dewy bottle coming through as he carried it back, smiling.

It was quite plain what he was going to do, apart from this afternoon. Somehow the girl had made everything much simpler. He *would* find out just what had been done to the figures. Put it on line. Tell no one. Just put the project all right and then vanish. He had done his bit. Vanish with Kyra. Why not? Why stay stuck in a miserable marriage forever? They would just *go*.

Back at the black front door he rang the bell. There was no answer. Then he remembered he had a key. He put it in the lock and opened the door.

Inside, the narrow hall was empty. Except for a broken plate smashed all across the carpet. He looked at it. *That wasn't there before.* "Kyra?" he called. "Kyra?"

The house sounded dead. He had come back to it feeling as if he were coming home. Now it was a place more foreign than if he had never been here before. Something was wrong. Very wrong. *"Kyra?"* he shouted.

He went into the kitchen. His coffee cup was still standing on the dresser. He suddenly realised his fingerprints were on it. He raced up the stairs to the bathroom. The shower was still dribbling. In the square basin below it was a stain still being washed away. Red paint, maybe? Clothes were scattered across the floor. He picked up a knotted twist; it was a small bra. Dropped it. He began to panic.

There was total mayhem in the living room. The bed had been torn apart. Ripped with a knife, it seemed, the stuffing bled out of the mattress. *"Kyra,"* he moaned. "KYRA!" She didn't reply. The idea hit him that she could be dead; Viktor's final joke. He raced frantically through the little house. Everything was in disorder. Strangest of all, were the dinner dishes, dirty, strewn across the kitchen. A half-empty bottle of wine. French wine. He picked it up, disbelieving. Then realised. He wiped the bottle with a tea towel. But that wouldn't do any good. There were two plates on the table. Pork chop bones and fat congealed on each plate. That hadn't been there before. *Jesus!*

He began wiping the door handles with the tea towel, retreating. It was plain now. The best trick of all. The bastards!

He raced into the street. The Ford Zodiac was gone; the green hose lay neatly coiled, exactly like a green snake. He turned back to the black door, made a jump for it—it closed on him. The click of the door's shutting was final. He hammered on the door. He was damned sure it hadn't blown shut. Someone was *in* there. He knelt down and tried to see through the letter box. He called her name.

The next front door opened and a woman in vivid pink bedroom slippers peered out. A cigarette was stuck between lips painted the same hue as the slippers. "Oh, it's *you*," she said.

"Did you see a girl leave? Did you see anyone come?"

She looked at him with infinite suspicion. "I told you last time," she said. "Any more bloody noise and I get the *police*. Bloody noise."

"What do you mean you told me last time?" he said. But he could guess, he could guess.

"Bloody banging about all night. I told you."

"Did you see the girl go?"

"I'm not spending my time hanging out the window. What you two get up to, that's your affair. But that record player was going all bloody night again. You need to do a day's work for your living like the rest of us."

His coat was in there. That was the best part of the trick. His coat and his wallet stuck in the outside pocket. That really was a bonus for them. He had really walked straight into it. He kicked the door violently. It resisted.

"All right then, that's it," said the woman. "This time it's the police."

He had a handful of loose change in his pocket. To get back to Cambridge he would have to borrow some money. It was bad, losing the wallet to them. And without his coat he was shivering. He went to the pub and took a half of Guinness over to the phone box. They were still playing that song. *I'm a going. I'm a going anyway.* It was a good melody, stupid words. The Guinness, the first drawn off this day, was mostly froth. There were no directories. He had to ring information to get the number of the Russian Embassy.

They made a real meal out of it. His pocketful of change diminished steadily as he pumped coin after coin into the box while they passed him from voice to voice. Ten times he said who he was, whom he wanted to speak to.

The last voice, he was sure, was Viktor's. "Professor Yeremenko is in Moscow. Why do you wish to speak to him?"

"When did he go back to Moscow?"

"Professor Yeremenko has not been in England recently."

"Is that Viktor?"

"I beg your pardon?"

"Is that you, Viktor?"

"Viktor?"

"Do you know someone in the embassy called Viktor? He's the man I've been dealing with. It's important. I've got something important to tell him."

"Viktor?"

He gave up. They weren't going to make it easy. They'd given him his chance. *We hoped to hear from you before then.* He had tried to be clever. What had they done with her? What had they done with that small naked body? When they had come for her they must have worked very fast. Did she blame him for persuading her to talk, under the shower? Maybe they *could* listen in even through the white noise of the running water. He'd only read that trick in a spy thriller, after all. How could they have done it all so fast? Maybe they were there the whole time; maybe the house was bigger than she'd told him. Maybe she was playing the game just the way they wanted. They weren't dumb. It would be the best ruse of all, her pretending she really wanted to escape.

He dialled another number. There was no other option now. Before the thing really got out of control, it was time to come clean and get some help. Professional help. He would look like a real fool, but that couldn't be helped either. He rang the number Science Service had given them at the last briefing. The people you were supposed to be able to talk to. The ones who would sort things out.

The man who answered seemed to hesitate when French identified himself. Then he said, "What sort of trouble, sir? Are you in immediate danger?"

"I don't know. Who am I talking to?"

"Patterson, sir. Where are you speaking from?"

"I'm in a pub. In Pimlico. Look, I think I better come and see you. It's a bit embarrassing. There's a woman involved. I think they are planning something really bad."

"Who's they?"

"I think it is Russian. Definitely."

"Blackmail?"

"It could be that."

"Has this incident just happened?"

"Yes."

"Then get yourself an alibi, fast. Go see someone you know. Come on here at four. You know where we are?"

"Is that the earliest? They might do something before then."

"What sort of thing?"

"I don't know. The girl's been taken away. They left the place in a mess."

"You come along at four and we'll sort it out. Is anyone following you, do you think?"

"I don't know."

"Pimlico. Wait a moment."

Michael could hear pages turning.

"Yes, of course. You know the British Airways terminal?
Go in the main entrance. Take the lift to the third floor. Go
down the corridor on your right and through door 224. That
leads you to the down staircase."

French supposed they had a list of such places. Curious.

On the way out to the Vauxhall Bridge Road and Victoria
he saw a police car, blue lamp blazing, pull into Moreton
Street. Maybe it was just a coincidence. He took the tube to
South Kensington and Imperial College, after going through
the ritual at the airline headquarters as proposed by the SS.
He was sure no one was following. He just hoped Professor
Cranfield was in.

The long walk up the ancient underground passage from
the station to the museums was chilling. Too many footsteps.
He found himself looking around, having to resist a temptation to quicken his pace. It would be good to be inside a
laboratory again, get his back against a familiar wall. He
stepped inside the gloomy entrance of the college with relief.

Duncan Cranfield was a long-time acquaintance. They had
begun in fusion physics together in this place long ago. They
had both put in for the job in Cambridge. But Cranfield had
hitched his wagon to the wrong star; he was on record as
deriding the laser solution. It hadn't, vis-a-vis his career,
been the best of moves.

"So this time you *are* here," said Cranfield.

Michael smelt hostility, tried to put it behind him as
another symptom of galloping paranoia. "I'm sorry?"

"People keep ringing up and asking if you came to see me
last week."

"What people?" asked Michael, his heart icing over.

"God knows. What do we do for the maestro anyway?"

"There were some postgraduate theses done here in the
last few years. One particularly on heat transfer through a
lithium blanket. I wondered if we could borrow your library
copy informally, rather than go through the system. It's the
new security. We can't have a lot of postgraduates knowing
we are reading their stuff and badgering us for jobs." It

wasn't, he realized after he said it, the most tactful thing to say.

"Yes," said Cranfield. "You want to pick the bones off the corpse. That's how it goes."

"I'm sorry," said Michael.

"Oh come on, Michael." Professor Cranfield's reddish eyebrows bunched into a continuous line across his chubby face. "We're understandably in a delicate state of health down here, thanks to you."

"I don't understand."

"You've scooped the jackpot, haven't you? Pressed the winning button. Proceed to Go and collect two hundred million pounds. What you *could* have done, Michael, if you don't mind me spelling it out, is to have spared a thought for the other poor sods labouring at the wrong end of the vineyard. Do you think there's going to be any CSSSA grants coming our way at the next grant review? We've been thrown right overboard, Michael. You get the lot."

"I don't see exactly what I could—"

"What you could have done, Michael, is to have thought your way around it a bit. There are a lot of useful things that have come out of Imperial College even if the ohmic-heating solution *was* the wrong horse. Suppose you had bothered to say to your bosses, 'Now that Cambridge is on top, there's room on our team for X, Y, and Z, whose help will still be invaluable.'"

Michael understood it. Cranfield was looking for a job for himself and his crew. "I'm sorry," said Michael. "I'm sure there *will* be plenty of opportunities if the thing gets moving. Bound to be."

"Oh, *good*. We should keep our eye on the Sunday papers appointments pages? Those of us who don't decide we are on a sinking boat and bale out for America in the meantime. I've built a good team here, Michael. They're feeling a wee bit sore. So am I."

"It didn't occur to me you'd see it like that. This thing took *us* by surprise, remember."

"I'm sure. But you've had time to swallow the champagne. And now you would like us to turn out our drawers and let you mine through the contents for any nuggets that could come in handy."

"I think this is a bit childish, Duncan. I know John Cox is looking into exactly whom we are likely to need."

"That slob," said Cranfield brusquely. "I heard. I heard he has been writing to some old pals in Canada. *Canada*, for Christ's sake!"

"I promise you—" said Michael.

"That would be nice. And there's one other thing. It's not going to be too good a joke if by any chance your ICARUS just blew itself to pieces, is it? I know we have a reputation for cynicism about laser acceleration down here. But if that should happen then we are *all* in the shit, aren't we? It won't be just your lot that goes up the spout. They'll wipe fusion research right off the map and start building bloody great windmills. It will be *proceed directly to jail*."

In the circumstances, it was an especially unpleasant remark.

"We do think you're staking a hell of a lot on a single throw, Michael," Cranfield went on, more reasonably. "I know it looks lovely on paper, but somehow we can't help feeling it looks too good to be true."

Michael decided to change the subject, fast. "Actually the other reason I came to see you is simpler. I lost my wallet over lunch. I wondered if you could possibly lend me a fiver."

Cranfield threw back his head and roared with laughter. "I *like* it," he said. "Two hundred million pounds and he wants to borrow a fiver."

"If it's not convenient," said Michael stiffly.

"No, of course you can. I apologise. You should be more careful where you have lunch." He looked at Michael with one eyebrow raised.

It was 3:00 P.M. Michael stepped uneasily into the street. There was still an hour to kill. A pretty dark-haired girl tourist was sucking a yellow ice cream with enthusiasm in the freezing cold outside the geological museum. *What have the bastards done with her?* came the question automatically like an ice bullet in his gut.

10

At 227 Artillery Mansions, five floors above Victoria Street, Robin Patterson was on his hands and knees under a cheap metal desk. He was looking for the red file on Michael French. Under the desk he was well out of reach of the single yellow 60-watt bulb. It was unlikely the battered file was down here, but Patterson had tried the likely places. He sneezed as his shuffling about raised dust from the ancient Belgian carpet. Cluffy's cigar ash, mostly. Decades of it. A hell of a way to die in the service of one's country, thought Patterson, to be struck down by the cigars Cluffy smoked back in the 1940s. They must have been something hideous even then. Coming out, the rim of the desk caught him on the back of the neck. Hard.

He swore vividly. In the next office, Vera's typewriter stopped hammering. Maybe she knew where the bloody thing was. He went in, still rubbing his head.

You could hardly see Vera's grey mop of hair behind the massive old machine. Its letters were about half an inch high, like the typewriter the Queen's secretary uses when she writes to old age pensioners when they hit their century. Rumour had it Vera cropped her hair with wire cutters. She certainly didn't waste time on the job. Which was a pity, because though she had to be sixty or more, she was still precisely what she had always been, a beautiful woman. The eyes were big, hawkish, and bright blue. She was very small. The other rumour had it that she was Cluffy's mistress in the old days, when the Science Service began. But anything was believable of those distant times.

Patterson was just twenty-seven. Most of the time, like the four other young men, he was on the road. This week was his time in what he and the others called "the Museum." Now that Benson had retired they were all having to do more desk duty.

"Vera," he said. "There was a file, A red file with green ribbons. On Dr. Michael French. It's gone."

Vera liked the young men. She raised a long finger, pointed to the green baize door of Cluffy's own office, then put it back to her lips.

"But French is coming *in*," said Patterson. "Any time now. A *Flüchtling*, Vera. When did we last have one?"

She almost mouthed her reply soundlessly. "Sir told you to stay out."

"God Almighty, Vera! The man was terrified. What am I supposed to say? The SS is asleep between twelve and two? I was just showing initiative." There was a fraction of a second between Patterson's seeing Vera's eyes focus above his left shoulder and the soft fall of a steady hand. Patterson froze.

Aloysius Clough could still move like a bat.

"I wish you wouldn't do that, sir," said Patterson.

The red file appeared under his nose. The dead hand squeezed his shoulder once, then released it. Patterson turned half around and looked into the eyes of the founder of the Science Service.

Aloysius Clough said, "You and I have time for just a few very important words, Patterson." His old bloodhound cheeks were livid. There was a flavour of gin in the air. But it was anger, not alcohol, glazing Cluffy's watery eyes. He directed Patterson into the inner sanctum. Quite rightly, Patterson concluded that this was not going to be the best afternoon of his life.

11

Not many people got to see Aloysius Clough's private room. Supposedly it was full of ancient secrets. The ones that went right back to the war. The ones that, even now, were best left alone. Like Clough himself. According to Hunter, one of the other "young men" (as Vera called them), the only reason Whitehall allowed Clough to keep the SS going was sheer fright that if they closed him down the secrets would start flying out of his cubbyholes like moths.

"Now you stay here," said Clough. He padded out, closing the door behind him.

In the distance, Patterson heard the doorbell ring. The *Flüchtling* had arrived. Patterson looked around him uneasily. Clough ate, slept, and worked in here, his only known activities; he did them indiscriminately and at all hours. There were a lot of chairs. Big old armchairs. Clough used them as filing cabinets when their bottoms gave way, piling papers on them until they slid onto the floor. Even Vera wasn't allowed to clear up in here. There was one picture: a sulky Virgin Mary standing on a greyish cloud. Patterson sat down. He wouldn't want Clough to come back and think he had been prying. But he would have given a lot to have the chance to open some of those files. Like that one on the shelf high up, labelled "Rudolf Hess."

Only once had Clough opened a chink of light into his past, Patterson recalled. Christmas before last, drinks for Vera and the "young men." Dismal occasion. Clough had revealed his ancestor was the Victorian poet who wrote "Say not the Struggle naught availeth," but that he personally thought the poet's best lines were, "Do not adultery commit; advantage rarely comes of it."

Patterson shifted in his uncomfortable chair. How long was he going to be kept in here? They said Clough had been here since 1940. Had moved in at the age of twenty-two when he got the place as a legacy of an uncle who missed the boat at Dunkirk. You could believe anything of the old man. Certainly the story of how he'd refused to move out for the Blitz even after another tenant had plunged to a messy death through a broken stair rail one black night. That was a Vera story.

Of course she *worshipped* him. According to hints from Vera, Clough had practically won the war single-handed by hounding down the first atom spies. Patterson wondered whether that was why Clough was so keen to keep Professor French to himself. It was said that even now, Clough had old scores to settle.

He looked at the ancient bed and began wondering if Vera and Clough . . . Then he tried to think of nothing in particular.

Outside the room, Clough sat Michael French down on the other side of a desk and looked at him with a curious lack of expression. "You are in trouble, Dr. French." It was said as a statement of fact, not of sympathy.

Michael watched, fascinated, as the old man, never taking his eyes off him, raised a large pale hand to begin picking his nose. There was a thicket of grey hairs in Clough's nostrils; he liked pulling them out, one at a time, when concentrating. It was painful, but he seemed to like it.

"Do you want me to start at the beginning?" asked French. He was less confident, having seen Clough. Maybe Henderson was right.

Clough raised his other arm in a one-armed shrug. "We help when we can," he said. "You seem to have left it until very late. Why?"

Michael looked at the sizeable red file to which Clough's hands now returned to rest. The office was very quiet, very dim. In the next room a typewriter was working, slowly. "You mean you know something about this? What do you know?" asked Michael.

Clough's expression changed slightly. Contempt. "The police have gone to your home, Dr. French."

The room was like a tomb. Clough had only a two-bar electric fire wedged into the fireplace. "Why?" Michael demanded. But he knew.

"They came here first. I thought that was very prompt of them. The point is, you'll appreciate, our job is to try to help you people before the police get involved. Once they are . . . well of course we'll do what we can."

Michael said, "You *have* to help. They've set the whole thing up for me. That's the point. Look. I was in that house half an hour. I've never been there before. Kyra asked me to get a bottle of wine—"

Clough quickly opened his file. "Who's Kyra?"

"The girl. The Russian girl."

"Oh no," said Clough, "that isn't the name. And you see she has been missing four days, hasn't she."

"Four *days?* I was there four hours ago."

Clough gave the impression of being embarrassed. "I'm sure the thing to do is talk sensibly and frankly to the police. You're married, aren't you?"

Michael nodded.

"Did your wife know about this lady?"

"Of course not."

Clough's eyes brightened as Michael tumbled neatly into the trap. "You see," said Clough. "You'd be surprised how often these misunderstandings arise. Scientists such as yourself. It's only human. One gets into trouble with a girl so easily, and the idea occurs that a good explanation might be that the Russians invented the whole thing. A genuine misunderstanding, of *course*. By the way, there were some bloodstains upstairs."

"My God."

"So if there is a *sensible* explanation, I shouldn't delay."

"I promise you I was there today, half an hour, never before."

"Well, that isn't how the police see it," said Clough reasonably. "It's not how the neighbours see it, either. You don't seem to be very popular with the neighbours. They certainly recognised you easily enough. From your picture."

"What picture?"

"I forget where the police said she kept it. By the bed, I think."

Suddenly the implications of a police car descending on Mary at home struck Michael. He stood up. "All right," he said. "So *that's* how it's done. And you're the one who's supposed to know how they operate. Or is that the point?"

"I do," said Clough with the palest of smiles. He stood up quite quickly and showed Michael out. "If there's anything we can do. *Do* get in touch," he said meaninglessly.

Michael did not even bother to reply.

When he'd gone, Clough released Patterson, made him sit down while he entered up Professor French's file, in small, neat handwriting. Then he slid it across the desk.

Patterson read it. Then read it again.

"Well?" said Clough.

"As I understand it," said Patterson carefully, "this poor sod is in the shit up to his neck and we are going to push his head under. It must have come as a nice surprise to him. I mean, maybe I don't inspire much confidence, but I was trying. He sounded terrified."

"Of *course*. Now, Patterson. Let me tell you what your job is about."

Michael stopped the car when he got to Royston. He had to find out. It was stupid, just letting them do their worst. He found a telephone box and fed money into it.

"Mary?" She had answered in the end. It had taken ages. But it often did. "It's Michael."

"Michael. Oh good, I'm glad. Listen, if I'm not in when you get—"

"Mary. Er. You're all right, are you?"

"What?"

"Look. I'm nearly home. I'm in Royston. Er. Look, Mary, it's just possible—"

"Michael?"

"Yes?"

"Can't hear you. I said I might go . . ."

"No. Listen. *Please.* I don't know how to say this. The police might call."

"Police! Why?"

"Well, I'll tell you. It's nothing, Mary. Really. But I wanted—"

"Is it the car? I *told* you to tax the car."

"No."

"What do you mean then, the police? Oh shut *up*, Jane, I'm talking to Dadda. Yes, of course he will. He'll kiss you when he comes in."

"Mary?"

"*Yes.* What's this—"

"Mary. I want you to trust me. If they do come. There's a sort of mess."

"I don't—*Jane!* Look, go away, will you?"

"*Mary.*"

"Yes. They are coming here?"

"Do you love me, Mary?"

Pause.

"Michael. I'm sorry, I can't concentrate. The children need their tea."

"Ok."

"Yes. All right? See you soon."

"I'm in trouble."

"Oh *Christ,* Nicholas. Michael. Look, tell me when you come home. All right? He's just taken the skin off his—"

He put the phone down slowly.

Why should there be any police waiting? Maybe it was OK. Maybe it would be a good idea to put a bit of perspective into all this. Take Mary, for example: a good solid woman, his wife. OK, maybe she didn't minister to every need. But there it was—she was his wife. They should be careful before they tried to break up a marriage, these people. Russians. He was driving faster now, through the little roads of the Cambridge hinterland. Going home. His little Honda hummed like a warm bee. The girl was just a picture on a box of chocolates. He had to remember that. She wasn't real. She was something they had dreamt up. She didn't really exist. *Mary* was real. That is what counted. And the kids. This was his life, Michael French's life.

He hadn't been unfaithful. He had wanted to be, but who wouldn't? He had escaped. The kids could be difficult at times, but it was his job to love them. He had done nothing wrong. And now he would really make sure it was going to be all right. With Mary. *Just give me one chance, God. Make it all go away. I'll forget the girl and the rest of it. Just let me have a quiet life.*

Suddenly he stamped on the brake and brought the car to a dead halt. The next moment, he jumped out and stood in the darkness of the February evening. He knew he was underneath Quex Hill, the village of Clothall to his right. A half-moon hung over the empty fields, and Michael French rested his forehead on the roof of his car. The metal was crusted with ice. He looked up at the half-moon; it was stained by grey patches. It was hideous. "Kyra," he whispered into the dusk. "Kyra." To say goodbye. Then he jumped back in and began driving.

He got to his own front gate. It was open. There was no car outside. Good, good. He drove carefully through the entrance and up the drive. Then stopped.

Ahead of him a blue Rover 3500 sprawled fatly across the front door step. It had a domed lamp on top.

The first thing he saw was Mary's face. It was like a raw wound, blotched. Dead flesh, all the muscles slack and hanging. Only the eyes violently alive.

"You *bastard*," hissed Mary French as he came in. Then she screamed it again, loud as she could, louder than he had ever heard her give tongue before. "You BASTARD!"

He was paralysed. She came at him, carrying something in her hands. He looked at fragments of torn paper, fractions of a human face. He recognised what she was holding, destroyed as it was. It was a picture of Kyra. A policeman stood against the kitchen wall. A man in motorcycle gear stood alongside him. Another policeman. It was embarrassing. "Mary—"

Addressing an invisible audience, she said, "I'm all right now. Go on. Ask him your questions."

Michael realised she had sat down so that the two policemen were behind her, one on each side. It made a formidable group. "I—" began Michael.

But the first policeman had started too, "Dr. Michael French?"

"Yes," he said, looking at Mary. She stared at the table.

"I understand you were rather expecting us, sir."

"What?"

"Your wife says you telephoned her to say we might be along."

It occurred to Michael that that had been a mistake to say

the least. "Yes," he said. "I visited a place called the Science Service. They warned me you were on your way. I phoned Mary to stop—"

"To stop what, sir?"

"Look," said Michael. "This is more complicated than you know. I think I am the victim of a plot. I'm a scientist, you know. My work is of interest to the Russians. They—"

"You know this lady, don't you, sir?" said the other policeman. He spread out the fragments of the photograph.

"Yes," said Michael.

Mary gave him a look of pure ferocity.

"But—"

"Daphne Hamilton, aged twenty-two. You have been to her home."

"I don't think she—yes, I went there today. The first time."

"Were you intimate with her, Dr. French?"

"*No*. Look, I told you. It's not like it seems."

"Do you know where this young woman is?"

"*No.*"

"Mrs. French recognises the young lady from pictures she has seen."

"They sent them to me in the post. Mary, I promise you I haven't—"

"I don't believe you," said Mary French. "God, you are a fool, Michael."

Michael began to shout. "Well, come *on!* What am I supposed to have done? Tell me!"

The motorcyclist leant off the wall and came forward. "According to the neighbours, Dr. French, you were a frequent visitor to the house. Miss Hamilton hasn't been seen for four days. Following a complaint by the neighbours and a request from the lady's mother, we effected an entrance this afternoon. The house was in disorder. There appeared to be signs of some kind of fight. The young lady has not been seen since last Saturday. We also found your wallet and a photograph of you by the bedside."

"That's very clever," said Michael.

"I'm sorry," said the policeman.

"OK," said Michael calmly. "The first thing is to ring up the Science Service. Here's the number. They'll tell you I came around to see them this afternoon." He pushed the card towards the motorcyclist, who hesitated. "Go *on*. Just ring the number. That will do for a start."

The policeman stripped off his white gloves and picked up the phone. Michael waited confidently. "Is that 01 692 8195?" asked the policeman. "This is Forster of the Cambridge CID. I am ringing on behalf of Dr. Michael French. He called on you this afternoon, apparently. Is that right?"

There was a long pause. Then the policeman put the phone down, slowly. He said, "They don't seem to have heard of you, Dr. French. They say you never called on them thio aftcrnoon."

From under the stairs the old grandfather clock began coughing its way towards striking the hour. It was very cold. Colder even than Cluffy's office.

"Right," said Michael French, understanding. "What do you plan to do?"

The policeman was quite young. He looked unhappy. "I think we ought to get down to the station and have a statement," he said.

"Mary?" said Michael, looking at her.

She looked back, red in the face.

"Don't you believe me?" Michael asked. "Do you think I have a mistress and I killed her? Do you rcally think that?" But he thought she really did.

She looked at him, very level, very hard, and said, "I am going to divorce you, Michael."

"Where are the kids?" he said.

"They're at John Cox's. They'll look after them."

"And that's it, is it?" he asked, in genuine curiosity. "I mean, you don't really *want* to know. You are not going to help me. You go along with all this."

"You love this woman, don't you!" she cried out fiercely.

He looked down at the fragments of the picture. On one of them was the curve of her upper lip, half a smile, puckered but strong. He looked back at Mary, then at the police. Then he said, "Do you mind if I just go to the loo? Then let's get this statement together."

He stepped out of the room, down the hall, opened and shut the lavatory door, grabbed a coat and went straight on through the kitchen and into the kitchen garden. There was a gap in the hedge beyond the rows of cabbages and he ran straight at it and through. Then there was a ploughed field and he ran all across that, hard and fast, his feet hitting the crests of the furrows. When he guessed they would be getting suspicious he dropped into the ditch and snaked along, up to the gate. He crouched by it, measured the jump, then lifted himself over in a quick fluid movement. Jacks Hill Wood lay ahead. He was hot in his town coat and threw it off, but trailed it after him, knowing it would get even colder later. The A10 lay ahead. He jumped out of the wood onto the roadway and stood in the middle of it, waving his coat as a pair of headlights cannoned towards him. The lorry slewed sideways to avoid hitting him.

"Fucking hell!" shouted its driver, winding the window open to shout more clearly.

"Thanks a lot," said Michael French. "Broken down. Just a ride to Gravely, OK?"

"I could have killed you."

"Thanks a lot," said Michael, climbing in. Five minutes had elapsed since he had left the living room. Michael French the survivor was beginning his career pretty well.

12

It took them some time to find Viktor Karpov, but this time only because they were not being very bright on the embassy switchboard. As usual at this time of the evening, he was sitting in the basement canteen. A half-eaten meal—boiled chicken—had been pushed to one side. A half-empty vodka bottle also. The Russian custom of packing vodka in foil-topped bottles is probably more responsible for that nation's chronic alcoholism than any other factor, since once the bottle is opened there is really nothing to do but empty it. A trifle unsteadily, Karpov got to his feet and took the phone from the wall.

"I want to come home," said the voice.

Karpov sobered up immediately. "The embassy is closed," he said. "If you would like to call at ten in the morning it will be possible to make an appointment."

"No. *Now*," said Michael French. "The police are after me. Where is the girl? I promise you, Viktor, if you've touched her—"

"The embassy is closed," said Karpov. "It opens for business at ten in the morning." He put the phone down. He would really have liked to have been more helpful, but there was always the chance French was being silly and taping the conversation to prove the Russians' involvement. Which wouldn't do at all.

Michael left the telephone box. A policeman was walking slowly towards him. Michael forced himself not to turn his face away. The policeman went straight by. It occurred to Michael, painfully, that he had two pounds in his pocket, no wallet, a bunch of car keys and no car, and nowhere to sleep for the night. It was amazing how completely and conclusively one's little world could fall apart, given a push in the right direction. He returned to the telephone box and dialled the London number of Jim Henderson. If anyone knew how to operate in this strange new landscape he had just entered it would be Jim.

"Good God," said Henderson when he'd heard some of it. "Where *are* you?"

"A crummy little village in the middle of nowhere."

"That's no good. Can you get a bus to a town? I'll drive up and get you."

"I can't ask you to do that."

"I know you didn't. But that's what I'll do."

"I don't want to go to Cambridge. Too many people I know. I can get to Royston, but that's where the police are."

"Are there any pubs where you are now?"

Michael peered through the dirty glass. "The Nag's Head."

"Then tuck yourself in there. *What* did they say you are supposed to have done?"

"Murdered my mistress. I'm afraid I didn't tell you the whole of it, either."

"*Have* you murdered your mistress?"

"Of course not."

"Jesus. What about Mary?"

"She's going to divorce me."

"You poor sod. All right. I'm leaving now."

Michael left the box feeling a good deal cheered. A small

corner of the nightmare had been lifted. But as he sat in the dismal public house, chewing a cheese roll left over from lunchtime, the future began to look gruesome.

It took Henderson an hour and a half to get to him.

"You look in one hell of a mess," he said. "Do you want to get out of here now?"

"Have a drink," said Michael. "I'm really very grateful."

"If you didn't do whatever you are supposed to have done," said Henderson, "you shouldn't be running. That's surely only going to make things worse. Now tell me the *whole* thing."

He started listening. He was a good listener, interrupting only to pick over the bits of the story that made no sense. Especially the question of Aloysius Clough. At the end of it he said, "Supposing you just let me print the whole story?"

Michael shook his head.

"Seriously. Otherwise do you know what I think could happen to you?"

"No."

"You could end up dead."

"I know. But it's the girl, you see. I want her. More than ever, funnily enough."

"She's in it up to her pretty neck. She has to be. You can't think anything else."

"No. She wants out. She's terrified. And even if you're right—"

"Yes?"

"It wouldn't really matter."

"What do you mean?"

"I mean they did a good job. I'm obsessed with her, Jim. They knew how to pick the one and only person."

"There's never a one and only person," said Jim. "You *know* it's a trap. They probably psyched you out for months. Probably had some guy taking pictures of every bird you ever looked at twice in the street. They do that sort of thing, Michael."

"It doesn't make any difference," Michael said flatly.

"Jesus," said Henderson. "Anyway, I'll tell you one thing. The Russians probably just saved your life, for the time being."

"Why?"

"Look. Clough and his friends; you believe me now. Trying to kill Niels Bohr is only a fragment of what that little outfit has done in its time. I can't tell you the rest of it. But it fits. Somehow they threw your research off line. When you've gone to Russia they'll put it back on line. The Reds will go off up the garden path using your phoney figures."

"But Clough couldn't have known I was going to be asked to defect."

"He could have guessed. But I agree. Much more likely you ended up as a nasty accident. ICARUS is under a security wrapper. The Russians have got your research even if they haven't got you. Maybe Clough would have risked just confronting you with the falsification. After all, what would you have done? If Clough had said, 'We know your figures are all wrong. But don't worry, no one need ever know. You mustn't publish any corrections because it's now a top security project. Just do it right and you'll get your pension,' you might have fallen for it, not done anything and taken the blame later."

Michael finished his beer. It made sense. Clough had struck him as the most cold-hearted little bastard he'd ever met.

"On the other hand," said Henderson, "the *Reds* may have put someone in to fuck up the ICARUS project. Clough may think you're on their side already. I mean, in this game you can never be sure. Now what you have to do is this—"

"I know what I am going to do," said Michael. "I'm going to get that girl back."

Henderson sighed. "Seriously, Michael. You can't fight the KGB and people like Clough singlehanded. You've got to leave the question of the girl out of it."

"Why? It's all right, Jim. My marriage, my job, my reputation—damned nearly my sanity for the last half year.

All gone. I've had enough. Now *I'm* going to start some action. Can we get out of here now?"

Henderson drove. He kept an unusually attentive eye on the rear mirror. As the welcome first streetlights of London began, at Mill Hill, he said, "I know people who could help, if you wanted to vanish for a time. Professionals. I think they'd trust me. It's not easy to stay out of sight, you know. These people could fix you up. There's a man called Crispin Bridge who specializes in it. He's what they call a Minder. On the other hand, when you get mixed up with people like him you really are crossing the Rubicon."

Michael was silent. Then he said, "It's no good. I've got an appointment at the embassy tomorrow morning. I'm going to keep it. I'm going to tell them I want to go to Russia. I don't want you getting more involved, Jim. I mean it."

"The damned girl," said Henderson. "Believe me, Michael. It won't—"

"Well, we'll see. Just drop me in town, Jim. Lend me a few quid."

"Look, even if she *is* a maiden in distress, that'll just be *two* funerals. God knows what they are planning for you, Michael. But they could stand her up against a wall and shoot her."

"Too bad," said Michael.

Henderson glanced at him. They were at the first traffic lights outside London. Michael's face was fixed and angry. "OK," said Henderson. "I'll start work on your obituary tomorrow. And promise me, Michael. When you want me, you know where I am. Any time."

Michael laid a hand on his friend's arm and left the car.

13

Four days later, at 6:00 A.M., Michael French checked out of a dim, damp hotel in one of South Wales' least lovely towns, Barry Docks. The night was still intact. It stank of coal smoke, an unusual smell for a resident of clean and windy Cambridge. He had a cheap suitcase in his left hand, and the vaguest notion in his head of the best way to his destination. He presumed the docks themselves would be downhill.

Viktor Karpov had been less than generous concerning the first part of Michael's proposals. Michael had demanded money, enough money to leave Mary and the kids in some comfort. Viktor wasn't having any of it. "People might imagine you had sold yourself to the Russians," he explained. "That wouldn't do at all." It seemed to be one of Viktor's favourite phrases. It also gave chilling support to Henderson's Second Scenario. That it was the Russians who had sold him up the river.

"The girl," said Michael. The second, most important part.

"The girl is just *fine*," said Karpov.

"I'm not going without her. I promise you that."

Viktor nodded. "She will be there."

"She better be, Viktor. No more tricks."

"Look at it this way," said Viktor. "We care about you. We had to give away a perfectly good safe house to persuade you to see where your bread was buttered."

Where did he learn that phrase? Michael wondered. "Were you in there?" he asked coldly.

"The house is maybe a little larger than it seems. Don't worry, Dr. French. You really have made a great impression on the young lady. Sometimes these things work out very happily. A romantic story."

"Just tell me where I have to go," said Michael.

Karpov decided that a certain change had come over Professor French since they had first met. He made a note to enter up his file carefully. Dr. French could, after all, prove a difficult customer, and if anything went wrong it would always be useful for Karpov to be able to say, "I told you so."

Small houses, fast asleep, lined the street around the docks. It was like stepping onto a film set, just closing down, for an old waterfront movie. Here and there the smell of coal mingled with that of red rust and foul water. Here, amazingly at 5:00 in the morning, lights were on, people were working. A crane was moving up and down ancient railroad tracks in the light of twenty yellow lamps. Beyond the crane was the coffin of a dock full of black water. It looked as if fifteen men were busy on the crane lifting a piece of yellow-painted ironwork into a small coaster moored in the dock. Three of them could have carried it between them. The crane screamed gently as its wheels were driven up and down the rusting track. The very earth was black with ancient oil. Here and there, fangs of broken cable stuck out of the earth like dragons' teeth.

His destination was the yacht club; it was lit up. It floated, brand new, like a raft over the murky black. Behind it, half lit by the dock floodlamps, was a huge barbed-wire fence. He read a sign saying KEEP OUT! HOLIDAY CAMP over rolls of the wire.

He climbed into the yacht's centre. Someone was brushing

the floor of the first level. In the Club Room there was definitely still a smell from the night before—old beer and cigarettes. Only this last year had they started opening the club at all in winter; the men liked to come here and drink to the future spring.

And there were always the enthusiasts, like the nature lovers. They stopped for nothing, especially this present lot, the Flat Holme Observation Society. When Michael opened the Club Room door, he didn't expect what he saw. He had come from the other end of England at an ungodly hour, and this place was lit up, waiting for him. And in this chilly concrete room in the Barry Yacht Club it still looked as if something were wrong.

There were about twenty people in the room. Sitting on benches, busy with thermos flasks and packets of sandwiches. Old people; well, none of them under fifty. They all turned to look at him. Old people, somehow with the same expression. Many of them with small iron glasses. Very sweet looking, some of the old women. All looking at him, intently.

One woman got up. She was wearing a strange kind of green dress, very saggy and homespun. Her hair was pinned back in a Quaker bun he hadn't seen since childhood. She came up to him. "You must be Dr. Quist."

He nodded.

"Well, welcome. We can go now."

He looked around the room. Kyra wasn't there. As he opened his mouth, she said, "There are some *very* fine flocks of Arctic terns just arrived, I am told."

The man with the broom was watching them. He shrugged and went on with his sweeping. Loonies, he thought, sailing around at this hour on a cold morning just to look at a lot of birds.

At a gesture from the woman in the homespun dress the rest of the party stood up, chattering quietly. They began climbing into anoraks and dragging on sea boots.

The boat was far down in the dock. One had to climb

down a vertical iron ladder. The old birds seemed to manage it pretty well. It was hard to see into the boat, a converted lifeboat from the look of it. Its diesel engine puttered quietly. There were two people down there. A man smoking a pipe, fiddling with the engine. And a slim figure in a gleaming black wet suit, helmet and goggles. He hesitated on the edge of the ladder.

"Your friend is there," said the woman in his ear. "You must go to the other end of the boat. You must put on a wet suit."

"Where are we going?"

"*We* are going to the nature reserve of Flat Holme, Dr. Quist. In the middle of the Bristol Channel. You and your friend are getting into a rubber dinghy some time before that. You will be picked up by a Russian cargo vessel coming out of the Avonmouth Docks. You must not worry. Everything has been taken care of."

He looked at the girl in the wet suit. It was Kyra. That beautiful, slender form. She glanced up at him and raised a hand in brief greeting. French felt a surge of excitement. Then he began to climb down the ladder.

He had to admit it was a sensible way to leave the country. No messing about with passports. No way even the most enthusiastic coast guard could pick up a rubber dinghy doing a transfer on the dark side of dawn.

The bird watchers took no notice whatsoever as, beyond the harbour, Michael French began the difficult task of climbing into a wet suit. It was obviously a sensible precaution. No one would last long in these icy waters if anything went wrong. He wondered who the old ladies were, and would have been surprised to know the truth. They were a loyal little bunch. People who had pledged their allegiance to the Russian Utopia up to half a lifetime previously. It wasn't necessary to call them out very often. But when they were called they came. Their eyes were flushed with excitement, to know they were still cared for.

Away from the lee of the land, the water was fast-moving and choppy. Michael sat uncomfortably on the anchor chain, smelling the aroma of damp neoprene. He surreptitiously opened his case to remove the knife he had bought in Soho. The first weapon he had ever acquired. Just in case. He slid it into a holster on his left leg. It fit snugly. He looked at the very small rubber dinghy bouncing along in the wake with some disquiet. Kyra had been taken into the diminutive wheelhouse in the middle of the boat. He wanted her.

The night was beginning to lift. A thin rain began falling; one could just make out the hulking grey ghost of the island of Flat Holme ahead. And a pair of lights, one red and one green, moving slowly from left to right. He presumed it was the trawler.

After half an hour the engine was throttled back, and for five queasy minutes the boat rolled uncomfortably in the swell. A dawn wind had come up, blowing offshore. It was not going to be a good trip in the dinghy. Upstream, the red and green lights were coming along almost in line.

From the wheelhouse, the pilot appeared, pushing the girl along by the elbow. He had a blinkered lantern which he kept on Michael's face, maybe by accident. He moved fast and efficiently, pulling in the dinghy painter with one hand, keeping Michael covered with the torch. Kyra was over the side smoothly, catching the small bundle thrown after her.

"Come on," said the pilot, jerking the lamp.

Michael went in clumsily, the dinghy skittering away from beneath him. They seemed in a great hurry to get him in. His suitcase bounced painfully onto his knees. Even as he looked up, the boat was pulling away from the dinghy. The bird watchers were gazing ahead impassively.

As he turned round to face Kyra he heard a click. She was sitting on the edge of the dinghy, and he was looking straight into the barrel of a gun. He was not very surprised, really, when she stripped off her head helmet and revealed quite the ugliest woman's face he had ever seen in his life.

"Nothing stupid, Dr. Quist," she said. The voice sounded like gravel being sluiced across corrugated iron. "I just deliver you. All right?"

He would have recognised the voice anywhere. She had been John Cox's last secretary! There had been a lot of jokes about Cox getting such a ferocious old battleaxe, so unlike his usual style. The story was that she was the wife of a lecturer in Slavonic studies. She lowered the gun a fraction and deftly pulled out the top from a tiny radio transmitter. It began bleeping softly.

"We are in the same boat," said the woman. "You will agree that we have to make the best of it."

The bird watchers were already a hundred yards distant, and vanishing into the mist. There was no outboard motor, Michael had noticed. The two tiny wooden paddles in the bottom of the dinghy might have been of some use on a duck pond.

"Where is Kyra?" he asked. But what did it matter? There would only be more lies.

"I am going to help you in Moscow," said the woman. "You will see."

Very slowly he reached his arm down his leg, as if rubbing a sore place. "No," he said. "I made the deal. No Kyra, no cooperation."

She looked up to the still-distant lights of the Russian boat. "This is a very special way out of the country, Dr. Quist. We can use it only for very important people. Miss Kruschev is coming later."

Suddenly anger began hitting the back of his skull in steady, pulsing waves. This brutish creature ahead of him, tricked out with a slim woman's body under a crabbed grey face furrowed by crow's feet, was maybe the one who had ruined ICARUS. He knew she was frightened. You could tell that by the way she kept looking for the Russian boat, willing it closer. He slid the knife out of its scabbard.

She cocked the gun again. It was not shaking.

"Throw that transmitter overboard," said Michael. "We're not going anywhere."

She risked half a smile. "We float out to sea together? Do you think that is sensible?"

"Do it," he said.

"I think not," she said. She raised the gun. Shaking slightly.

"And what are *your* chances of promotion in the KGB if you shoot me?" asked Michael. He really did want to know. If she had said they would be very good indeed he would have believed her.

"There is nothing you can do," she said tightly. They must have told her it was going to be easy.

"Throw it overboard," said Michael. "Or I put this knife through the bottom of the dinghy." He held the knife, point down, over the floor.

"That would be very stupid," she said.

With a decisive plunge, he brought the knife down. The woman gave a shrill gasp of pure terror as dark water bubbled up around their feet. She came plunging forward, scrabbling, trying to see where the hole was, still waving the gun. As the water surged up he kicked out, catching the gun hand with his left foot, and as he overbalanced and fell back into the water he heard the gun fire.

It was 9:00 in the morning before the Russian dinghy found the transmitter. The rain was lashing down now, straight and mean. Visibility was less than fifty yards. The transmitter was bobbing up and down, still bleeping gently, and they fished it aboard, cursing. Three men on board looked around in the tumbling seas. They were very puzzled, very angry and very wet. There was a great deal of water out there. Fast moving, treacherous, and empty.

"Not a chance in hell," said the biggest of the three men.

From the mother ship came urgent, crackling orders on their own radio. There was no point in staying any longer. Not unless they wanted to attract the curiosity of people ashore. And they didn't.

PART TWO

PART TWO

14

Everyone agreed. John Cox proved a real tower of strength after Michael disappeared. Coped wonderfully with poor Mary French and the kids. Fought off the bloody newspapers and their "Atom scientist in missing girl riddle" stories, too. Cox got the entire team together two days after Michael's disappearance and was very frank about the whole thing.

Afterwards, one or two felt the Team Meeting had been maybe just a trifle callous. But it's a tough world. It wouldn't do at all for anyone to get the idea that just because Michael French was missing, the ICARUS project couldn't go ahead under the rest of the team. Little Susan Hill, one of the laser programmers, was the only one to ask, "If he comes back, and all this sorts itself out, he will still be running it, won't he?"

John Cox shifted easily in Michael's old chair. "We have to be *realistic*," he said. "Time is limited. I think we have to present a very firm picture, with no ifs and buts. Quite apart from anything else, whatever has happened, poor Michael has obviously been under very great personal stress. He'll need to have time to get on an even keel again. Even if—"

"I just don't believe Michael French would ever—"

"Susan. We can all speculate."

Young Peter May, Michael's ex-student, was restless too. "Look," he said. "I think we could still make some sort of collective statement of confidence in Michael. He was a damned good boss. As straight as they come. What we're doing is shuffling him under the carpet. It makes him *look* guilty."

From the filing cabinet behind him, John Cox produced a stack of brown envelopes. "The police asked me to let you see these," he said. "Believe me, they are being as sensitive about this as they can. They appreciate the problems we all have. Have any of you ever seen this girl, anywhere in Cambridge?"

As the photographs of the woman circulated and the scientists turned them over to read the love messages on the back, an embarrassed silence fell on the room. Susan Hill blushed brightly as she was passed the picture of the girl naked on the chair.

"Good looker," said the Welshman Derek Sewell, studying the picture with interest. Peter May twitched it away from him. "Oh, steady," growled Sewell. "I agree with John. We've got a job to do. If poor old French flipped his lid then the sooner we get back to work the better."

But the feeling remained for some in the room that something dirty had been done between them.

"Anyway," said John Cox, "Michael ran this project. He did his part. He did the theory. We have to get on with the nuts and bolts of putting it in action. Remember, we've still got to get ICARUS running on May 1. The ministry's been getting restless about the delays. And quite frankly, now Michael's gone, I want to move things faster. Now I'd like to move on to—"

"Just a moment," said Sewell. Cox looked up at him, surprised. "I don't want to make any problems, but my personal position is a bit different. Aloysius Clough, the Science Service people—I have to keep in touch with them.

You know that. They want to look at the books before they give us the go ahead."

"What on earth do you mean?" said Cox.

Sewell grinned. Once again Cox noticed how hideously discoloured his teeth were. "Well, I suppose," drawled Sewell, "our masters have a certain reluctance about wrapping up millions of pounds in brown paper for a project that has apparently been run by a guy with half his mind on bopping pretty ladies on the head."

Paul Crockford said, "Will you cut that sort of talk *out*, Sewell?"

But Sewell didn't even bother to glance at him. He said, "They want Duncan Cranfield of Imperial College—and Clough and myself to go through the figures. That's all."

"Cranfield?" exclaimed Crockford. "He'd take forever. If Cranfield had the chance to run this project into the ground he'd give his eyeteeth."

"Why didn't you refer this to me?" asked Cox icily.

"Because they wanted to speak to *me*," said Sewell. "Maybe they hadn't appreciated you were now in *total* charge of things up here, John."

"Right," said Cox. "And maybe this shows exactly the sort of thing I mean. If we let this degenerate into a scrapheap where anybody at any time makes arrangements none of the rest know about, they'll pull us to pieces. In future, *if* everyone agrees, *I* will talk to our friends in the ministry and elsewhere. And *I* will keep you informed and ask your help as necessary."

"Hear, Hear," said Crockford.

Sewell's little bid for power seemed to have been cut off smartly at the root. He didn't seem unduly bothered.

They went on to discuss the delivery schedule on the lasers.

15

Early March. Still very cold. Michael had been gone ten days. Mary French was beginning to look quite buoyant again. Good old John Cox was so busy, but he had really pushed hard over the question of Michael's pension and superannuation rights; the sensible thing to do, it turned out, was to get Michael declared redundant for health reasons. What's more, if Michael really did stay vanished, there was a pretty good chance you could get an assumption of death in a year or two, and the insurance on the mortgage would be paid off. John had been very gentle about broaching the subject of assumption of death, but she had taken it on the chin.

At night she lay awake a lot, and when she slept she sometimes woke up to find herself reaching for the empty space alongside her. Quite often she got back to sleep again by doing sums in her head; like counting sheep. On the whole, things would probably work out.

The one thing she liked least was Michael's old clothes hanging up in the wardrobe. The children were surprisingly easy about it all—the boy took it worst; he had gone rather quiet and secretive—but the two children seemed to have stopped fighting. The house was definitely more peaceful.

The weather was clear, bright, and hard. Yellow and blue

crocuses were appearing in the garden. Sometimes Mary felt sentimental and lonely. But a lot of women friends rallied round; she basked in their collusive sympathy. She heard a new batch of tales about how difficult *their* marriages were. When she got really low and angry she got out the picture of that damned girl, which she had stuck together with cellophane tape, and studied it. Bloody little whore.

One day a rag-and-bone man called and asked if there were any old clothes. On an impulse she had let him loot Michael's wardrobe. The man seemed surprised but asked no questions. He flicked small oily hands through the pockets. There was often trouble if you took something away in the pockets. He laid down a small pile of bits of paper: bills from filling stations, the tab from a restaurant dinner she didn't recognise, a letter from Michael's mother. And a big Swiss army penknife, bright red and full of gadgets. Michael had bought it for the summer holiday; it was full of gadgets like saws and tweezers and it must have cost at least twenty pounds. A sign of second childhood, she had joked at the time. Nicholas had come in early from school as the dealer was finishing his task. The boy stood there, saying nothing. Then he picked up the penknife and slipped it into his pocket. She called after him, but he stomped out.

In Cambridge this same afternoon they were also picking over the pieces. John Cox had decided that the small man with watery, bloodhound eyes, called Aloysius Clough, was one of his least favourite people. The feeling was mutual. Even over a very good lunch of lamb in Trumpington, Clough had not warmed at all to John's brand of bluff managerial charm. Cox could put the drink away as well as anyone, but Clough just soaked it up with the emotionality of a sponge. And Cox didn't like the way that whenever he glanced up, he was being looked at speculatively by Clough.

Clough downed his second cup of coffee and said brusquely, "Can we sit in the car and talk?"

Cox summoned the bill. He knew that Clough and his
three friends had been busy. Very busy indeed. He knew
they had been staying in Cambridge at the University Hotel;
that must have cost someone a lot. After a violent behind-
the-scenes effort, Cox had managed to get Professor Cranfield dropped from the investigating team. But he suspected,
rightly, that Clough and his friends were still talking with
Derek Sewell behind his back.

In the car park Aloysius Clough put a briefcase on his lap
but did not open it. He stared straight ahead at the view,
which was a whitewashed brick wall, and said, "Did you ever
know Niels Bohr?"

Cox was surprised. No, he hadn't met the Nobel Prize-
winner, the Norwegian giant of early atomic research.

"I did," said Clough. "What a problem *he* was. I suppose
you know it very nearly became necessary to have him
murdered."

Cox turned to the old man in amazement. "Really?"

"Really. A classic example of the sort of problems you
people have. There he was, under Hitler's wing, with a
heavy-water factory in full production. And he still couldn't
see that what he was doing wasn't Pure Science. He was busy
making an atom bomb for Hitler, and he wouldn't let us stop
him."

Cox remembered. Something about commando raids on
the heavy-water factory, about blowing up a ferryboat with all
the heavy water on board.

"Strange how history repeats itself," said Clough.
"Thanks to the king of Norway, we got him to see sense in
time. It looks as if we were too late with Professor French."

"I don't understand."

"Don't you? Professor French seems to be the last in a long
line of heroes. Perhaps I understand their agonies better than
you, Dr. Cox. You remember the people who gave away atom
secrets in 1945, Klaus Fuchs, so forth?"

"Yes."

"Fine men. Highest motives. Like your friend Michael."

"Colleague really. Not friend," said Cox carefully.

"Well, of course. You and I know how the real world goes on," said Clough with an almost invisible sarcasm. "Are you going to believe me when I tell you Michael French was faking all the latter stages of his research?"

John Cox's head went into double time. "Go on," he said.

"It looks like it," said Clough gently.

"But everything has been printed. It couldn't be wrong."

With two snaps Clough opened his briefcase. It was full of computer print-out. Here and there were rings in red ink. John Cox could recognise that the marginal notes were in Sewell's sprawling hand.

"If you build this thing it will simply blow up," said Clough flatly.

Cox reached across for the printed folds of green paper. Then he reached into the glove compartment and pulled out a sophisticated pocket of calculator.

Clough watched him, maybe with a flicker of amusement on his ravaged face. "It will take more than that, for *you*," he said. "I'm afraid Michael French was really a very clever man."

"You mean he was trying to wreck the project? You mean that's why he has gone? Where is he?"

"Safely in Russia, I imagine. Are you ready to talk practicalities, Dr. Cox?"

"Go on."

"If it were just a question of getting things wrong one of you would have discovered it already. Michael knew the right answers. That's why his mistakes are so convincing. What we have discovered, the last two weeks, is what those right answers are."

"You mean he's gone off to Russia to put them ahead? He thinks we will build this thing and watch it blow up?"

"So we are going to put it right. That young man Sewell. You don't much like him, do you?"

"No. Actually."

"Nevertheless, you are going to have to work with him.

Don't worry. We employ him. We have been right through the whole job. There is still time to put Michael's *correct* solution back into the programme. You will get all the support you can imagine, Dr. Cox. There will be no trouble from Sewell. In two years' time we will allow you to publish a paper showing how you entirely redirected ICARUS and found the correct solution. Michael French is not going to get a posthumous Nobel Prize. That has already been taken care of."

Cox thought about it. The brick wall ahead seemed very solid. "You mean I am going to take the credit for research Michael did? That goes against quite a few of the books."

"You have come into a new world, Dr. Cox. Just as Niels Bohr had to. We are talking about *real* time, real problems. Michael French is a traitor, let us be blunt. You are a very brilliant man. You have taken over this project beautifully. Look on this as an accident of time and chance. See it as helping the country. We *need* the ICARUS project. We need it in going order. We paid Michael French to do the job. Now we are paying you. We'll give you the correct answer that Michael worked out. You carry it through. That is a reasonable request."

Cox thought hard. Then he said, "You're absolutely sure French falsified his own results? And has gone off to Russia with the right ones?"

Aloysius Clough looked at him patiently and snapped the briefcase shut. "We know how things work. Dr. Cox. Believe me, if I had ever met him, I am sure I would have liked Professor French very much. I *admire* idealists." The sarcasm was more evident this time. He went back to staring out of the window.

Cox couldn't imagine what was going on behind those pale, cold eyes. If he had known that Aloysius Clough was thinking about the white, haunted face of Rudolf Hess he wouldn't have known why. "OK," said Cox.

"Good. I'll let you have the papers when we've worked on

them. And don't worry about Derek Sewell stabbing you in the back. He knows what he is up to."

"It's still not ethical," said Cox, "using another man's research. Even if he is a traitor."

"Well, unfortunately, and I've never understood why, it is you scientists who believe an ethical world is possible," said Aloysius Clough in a rare burst of candour.

They drove back to Cambridge without speaking.

16

In the laboratories the three hatchetmen in Aloysius Clough's employ were waiting for his return from lunch. When Clough arrived, they came up in a hurry, almost tugging at his sleeve.

"Do you mind if I have your office a moment?" Clough asked Cox.

Cox shook his head. The collusion had begun.

The four men left Cox and shut his office door. On his desk more computer print-out lay unravelled. One of the young men simply pointed to an entry dated just two days back. Clough studied it impassively. "Yes?" he said.

The young man's finger was shaking. "You know what that is?"

"You tell *me*," said Clough, with one of his half smiles.

"These are the central records of the ICARUS project. Right? Held in the Hewitt-Packard Computer in Texas, right? Do you know what that number is there? That is *Michael French's* private access number to the computer. The number he dials in from any telephone he likes to get access to the computer. And that's what somebody did two days ago. They ordered a full print-out of the entire data store on ICARUS. Why in hell wasn't the number blocked? That guy is still in Britain. Or someone who knows his code and all the supplementaries. They've just picked the whole thing clean."

"Good," said Aloysius Clough. "So what have you done about that?"

"I waited for you to come back." The young man looked nervous.

"*Very* good," said Clough. He laid a hand on the young man's shoulder. "For a dreadful moment I thought you might have taken it on yourself to tell the computer to wipe out Michael French's number."

"You mean it's all right?" said the young man cautiously, beginning to breathe again.

"Well, that *would* have been a mistake, wouldn't it?" said Clough. "We wouldn't want Michael to go away without all the facts at his fingertips. The *wrong* facts."

"I thought he was in Russia. You can't contact the computer from Russia."

"Then his new friends in the Russian Embassy in London must be giving him a hand."

"I asked Hewitt-Packard to check the source of the call," said the young man, "but you know how it works. Anyone with a paid-up terminal can just plug any telephone in the world—except the Iron Curtain countries—straight in. It's probably from a hotel. These things go in an attaché case nowadays."

"So you can find out who has rented a new terminal in the last month?"

"Yes, sir."

"Well then, the main thing is just to keep an eye on what goes in and out of the ICARUS account. I'm a bit rusty on these things, Lewis. I presume whoever has hold of this access can't do anything dramatic like wiping out the record?"

"Oh no, sir."

"Then it should all be quite interesting." It really was like the old days. For Aloysius Clough the good times had definitely returned. He had always liked atomic scientists. Such a devious class of people.

"Oh, there was something else," said Lewis, more confidently. "Phone call from your man Patterson in London. Someone named Henderson after you. A journalist."

Clough shrugged. The name meant nothing.

17

John Cox drove thoughtfully back to Mary French's house. There were some papers she had to sign. He quite enjoyed playing the Good Samaritan. The kids were over at his own place. Mary had said she wanted an afternoon to herself. To be alone. He knew he was imagining it, but he thought she had flushed slightly when she told him, though her big cheeks were often rather red. They had definitely got to know each other much better the last few weeks. He was a shoulder for her to cry on, after all.

He parked the car well inside the front hedge. One didn't want the neighbours getting any wrong ideas. The back door was open; he pushed it and called up. The house was quiet except for the lurching clock.

"Mary?"

She called from upstairs, "I'm up here."

He climbed heavily up the narrow black wood stairs, humming cheerfully. He was a bit surprised to find her lying on the bed flat on her back. She seemed a little doped. He knew the doctor had put her on Valium, but there was a smell of something in the air.

"I'm sorry, John," she said. "Not a good day." She turned her head rigidly, looked at him.

Rather awkwardly, he rubbed his hands on the flanks of his trousers. "That's all right, old thing. Children back at my place?"

"Do you mind if I don't get up?"

"Of course not."

After a moment he sat down on the bed. "You all right?" He put his hand on her forehead. It felt hot.

She moved her head appreciatively under his hand. Went on looking at him. "You've been very good to me, John."

He moved his hand and chucked her under the chin. "You've had a rough time."

"I keep thinking of him and that girl," she said. She went back to staring at the ceiling.

"Well, there it is," said Cox. It was getting dark. The cottage windows framed a single yellow lamp from the nearest neighbour's house, across the lawn, which was hard frozen again.

She raised her chin stiffly. "Would you mind drawing the curtains?" she asked. She watched him as he did so. A little warily, he came back to the bed and sat down again. She stuck out a hand and gripped his. He gave it a little squeeze.

*　　*　　*

The children came back sooner than expected. Cox was in the kitchen just putting the kettle on. Mary was in the process of coming downstairs.

"Hallo young man," said John Cox. "Good day at school?"
Nicholas put his schoolbook on the table, said nothing.

"Hello dear," said John to his wife, who was carrying Jane, who had lost a shoe.

"What's this, then?" asked John, opening the schoolbook. There were a lot of heavily pencilled sketches. After a moment John saw they were several versions of three crosses on a hill. Easter was early this year. The village schools were strong on religion.

"We have been learning all about Judas," said Nicholas, looking at John Cox coolly.

18

"That's right," Henderson said. "Dr. Michael French. He may have called here. If he was in trouble. He told me that's what you people are for."

Robin Patterson glanced at Vera. "I don't think so. I'm sure not," he said. "We're an advisory service, but . . ." Vera gave the smallest, almost invisible sniff.

Henderson looked around the wierd office. Crummy. Very strange. But he'd been in such places before. He knew the crumminess didn't necessarily mean a thing. The young man looked nervous. "Listen, sonny. Do you mind if I am perfectly frank with you?" It was a question designed to get the answer No, as his old Latin master put it.

"Go on," said Patterson.

"Michael French is one of the best people I know. A straight, honest guy. If he came here looking for help, what happened to him?"

"I don't know," said Patterson. "I mean, I don't know what you are talking about."

Henderson gave him a big smile. "Where is Mr. Aloysius Clough?"

"Not here," said Vera, studying her typewriter.

"Then I'll just have to go and write it all up after all," sighed Henderson. "It is spelt C–L–O–U–G–H, isn't it?"

"I think—" began Robin Patterson.

"That's right," said Vera. "C–L–O–U–G–H. Would you like a card?"

He took it gracefully. "Thanks. Tell Mr. Clough, won't you? Tell him Fleet Street leaves no stone unturned."

At the door, as Patterson pressed him out, Henderson said, "I hope it wasn't you who landed Michael in the shit, son."

Patterson stared at him. Once again, it was all Henderson needed. "Think about it," said Henderson. "You've still got time to join the human race."

He was well pleased, in the circumstances. They definitely knew something, that pair.

19

At No. 75 Barrow Point Hill, Pinner, Middlesex, this March evening, the new lodger was obviously making a small meal. He was really no trouble at all; in fact, Mrs. Grainger, sniffing the plastic scent of spaghetti rings from the bottom of the stairs, would have been perfectly happy to make him a *decent* meal. Though she always gave him a good breakfast. You have to give a lodger breakfast, their solicitor had told them, when they had said they wanted to let a room, what with the rates going up and up, because under the Landlord and Tenant Act you just can't get rid of anyone unless it's a bed and breakfast deal. She had put the postcard up in Maynell's window in her best handwriting, a little wobbly because of the arthritis, and the young man had called her the next day.

Well, not so young. About forty. What Mrs. Grainger would call a "fine, sensitive face." A bit sad looking. All he wanted was somewhere quiet and a telephone. The telephone was important. Jim had been a bit doubtful of this, but the lodger had explained it all very carefully and authoritatively, as if he were used to explaining things. He said he would pay the whole telephone bill, and unfolded a bunch of ten-pound notes there and then. The big brown notes were a pretty welcome sight.

The new lodger wasn't a talkative man, not at all. But he met Mrs. Grainger on the stairs the morning after he had moved in and they had had a very good chat about how quiet Barrow Point Hill really was. And Mrs. Grainger had told him they had a real river at the bottom of the garden. The River Pinn. And when her children were young—quite a long time ago, she joked—they used to catch minnows there. The children lived in Australia now, she explained. *All* of them.

"Yes," he said. "That's a long way."

She wondered if he had ever had children. Somehow she guessed so. But of course she didn't ask. You respected people's privacy.

"More telephoning?" she asked sweetly, as he went off upstairs again.

"Afraid so. Do tell me when you need it."

Once she had dared pick the downstairs phone up when she knew he was on it. But all she had heard was a strange chattering noise, kind of dim rattling, a tumbling over itself. It was nice to know a man was upstairs. Since his retirement, Jim spent more and more time just sitting in that shed on his allotment; you'd think he wanted to get away from home, though she couldn't think why. Even though things were more difficult on a fixed pension, she had never nagged, she was sure.

This March evening Michael French did not dial the computer in Texas; he rang Henderson instead. It was time. He had survived three weeks, but the money was going, fast. And pretty soon there'd be a visit from the telephone engineers.

When he had picked himself out of the bottom of the dinghy, he had come face to face with the most horrifying thing he had ever seen in his life. Michael had never seen anyone die violently. Let alone been responsible for such a death. The creature crouching in the dinghy in front of him was black-suited jelly with a face masked by throbbing blood; the gun, when he had kicked it, had fired and shot the creature's throat away. Its death didn't take long. On hands

and knees, the rubber-coated figure subsided, raised a hand
feebly to its neck three desperate times, the eyes going hard,
and lost. He backed away; facedown in the water in the
bottom of the dinghy, it began to wash to and fro. Once, he
tried to raise the corpse out of the reddening water, to try to
turn it over. Inside his own wet suit, he could feel sweat
trickling down to his crotch. "Jesus," he kept saying.
"Jesus." After all, her body had looked like Kyra's. Still did,
upside down.

The dinghy did not sink. Unlike the Russian, he had
known enough about physics to know it wouldn't. Inflation
chambers kept the craft afloat, not the floor. When he looked
up, the twin lights of the cargo boat were coming straight at
him. The transmitter was still in the dead woman's hand. He
took it out easily enough, then threw it as far as he could
upwind. It was not pleasant, picking the tiny oars out of the
purple pool in the bottom of the boat, lifting the dead weight
of the woman to get the right-hand oar out. But he did it, and
he began to paddle hard. In a very few minutes, the dinghy
was out of sight.

In all his musings, Michael had never thought about the
question of operating small rubber dinghies on tidal waters.
He began thinking now. Paddling was quite obviously a way
of keeping warm. But even that was an illusion, he knew,
since he was simply transferring inner body heat to the
surface and losing it in sweat. The wind and the tide were
going to take the dinghy scudding wherever they wanted.

He tried to reconstruct a map of where he was. The tide
had seemed high when they embarked. So it was ebbing.
Also, the wind was pushing southwestward. A damned sight
harder than the tide. There was clearly no future at all in
being swept out to sea. Except in the long-term view.

After half an hour, Michael worked out a crude but
effective mechanical solution: he invented a sea anchor. It
consisted of the woman's body, tied by one leg to the dinghy,
which the corpse slowed and also made less ghoulish. The
water washing through the hole he had made had cleansed

the grey rubber floor. He was still shivering in his wet suit.

The landfall came fifteen hours later, into mud of bottomless depth. He had never been colder in his life. It was dark again. When he put a foot over the edge, his sleek neoprene leg vanished into clinging mud. It took an hour's work to push away with the oar and fumble around the mudbank until he was in still water.

He climbed out, clinging to the first of a row of rotted wooden poles, and was just beginning to feel a firm bottom beneath his feet when he realised his error. The dinghy he had left behind him had a dead body hanging on to it by a short piece of string.

He hooked the suitcase over the jagged point of the pole he had reached and began wading back. The chances were less than even that he could get back to the case again. Wearily he clambered in and paddled out. One hundred yards away, or as near as he could estimate it, he cut the cord. The unseen weight sank without a trace. There was still the bag they had thrown her, a black plastic holdall; he hung it round his neck. Then, in sight of the row of posts, he began slitting the buoyancy hull of the dinghy. It took a long time to go down. First the bow, then the stern where he sat. As it vanished beneath him, he began swimming, clumsily, noisily. But there was no one to hear.

There was just one train through the small town of Highbridge, Somerset, that night. It drifted through the pollarded willow fields at the edge of Sedgemoor and many of the train's inhabitants were asleep. Certainly Angelo Caccia, travelling salesman for the Italian firm of Moto Guzzi was asleep, and never felt his jacket being lifted from the back of his seat or heard its soft fall out of a lavatory window ten miles west of Bristol Temple Meads station, minus its wallet and two hundred pounds sterling. In cash. No doubt about it, Michael French was learning all the time.

20

"Good God!" said Henderson. *"Michael."*

"How are you?" said the voice.

"Fuck that. How are *you?* What happened?"

"Will you help me?"

"You know I will. Where are you?"

"I'll tell you what I want," said the voice. "I've been thinking about it. I'm new to this. I want that bodyguard you were talking about. You know someone like that, you said. Someone really hard. I've got to stay out of sight. But I'm going to need money. I need some help on that."

"Are you all right, Michael? This doesn't sound like you." There was a pause. "You there? What happened?"

The voice said, "I killed someone, Jim. A woman. Not *her.* The Russians think I'm dead."

"Killed someone?" Maybe Michael French really *was* out of orbit. Maybe one would have to think again about all this.

"It's all right, Jim. Don't worry. I'll tell you when I can. Do you know someone who can help?"

"Crispin Bridge was the name."

"Look," said the voice. "I got away from them. I got ashore in a rubber dinghy. I stole money. I have a room in Pinner. I am working on the computer. But they'll catch up with me if I stay here, Jim. Unless I get help they're going to get me."

Henderson digested it, though it was getting beyond him. In particular he couldn't quite recognise the cold, factual voice at the other end of the line. "You want to stay out of sight and sort things out?"

"Yes. Next time I'm going to win."

Henderson thought about it. In a job like his, he knew villains. Most of them had horizons that stopped short about three feet in front of their flat noses and about six feet in front of an early grave. They were a hardworking lot, but like all businessmen they were busy with the next job at hand. Not since the Richardson gang was there anyone to go to with a speculation. Except, maybe, Bridge. If he could find him. "Have you got *any* money?" he asked. "If you haven't, I'll help."

"No. And I don't want you to help. I've got a proposition."

Henderson found himself getting cross. "Look," he said. "Explain it. Bridge doesn't work for charity."

The voice suddenly sounded ironic. "Of course. Offer him a bent computer scientist. Someone who can extract money from a company's bank account by pressing the right buttons on an acoustic coupler."

Henderson frowned. Michael French was definitely different. "OK," he said. "There's a pub called the Londoner. Corner of the West India Dock Road. How about eight o'clock?" He could still show Michael French a few tricks too.

The pub was full of American tourists. They came by the busload. The jellied eels were authentic. Few of the tourists came back for a second helping. In the middle of a cloud of phony East End nostalgia a local girl band bashed out a disco number, shaking large drops of perspiration from their creamy breasts. They were really working at the popular song.

"Don't tell me," the biggest blonde sang. Half the men in the pub looked up. "I'm a going"—she winked all around and waved her hips—"I'm a going. *Anyway.*" The *anyway* was high, like a girl wolf's howling. The audience began clapping. DON'T TELL ME. She crouched down over the mike. Then she backed off as it began an electronic scream: "I'm not staying. I'm not staying. Anyway."

Michael French appeared, apparently out of nowhere, and sat down at the small round iron table at which were his friend Henderson and an old man in front of a full pint of beer.

"Wally," shouted Henderson. "My friend Michael French."

The old man glanced up mildly, then back to the music. He must have been the same age as, say, Aloysius Clough. But had reached his mid-sixties by a different route. A life sentence in Wormwood Scrubs. Wally Bright looked at the cavorting girls with lively appreciation. "How are you, Michael?" he said absently.

Michael nodded. He had lost at least fifteen pounds, thought Henderson. Plus the new beard. He let the old man watch out the song. Whether or not, back in the fifties, Wally Bright had fought off the Chicago Mafia's attempt to move in on the East London waterfront had been often chewed over by Fleet Street journalists. But there was no doubt he still knew all the young people who mattered.

"My friend here wants help," said Henderson, looking at no one once the song was over. "Another pint, Wally?"

"Thank you very much," said Wally. He was a tiny little man. His hair was the biggest part about him. A big salt and pepper bush.

While Henderson was away at the bar, Wally said, "You in trouble?"

"Yes."

"You shouldn't be in trouble. Who's doing it to you?" Wally could tell an amateur a mile off.

"The Russians and the Science Service," said Michael simply.

"Christ," said Wally. "Then you *really* need help." He cast a bright blue eye at Henderson's back. "Between you and me—" he said.

"Yes?"

"He's your pal, isn't he?"

"Yes."

"Thought so. I'd go pretty far for young Henderson. He did a lot for my son, you know."

Michael nodded.

"You want a Minder, he says."

Michael nodded but didn't understand.

Henderson came back, carrying drinks. A bunch of Americans were trying out "Knees Up Mother Brown."

"What you bring me here for?" asked Wally Bright.

"Come on, Wally. You love it. What can you do for our friend?"

"Bloody awful pub," said Wally, and sank his upper lip into the pint. After a moment he said, "Suppose you want somewhere to hide up, too. You haven't killed anyone or anything heavy like that?"

"Yes," said Michael.

"Give me an honest man," said Wally, "any time."

The rest of the round of pints went down in silence.

It was 9:00 in the evening of a cold March night. At 75 Barrow Point Hill, Mrs. Grainger was just watching Angela Rippon give a resumé of the news when there was a ring at the bell. Though it was early for Jim to be back, she got up as fast as the arthritis would allow and went to the door, because Jim was really spending far too much time at the pub since his retirement, for his health apart from anything else. But there were two men at the door with small plastic-covered cards in their hands.

*　　*　　*

"Just a minute," said Wally. He got up and walked steadily away.

"He's a great character," said Henderson. "One of the real people. Ex-docker of course."

"Thanks," said Michael. He looked at Henderson and smiled. "Really, I mean it. Thanks."

"What happened to you?" asked Henderson urgently. "I've seen that look before, you know. On people who have been at war. Don't lose the hang of it, Michael."

Michael went on looking at him.

"What happened to the girl?" asked Henderson.

"I don't know. Yet. That's on the agenda, too."

Wally was coming back. "He'll be here in half an hour," he announced. "You're a lucky man, Michael. Cris is one of the best."

In precisely half an hour the door swung open. The man had arrived. He stopped just inside and ran his eyes over the entire pub, very fast, before coming further. Then he came straight up to the table and laid a big hand on Wally's brush of hair. "Nice to see you, Wally. You look good enough to shave with." His eyes were on Michael French now, unblinking, very steady. Extremely blue, attentive eyes, with a lot of cold weather behind them. Something like the kind of look Michael French was beginning to get back from his mirror in the mornings. Michael returned the gaze.

"You seen that man over at the fag machine before?" asked Crispin Bridge.

Michael waited, then turned. "No."

"Well, he's trailing *somebody*."

"I took good care," said Michael.

Bridge smiled. It was funny how people were convinced they could get around without being followed. "Let's hope so. I hear you need looking after."

"It may be more than that."

"What do you mean?"

"There are some other people who need looking after, too. Is it all right to talk here?" Michael asked.

"What have we got to talk about?" asked Bridge. He was impressing Michael so far. The face looked rock hard, a soldier's face. The blond hair was expensively cut. Obviously a good brain and fast reflexes behind those chill eyes. "What are you into?" said Bridge.

"Yes," said Michael. "Well, I'll tell you. We have one month to smash up a top-secret scientific project. We have to sell a major atomic secret to the Russians. We have to get a girl out of Russia in return and I have to not get killed by the British Secret Service and/or the KGB in the meantime. Especially as I've just killed a Russian agent."

Bridge looked at him very carefully indeed. "Then we definitely don't talk here," he said.

"Michael—" began Henderson. "You can't mean all that."

"I mean it. Oh, and there's one other thing. We don't have the secret to sell. Yet. That's going to cost about one hundred thousand pounds in computer time."

"And of course we have to steal a computer?" asked Bridge.

"No. I've got that. Here, take a look. In the gents'."

Michael passed him the small black attaché case. Bridge took it to the lavatory, locked the door, and opened the case. As he clicked it open the neat little visual display screen slid up. There was a keyboard. And two cup-shaped cavities. He shut it and returned to the table.

"You put any telephone handset in those two holes and dial a number in Texas. With the right code number and the right answers to a few questions."

"That's neat," said Bridge. "OK. You have the right kind of toys. By the way, I'm expensive. Very."

"Then we'll also have to find a way of getting some money together."

"You haven't got any *money?*"

"About ten pounds."

Wally looked upset. "Christ," he said.

"That's all right, Wally." Bridge looked at Michael French with some respect. "Just out of interest, how do you think you can find a way of getting fifty thousand pounds? Or would you like me to rob a bank?"

"No," said French. He patted the attaché case. "We ring up the Cambridge University Central Accounts office and they send us a cheque."

Bridge nodded.

"I'm not sure I heard any of that," said Henderson.

"Who are *you*?" asked Bridge.

"Henderson. Journalist. Friend of Professor French. And I've heard of *you*," he added.

"Journalist? You be damn sure you didn't hear any of it. Wally. You *are* a crazy buffer, aren't you, Wally? This guy is the original mad scientist. Come on, Professor. We are going to have a think about all this."

"Keep in touch," said Henderson. "I went round to that Science Service place. I hope I put the fear of God in them."

"This something to do with his problems?" asked Bridge, standing up. "Don't you do a thing until you're asked to. All right?"

"Where are we going?" asked Michael, standing up too. "It may not be safe to go back where I've come from."

"You bet it isn't!" said Bridge. "You're not safe to take a pee by yourself from the sound of it. Even with me around. I hope you're not planning on a long life, Professor."

Crispin Bridge, ex-SAS, Belfast. Ex-long distance truck driver on the Middle East route. Ex-consultant to the Dirty Tricks department of the Northwest Aerospace Corporation. Not quite ex-consultant, for the monthly cheque from Hector Rose still arrived promptly. There was only one word for that money: blackmail. Or maybe it would sound nicer to say it was Hector Rose's penalty for a very ugly affair that had gone seriously wrong.

The scars on Bridge's hands, collected in that last wild

escape over a perimeter fence constructed out of a million razor blades, had healed up. It had been one of many interesting things learnt on that assignment, that barbed tape was a damned sight nastier than barbed wire. There was still some stiffening of the fingers which diligent practice at the Royal Kensington Small Arms Society was putting right. The other scars were inside; Bridge had been lying low a whole year, waiting for *them* to heal up.

There had been plenty of offers of employment. Some of them would have been OK a few years back. But at thirty-four, Bridge was getting wary. The bunch of mercenaries who wanted to get him to Rhodesia—six years ago it would have been attractive. But all he saw now was kids with big muscles and small brains who were obviously going to get themselves killed in almost no time at all. As for the villains who occasionally propositioned him to take part in the usual jobs—the bank robberies and general mayhem of East and South East London—well, they were dedicated pilgrims in search of a long, long jail sentence. As for the hit jobs on offer from the Middle East—no expense spared and very efficient support services—this was where Bridge had changed most, inside. Since his encounter with the French plane makers of Super-Céleste, killing had somehow changed for him. A psychiatrist could have explained it to him: at twenty-five, Bridge had been classifiable as a psychopath, if cold-blooded killing for cash is a sign of psychopathy; sometimes this curious medical condition burns itself out as the years go by. Certainly Bridge hadn't been making plans to kill anyone for at *least* a year.

Michael French intrigued him. It was interesting to deal with a man who was supposed to be brilliant. Way back in Bridge's head were memories of a run-down slum school where half the kids could scarcely speak English; he had got out at the age of sixteen, much to the general relief of the staff. Since then his life had furnished its own kind of specialised education, but Bridge had often wondered what the real thing was like.

He drove Michael French back home. Grinned privately as
he saw the wary eye his guest cast on the jungle he unloaded
him into. A private, icy whirlwind was chasing its way around
the foot of the high-rise block; it went straight up forever.
Michael knew he was on the south side of the river; further
than that, he was lost.

"Don't hang about," said Bridge. "They drop things from
the windows."

There was not a living soul in sight. Solid concrete though
it was, the building looked somehow as if it had been in a
war. Everything breakable had been broken; everything
uprootable had been uprooted. The lift was open and lined
with steel, but even this had been dented as if by frenzied
hammer blows. Also, it was not working.

"All right," said Bridge equably. "Keep fit time." He led
the way to the steps, which smelt gruesome. "Twenty-
second floor," Bridge. "You'll be OK up there. You can die of
old age up there and no one will bother you."

The stairs were sprinkled with debris all the way up. A
charred mattress on the fifteenth floor was still smoking. The
only person they passed was a young woman with a white
face, climbing down. There was no sign of recognition. The
woman hastened her steps when the two men had gone by.

When they got to it, Bridge's apartment was impressive.
By day there must have been a fine view. The rooms were
clean, masculine. Michael noticed a huge deep-freeze, a neat
stack of *Soldier of Fortune* magazines, a collection of extremely damaging-looking knives displayed on the wall.
There was no sign of a woman's presence. It was the kind of
place you could camp out in, comfortably, indefinitely. It was
totally impersonal.

Bridge showed him a small room with an iron bed and
three khaki blankets. Then he began making a meal.
Michael was surprised to watch him: he was making
omelettes, and he was doing it with an unfussy professional
skill. With herbs, too.

They ate. There was no small talk. Michael started

apologising for throwing the whole story that way at Bridge in the pub. He wanted to say how much a relief it was. Bridge cut him short. "Tomorrow," he said. "After you've robbed your bank." He looked at Michael with amusement. *"That* I have to watch," said Bridge.

Michael nodded. Obviously the deal was professional. No money, no service.

So they chatted about the block of flats. Bridge didn't seem to have much time for his neighbours, his landlords, the planners. He spoke about the place in a detached way as if he were a visitor from another planet. Bridge couldn't understand the fellow residents of the Inigo Jones Tower. They seemed to go out of their way to make life even more uncomfortable for themselves than necessary, what with wrecking the lifts, tearing out the light bulbs, mugging each other on the stairwells.

Michael French was beginning to get the picture. Bridge was a loner. A professional survivor. It looked a good combination.

21

He awoke early. As usual, he thought first about his kids. That was always the worst pang. Then about Kyra. Where she might be, if she were still alive. Then about Mary. He hurried to get up. Otherwise the whole bag of misery and troubles would spill out. Some days in Pinner he hadn't been able to get out of bed at all, when it seemed particularly hopeless.

Bridge was on a small balcony, stripped to his underpants and doing a complicated routine of exercises. The view *was* extraordinary. A great empty space, the size of a small town, lay underfoot. Beyond it, rising clear and sunlit, was the fretwork skyline of the City of London. "Surrey Docks," said Bridge, pointing down, "once upon a time. Until they all went on strike for about twenty-five years. I don't eat breakfast. Help yourself."

Michael made coffee. Bridge waited while he drank it, studying the brochure for Volvo trucks that had come through the post. He'd had his own once. It earnt him four thousand pounds each trip, until it ran off the road in the middle of Turkey one night, thanks to a rearrangement of road signs by a particularly vicious bunch of bandits. "OK, Maestro?" he said when Michael had finished, not looking up. It was bankrobbing time.

"We have to open a Building Society account," Michael said.

Bridge looked wary. "Is this going to be a long job?" he asked.

"No. Come on."

They climbed down the stairs and drove to the nearest shopping centre. Opening the account took three minutes and a five-pound note. No identification was required. It was just a question of giving a fictitious name and address and collecting a book and a number. Then they went back to the flat.

Michael dialled information and obtained the number of the University of Cambridge Central Accounts Office. Then he rang them and identified himself as from the accounts department of Imperial Chemical Industries, asking for details of recent invoices from that company. There were quite a few. He needed to check them, he said, because some things had gone astray in the ICI systems recently. ICI

did a lot of business with the university. He noted down a list
of dates and figures, then stopped the girl.

"March 18. Fifty-nine thousand pounds, ninepence.
That's the one. What's the number there? The invoice
number. And what's our account reference number—was that
on the new system or the old one?

The girl didn't know anything about new systems and old
ones. She just read off the account number and the invoice
number and was glad to get off the phone.

Next, Michael got out his little attaché case and dialled the
university computer. Bridge watched, fascinated, as the little
print-out screen chatted with questions and figures. The job
went wrong once and the screen went dead. But Michael just
began again.

"Can they check this back to this number?" Bridge asked
quietly.

Michael laughed. "No one's listening in. We can play at
this all day. We are talking to an idiot, remember. There you
are." He removed the telephone handset and closed up the
case. "What do you mean?"

"You're fifty-nine thousand pounds richer. Plus ninepence."

Bridge stared at him.

"Look," said Michael. "The university owes ICI fifty
thousand, right? It pays out when someone punches in the
accredited account number and the invoice number. Now
what we have told the computer to do is to cancel this
particular transaction as soon as it gets fed in. You often have
to scrub an entry out if you punch it up wrong. Then we've
told it to pay out exactly the same amount of money against
that account number and reference number to the Building
Society we've just been to see. At the end of the day the
books are going to balance, because there's an invoice for
fifty-nine thousand and a payment against it. The cheque
gets written automatically. Even if someone is looking at the
people the cheques are paid to, no one is going to worry

about a Building Society. The university is always investing in Building Societies. As soon as the cheque is cleared through the bank, the bank advises the university and someone punches in the good news. The second they do that, the computer wipes out the record of the entire deal and reinstates the original record as a payment to ICI. Of course they find out eventually. But that just leads them to a false name in a Building Society account which you cleared out long ago."

Bridge just went on looking at him. Then he said, "How the hell did you get all that together?"

Michael looked pleased. "We were sitting around talking about it one day with some people on the Accounts side at Cambridge. They were maybe a bit indiscreet."

"You've just lifted fifty-nine thousand pounds? Just like that? People go out risking their necks and waving guns about for that money. You mean you just ring them *up?* You needn't have got out of *bed*."

"Well," smiled Michael, "in America they fiddled one hundred million dollars with a computer one time. A racket called Equity Funding."

Bridge nodded appreciatively. "I like you, French. You and I could do well. Why don't we just forget the Reds and the atom secrets and concentrate on making some money?"

Michael was pleased. He felt he had passed some initiation test. "Do you want to wait for the cheque to come through?"

"That's OK. I'll believe it. Now we'd better have a long talk, Professor French. We're in business. Tell me what we're supposed to be doing."

It took five days. Some of them Michael French worked seventeen hours. Bridge had to admire his tenacity. Michael sat, hunched in front of the television screen, scribbling the figures that poured onto it via the acoustic coupler. He covered the floor with papers, occasionally shouting absentmindedly at Bridge to share some new triumph or setback.

On day three it occurred to Bridge to ask, "You sure nobody else can listen to all this stuff?"

"I hope so," said Michael. "Because that's the only reason I'm doing it."

In Cambridge, Derek Sewell looked up in horror as his own terminal display came to life. He had left it on alert for Michael French's access code. Every day it stayed mute he had breathed a little easier, felt safer in the conviction that French was by now in Russia or dead. Preferably both. Because an unpleasant fantasy kept occurring to Sewell. That French might, appallingly, reappear one dark night in an alley and take violent personal revenge.

It had been bad enough when French was still around. There had been extraordinary risks—removing the entire research record from the computer bit by bit, erasing memory segments, replacing them with the false information. And though Clough had provided him with a backup team to do the spadework, only Sewell was sufficiently equipped in fusion physics to take the brunt of it. *Operation Penelope*, Clough had termed it: unpicking by night the tapestry woven each day.

Now Sewell was looking at the visual display on his computer terminal and digesting the hideous news it brought. Michael French was neither in Russia nor dead. He was alive and well and talking to the computer. What the hell was he *doing?* Sewell watched, mesmerised. He knew he was supposed to inform Clough, immediately. But he couldn't tear himself away. After two and one-half minutes, Sewell suddenly realised exactly what the hell Michael French was doing. He felt the sweat prickle on his scalp.

Now he *had* to tell Clough. Urgently. So they could terminate French's access code at once, before he got any further. Because what was going on was the worst imaginable eventuality of all. Somewhere out there French had homed in on exactly that part of the research memory that had first been falsified, probing it like a dentist's drill. He was *reworking* it. Which meant he knew that the thing was wrong and was trying to put it right.

Still Sewell hesitated. He could see that French was going to have a long, hard time of it. Obviously, from the hesitancy of the progress he was working alone and probably without a written print-out facility. Sewell began thinking, hard. Michael French, Clough had told him, was on the payroll of the KGB, was planning to defect. Clough had appealed to Sewell's patriotism. He had also deleted Sewell's sizeable bank overdraft. OK. So now French *hadn't* gone to Moscow. Why? Because presumably he and his damned masters knew all about Operation Penelope. Probably the Russians had told him, We're not buying damaged goods. You get it right, then you can come over. If Sewell cut Michael's access off, Michael would stay right here in Britain, with nothing to lose and a powerful grudge against Sewell to settle. If, on the other hand, Michael was just left to get on with it, well, the Russians would get a fusion reactor. Personally, Sewell didn't mind too much about that.

And then there was the other good reason. Sewell was clever. But not as clever as he had hoped. He had been confident, talking to Clough, that he had the brains to get the research back on track. But recently he had had some hideous doubts. He watched the display panel with increasing fascination as the unseen operator started picking at the heart of the matter: the mathematics of what went where when those pellets were hit by twelve lasers and their outer atoms started imploding at two million miles a second. Sewell had a burning curiosity to know if Michael would come up with the same answers he had provided to John Cox.

He left the terminal running. Put on his coat, locked the door behind him. It was a No Access office. It was safe enough. He said to his secretary, "I think I've got a bout of flu coming on. Don't let anyone in there." He stayed away five days. On the fifth, he was telephoned as usual by

Clough. The little man had been on to him morning and night. Sewell had detected a growing scepticism in his unemotional voice.

This time Clough came over the line like frozen fog. "I am in your office, Sewell. Get here."

With a sinking heart, Sewell trudged back for his day of reckoning. Clough was sitting at Sewell's desk, a huge pile of print-out in front of him.

"Did you know about this?" he asked. Two of his experts stood behind him looking at Sewell sharply.

"What is it?" said Sewell.

"Michael French," said Clough. "He seems to have been busy."

"Busy?"

Clough's hands trembled in anger as he slapped at the pile of paper. "It was essential to stop him doing this," said Clough. *Essential.* I just hope, Sewell, you were being incompetent." He cut off the scientist's protests. "Just look at it, will you?" he demanded. "Go on. I'll give you half an hour. I want to know if he's put the thing right. If he has, and we don't find him, we've just given the whole damned thing to them on a plate. You get into that and then tell me. Do those calculations fit with yours?"

They waited while he studied it.

Eventually Sewell looked up and said, "Yes. I'm afraid so. That's exactly the alignment of the lasers I'm going for."

Clough stared at him a long time. "You *are sure* of that, Sewell, aren't you?"

"Yes!" Sewell lied.

22

On the twenty-second floor of the Indigo Jones Tower, Michael's TV screen went blank. With a whoop of triumph, Michael shouted out to Bridge, "They've bought it! I've got them. They just shut off my access."

"You mean we've finished with all that?"

"Finished."

"We can tidy this damned mess up?" Bridge gestured at the chaos on the floor.

"Sure."

"And what *exactly* have you done?"

"I've told my dear colleagues in Cambridge how to build a fusion reactor. Now all they need to do is screw it together."

"I thought you said they had messed your work up."

"Yes."

"Now you've told them how to do it."

"That's right."

Something about Michael's elation disquieted Bridge. "Tell me," he said. "What actually happens if you build one of these things and some crazy scientist has made the wrong calculations?"

Michael smiled, a can of beer from the fridge in his hand.

He was relaxing. He collected a drop of moisture from the condensation on the can and transferred it to a plate. Then he put another drop on his fingertip. "Look," he said. Very gently he brought his finger to the plate. The drop of water on it shook, swelled, as the water on his finger joined it. "That's fusion. First there were two drops. Now there's one. *Now* look." This time he shook the water from his finger, and the drop on the plate shattered at the impact. "If you hit it too fast, the thing breaks up. In atomic terms you get a shower of subatomic particles. It's called scattering. It makes holes in your lithium blanket. And you get quite a lot of fallout to worry about."

"People get killed?"

"Don't worry," said Michael. "We'll let them know in good time. It's up to them, isn't it? Come on. Now let's sell it to the Russians."

"It's a hell of a lot of trouble to go to for the sake of a girl," said Bridge. He gestured at the blank screen. "Also, you just lost a good reason for staying alive. They wiped you out on the magic box. Now they'll terminate the rest of you. If they find you."

"That's your department," said Michael brusquely. "Come on. Ring up the Russians."

Viktor Karpov, until the horror story in the Bristol Channel, had been a rising employee of the *Glavnoye Razvedyvatelnoye Upravleniye,* or GRU. Now, however, he had fallen on hard times: he was demoted to the thankless task of salesman for LADA motor cars in southeast London. Few people had so decisively blotted their copy book. The KGB, which has been trying to stand on the GRU since 1925, made a big case out of Viktor's disasters. A romantic, they called him. Viktor had cost Russia not only Michael French but also Lydia Khovanskaya. Plus an expensive safe house in Pimlico.

Plus one of the best potential "swallows" in the last few years, Kyra Kruschev. Viktor was kept in Britain only in case someone, one day, rang him up.

Which was what Bridge now did. Viktor got the call routed to him just as he was explaining to an unhappy customer why his new LADA, built on licence from Fiat, was making funny noises.

"That's handy," said the voice on the phone. "There's a swimming pool just near you. In Laurie Grove. Cubicle 20, three o'clock."

"You want to buy a car?" said Viktor. He had lost track of things lately.

"I don't want to buy a car, Viktor. I want to talk about Michael French."

Suddenly Viktor's world lit up. He forgot all about the recent troubles. He thrust his left hand in his pocket and felt the platinum cigarette lighter. He wished Joe Asimov could see him now. But they'd sent Joe to Mozambique. "I don't know what you are talking about," Viktor said, affecting disinterest.

"Oh dear," said Bridge. "One of *those*, are you? Never mind. Cubicle 20. Bring a swimsuit."

Viktor Karpov waited until the telephone was dead. Then he re-dialled. Straight to the top. He identified himself with measured dignity. He could tell the voice recognised him; it was cool. "I have direct contact with Michael French," said Karpov. "As I said when we last met, this is an ongoing operation."

"He is alive?"

"I never doubted it," said Karpov unctuously. "Obviously, things are more complicated than they may first appear."

"He has talked to you?"

Karpov took a sensible risk. "Not yet. I don't take undue risks, Colonel."

"So what do you want?" The voice was hard.

"I want my number back. I know what I am doing,

Colonel. I just want a little bit of trust, a little bit of cooperation."

It was a smug and buoyant Viktor Karpov who took himself to the ancient Victorian swimming bath in London's New Cross area that afternoon. He had liked the sound of the man on the phone. A *professional*, you could tell. Viktor planned on writing a full report. He would show the bastards. They had assumed he had just managed to lose a damn scientist out of a rubber dinghy. He would tell them that wasn't the way things went; there was a lot more to it. The British Secret Service weren't so stupid. Karpov began working out his plan in his head. His report would began:

> While, plainly, my original recruitment plan for Michael French was satisfactory, in that we got him on board, I personally never underestimated the degree of problems involved, particularly following the loss of Kyra Kruschev, for which I was not responsible. Nevertheless, given the necessary confidence it is reasonable for a senior GRU officer to expect, there should be no problems in handling the next stage. Naturally, I will . . .

Viktor Karpov stepped inside the marbled door of the swimming bath. The place was shrill with children's screaming. Karpov queued patiently, sniffing the fetid warmth of chlorine nostalgically. Just like home. He bought a ticket.

"You got a towel?"

He hadn't. With a flourish, he hired a towel for 25p and tucked the harsh cotton roll under his left arm. There were two minutes to go till 3:00.

Cubicle 20 was empty except for a pair of canvas sneakers neatly laid on the simple wooden slat that served as a seat. Karpov smiled. He liked the old-style intricacy of the way the

British did this sort of thing. He pulled the plastic curtain over the top half of the stable door of the cubicle and began undressing. He took off his orange and black underpants and reversed them. British underwear was one of the things every GRU man learnt to appreciate. Very stylish. They would serve as swimming gear on the Black Sea any day. Viktor folded his socks neatly and laid them inside his shoes next to the canvas sneakers.

He straightened up as the shadow came in behind him. A big young man entered. "Very punctual," said Karpov. He smoothed his hands over his belly. The young man pulled the plastic curtain behind him and bolted the door. Then, very expertly, very painfully, the young man hit Karpov in his kidneys, twice.

The Russian doubled up with a soundless howl of agony. When he came up, gasping, his eyes were misted with pain and disappointment. This thug could *not* be a professional. Professionals never did this sort of thing. It was one of the rules of the game. If people went around hitting each other it only made an already difficult job more uncomfortable. Besides, it hurt like hell. "What was *that* for?" He decided the young man had the hardest blue eyes he had ever seen.

"You've been upsetting Professor French," said Bridge. "He doesn't like it. *I* don't like it."

"Have you got him?" You never knew. They could have found him floating somewhere. The British had a funny sense of humour. Only last year they had sold the GRU one of their most valuable agents, having forgotten to mention the man was dead.

"You're lucky he's such a nice guy or you would be dead already."

"Be reasonable," said Karpov. "We did everything correctly."

"Then where was the bird? He wasn't asking much, was he? You don't seem to know how to do business, Viktor."

"Of course the girl was on the boat," said Viktor.

Bridge hit him again. This time Karpov slid all the way down the wall and sat there on the wet floor moaning.

"My *kidneys*," he exclaimed.

"Sorry. You planning to donate them? Next time I'll hit you somewhere else. Of course she wasn't on the boat. If you got *her* on the boat you could have got *him* on the boat without the splashing about. Now, when do we do this thing properly? I'm trying to educate you, Viktor. Or would you prefer I dealt directly with your boss?"

The plastic curtain twitched away behind them. A small man with a bristling moustache that scarcely came over the top of the half-door glared in. Bath attendant Prewitt didn't miss much, certainly not two men going into the same cubicle. Disgusting. "Come on," he barked. "Out!"

"My friend has had a heart attack," said Bridge. "Get an ambulance."

"No, *no*," moaned Karpov.

Prewitt looked at the grey heap on the floor, then went off, running and blowing his whistle.

"*Please*," said Karpov, trying to rise. "I promise you. The girl's back in Russia. She was getting difficult."

Bridge stirred Karpov with his foot. "Then you and Orlov better think of how to get her out again," he said quietly. "Or my friend is going straight back to Cambridge to mend his fusion reactor and sell his memoirs to the *News of the World*. I read *The Times* myself. The personal column. Every day. I've a girlfriend called Daphne."

People were crowding around the door. They had brought a stretcher.

"*I am all right!*" Karpov shouted. He still looked grey.

Bridge picked up the Russian's clothes. "He's an epileptic, too," he informed the four young bath attendants. "You might have to tie him down. Don't worry, Viktor, I'll bring your clothes on afterwards. It'll be all right."

As the soothing injection slid into his vein in the ambulance, Karpov closed his eyes and stifled a sob. It looked as if he had been wrong about the young Englishman, who would by now, Karpov was quite sure, be well on his way to Karpov's new and humble apartment to turn the place upside down.

23

Alone in her kitchen this March afternoon, Mary French was making bread. Steadily, powerfully, her broad reddish hands pounded the dough. She worked off a lot of aggression hitting bread. Today had been one of the bad days. She had burnt the picture of that damned girl long ago. But then there had been the others. She hadn't stopped pestering John Cox until he showed them to her. And she had made herself thoroughly miserable one whole afternoon just sitting and looking at them. She had stared at those slim arms and imagined them wrapped around Michael. She thought of Michael and tried to imagine him dead. Then she thought of that stupid half hour she and John had made love. Life was *not* simple.

The front doorbell rang. She shouted at Nicholas to get it. Her hands were heavy with dough. The kids were watching TV. She shouted again.

Last night had been a bad one. A bad dream had come on like a green fog. It kept coming down in her waking hours.

Like now. She was a diver working on an oil rig in the North
Sea. Deep down. Suddenly the girders of the rig began
melting, falling all over her. She was trapped in the girders,
which were wrapping themselves around her like the legs of
an iron octopus. They were greenish yellow in a pea-soup
sea. And then there was the girl. Naked as a fish, laughing,
swimming dextrously in and out of the cold girders. Laughing
at Mary as she tried to escape.

The doorbell rang again. She shouted angrily for Nicholas
to go. At least he could do *that*. He was old enough to answer
the door.

The girl had a knife. She could cut Mary free from the
girders if she wanted. But she didn't want to. She just circled
Mary like a beautiful fish. Every time Mary cried for help a
bubble came out of her mouth with the word HELP in it, as
in a cartoon strip. And the naked girl swam up and, laughing,
knifed the bubble until finally there was no more air to
breathe.

Mary had woken up choking and screaming. Jane was in
the bed too; she had started coming in each night, into
Daddy's old place. Nicholas never woke up.

"What's the matter, Mummy?" Jane was standing in front
of her now.

"The door. Just tell Nicholas to open it, will you?"

Then Nicholas came in. Sucking his thumb, as usual,
clutching his small blanket. He looked at his mother without
expression. "Lady," he said. "To see Daddy."

Mary began wiping the dough from her hands. "Hmmmm?"
she said.

The small boy's eyes were cool. *"That* lady," he said. He
pulled his thumb out of his mouth with a pop. He looked,
thought Mary, about a thousand years old.

Still wiping her hands, she went to the front door. Nicholas
hadn't learnt the front door slammed shut if it was left to
itself. She opened it, smiling. A Mrs. Gardiner had lately
been making the rounds to buy some old clothes for the
church jumble sale.

Out on the step was the slim, shivering figure of Kyra Kruschev. Mary met the dark eyes of the girl in the nightmare and breathed in with a gasp. She was as beautiful—more so—than the pictures, in spite of the bruise across her left cheek and the way her mouth turned down with fatigue.

"Is this where Michael French lives?" asked the girl.

Mary looked at her, the white face above the shapeless brown coat. She was still looking at her, dumbfounded, when Nicholas, age six, took the girl's hand and brought her in over the doorstep. "She is cold, Mummy," he said.

Mary wiped her hands down her skirt, rubbing them until she could feel the dough crumbling away from the skin. "Nicholas," she said, "I want you to go and watch television. I want you to be a good boy and stay in that room and don't come out."

He left. Mary folded her arms and waited. Then she said, "How *dare* you?"

"I'm sorry," said the girl. "I wanted to say goodbye to him. I know what he must think. He's all right, isn't he? I went to look for where he would work, but it is a big town." She seemed bedraggled, not even very clean.

"You *should* be sorry," said Mary. "You little *whore.*" She liked the old-fashioned word.

"Is he here?" asked the girl. She gazed at Mary with mild confusion.

"He's left *you* then now, has he? Love in a cottage is cinders, ashes, dust, is it? Well it is in *this* one. He's not here. Where do you want him sent to? It's too late for him to come truffling back *here* for a bed. Got it?"

The girl looked at the angry middle-aged woman as if it were hard for her to focus. Mary wondered how she could have got here. Walked? Six miles? The idea of such devotion was an insult in itself. Somehow she kept seeing the pale-faced girl naked. She shuddered.

"*Please,*" said the girl. "I know what you must think. You don't know. Neither does he."

The living room door opened. A blast of Disneyland came out. "Jane wants her tea," said Nicholas, looking at the two women.

The girl turned to look at him, then apparently lost her footing on the red tiles and fell into a chair. She sat there, legs apart, her dark hair lying wetly across her forehead, eyes closed.

"I'll get your tea, darling. Now you just go back and do as I told you."

"Is the lady all right?"

"No," said Mary. "I don't think she is very well. Don't worry."

When he had gone again, Mary was perplexed. The girl was leaning her head against the wing of the chair. Her face was pale as moonlight.

"Please," she said. "When is he coming back?"

Suddenly Mary understood. "So when did you see him last?" she asked.

The girl raised her head. But she looked wary.

"Well, just a moment," said Mary. "I am going to ring the police, Daphne. I think that is the best thing to do, don't you? You got the two of you into all this and you've now got *your* problems and—I'm sure this hasn't crossed your mind— I have mine. Like getting tea for my children. All right? You sit there and we will get all this done properly. I'm sorry if I sound unsympathetic, but I'm a bit old for lovelorn young women."

Mary got up for the telephone. Then she saw the girl was weeping, in great shuddering sobs but quite silently, into the wing of the chair. She couldn't be more than eighteen. She began murmuring in a strange language. "What?"

The girl turned her head away from her and drew up her knees until she was curled up on the chair.

"Oh come on," said Mary. "We'll all survive. Michael and I wouldn't have lasted much longer, probably. What was that you said?"

But she was silent. So silent Mary became alarmed. Puzzled, too.

"What language was that?" said Mary. She put the phone down and came closer to the girl. Curled up like that, she looked as if she could have been her own daughter, Mary thought with a sad pang. She saw the way Michael used to cuddle his daughter. He never cuddled *her*. She remembered a row when he had mysteriously said, "You are not the same *shape*." She put out her big hand and touched the girl's thin shoulder. Touching the same flesh Michael had touched. Mary drew her hand back, then patted the girl's shoulder. That was one of Michael's gestures to her, the comradely pat. "Come on," said Mary. "I'll make you a cup of tea. Let's sort it out with the police."

"The British police?"

"The British police? Of course!"

The girl nodded. "I never wanted to hurt him," she said.

Mary picked up the phone. "Oh, we never do, any of us, do we? When we get into these things."

Mary did not dial the police. She dialled the number Aloysius Clough had given her to call if by any chance she got contact from her husband. She counted the girl as a contact.

Clough was attentive. "Can she hear you?" he asked.

"Yes."

"Can you keep her there until I come?"

"I think so."

"You must. If you have to, lock her up. Are you sure she is alone?"

"No. I think so."

"I will be there in forty minutes."

He threw the phone down and ran down the hotel corridor to the room of Patterson's, who was watching television and yawning.

"The girl's at Mary French's place. Get the car. *Now*."

*　　*　　*

As Patterson urged the car through the last of the Cambridge rush hour, Clough said, "Now you see why we hung around."

"What's she doing?"

"I don't know. Fortunately, Mary French doesn't either. Yet. Let's hope they keep the conversation on a simple hysterical level. Between a wronged wife and a mistress."

"But what *can* she be doing, sir?"

"Looking for French on her own account. Looking for French on the Russian account. Telling Mary French her husband is dead. Telling Mary French her husband is in Russia. One of those things." The words were dry as pebbles far beyond the highest tide.

Patterson sifted through them, peering into the black lanes while Clough barked road directions.

"You think the Russians have lost him?" said Patterson. "Then where is he? Why hasn't he come back? Why's he working the computer on his own account?"

"It makes one more damned good reason to find him," said Clough.

In the cottage, the two women and the two children were sitting around the kitchen table drinking tea and eating homemade bread. There was no conversation. The children, puzzled and subdued, kept their noses down. The family cat pushed through its hatch in the door, made its way unerringly to Kyra, and jumped on her lap. The girl sat, head bowed, stroking the cat. Mary watched the sensuous flow of her hand over the animal's head and averted her eyes.

The sound of a car on the drive brought the tension to an end just before it reached the snapping point. The two men entered quietly, eyebrows raised. It was like calling in the doctor, thought Mary.

"Is it all right?" asked Clough.

"She's in there. Children! upstairs in the bedroom. Go on. I'll come up in a moment."

Kyra was sitting alone in the kitchen. She turned her head around to see the men come in. She looked very afraid.

Mary hesitated. There was a finality about the moment. She knew somehow she would not see the girl again. And that, when she went through it, another last link with Michael would be broken. She said, "I can't forgive you. Or him. Tell him that."

Suddenly the girl raised her chin and coloured. "You don't understand *any* of it. You're as bad as the rest of them. They *used* us. Like a game. You don't *want* to know what happened! You never—"

"That will do," said Clough drily.

"If you'd loved him better he wouldn't *be* in this trouble."

"That will *do*. Mrs. French, would you?"

But Mary was storming forward, hands on her hips. "You tell me about loving my husband? You have a bloody cheek. *My* husband!"

"Patterson," said Clough crisply. "I want this stopped. Now. Get Mrs. French upstairs. *Go.*"

When the door shut, Clough sat down at the other end of the table. The girl's condition interested him. She looked as if she had been on the run for some time. "Who sent you here?" he asked.

"No one."

"Who knows you are here?"

"No one."

"You mean you made a run for it? When?"

"Three weeks ago. I knew what they were doing."

"But *surely*. You could be in Russia with him now."

"He is not in Russia. They lost him. They said he was dead. I do not believe them."

"Why do you believe them when they say he is not in Russia?"

"They meant it. They were very angry. They were hurting me for days. They heard us talking when he came to the house. They thought we had planned something together."

"What kind of thing?"

"To get away from them. Together."

"Why would you do that?"

She looked at him with curiosity. "Because I love him."

"Oh, I *see*," said Clough. He smiled. That was clever of them, he thought. To get them *both* in it. "And what do you want to do now?" he asked.

"I want to stay in England. I want political asylum."

Clough put his fingertips together. "Did you have any rank in the GRU? Let me give you a bit of advice. It will help with my colleagues. They're much more likely to let you in if they think you can tell them things. You know—names, addresses. How do you feel about that?"

"You mean they might not let me in? They *must*. They could kill me in Russia. You must let me stay. I would die there."

"Don't worry," said Clough. "I will do everything I can. But you must be very honest with me. What did you do before they got you involved in this?"

"I was a student, at the Kirov."

"You mean the ballet? You are a dancer?"

"Yes."

He nodded. It was one of the usual cases. They picked up these poor kids from the backwoods. Offered them the world. Took them to Leningrad and promised them a place in the ballet school. Then began explaining the conditions. Like servicing some overweight KGB colonel.

Clough stood up. He opened the door and called for Patterson. "I'll come up," he warned. "Take the young lady to the car." He turned back to the girl, who was tense with anxiety. "Don't worry," said Clough. "Everything is going to be all right."

The two men passed on the stairs. Clough whispered, "They *have* lost him, I think. Promise her everything she wants." He paused at the bedroom door and knocked.

"Come in," Mary said. The trio were sitting on the bed, the children sucking their thumbs.

"Where are you taking the lady?" asked Nicholas suspiciously.

"Home," said Clough. "She is not a very *well* lady. Thank you for looking after her."

"She's the one my daddy went off with, isn't she?" pursued Nicholas.

"No," said Clough.

"Go and watch television," said Mary.

The children left. Clough closed the door behind them.

"This must have been very upsetting for you, Mrs. French."

She did not look at him.

"Did she tell you some wild stories?"

"No. I didn't give her much chance." She looked up. "Perhaps I should have." She looked uneasily at Clough. She didn't like this pallid little man. She wasn't quite sure why. "Tell me," she said. "She murmured something—in a foreign language. I think it was Russian."

"Yes?"

"My husband was trying to say something about being in trouble with the Russians. Is there something in this I don't know about? Is *she* Russian? I need to know."

Clough sat down on the bed beside her. "Tell *me*, Mrs. French. Did you love your husband very much?"

She hesitated.

"I don't want to *pry*."

"No," she said. "It wasn't a very good marriage. He was a romantic. I'm afraid I'm not."

"Then perhaps that will make it easier to explain," said Clough. "Mrs. French. I expect you know—we have tried to make things easier for you. I mean in questions about your husband's pension rights. I'm afraid there is rather more to all this than we wanted to tell you. For your sake, for your children's sake. I now want to tell you something. I am going to ask you to keep a secret for the rest of your life. Again, because of the pension and all the kind of trouble this sort of thing can bring: the publicity, the gossip. Sometimes ugly gossip which can be aimed at a perfectly innocent wife."

"For God's sake," she said. "What are you telling me?"

"Your husband was involved in espionage. For much of his adult life. He was a brilliant scientist. But as you say, a romantic. I cannot tell you much more. As you can see, things came to a head. This girl, his mistress, was his contact."

"He's gone to Russia?" she asked calmly. She was quite cold all over. Quite unemotional. As if she were a million miles away. So he hadn't just betrayed *her*. But *everyone*. Friends, colleagues. All those secrets behind those grey eyes, when she had thought he was just absentmindedly daydreaming.

"Whether he went or not we are not sure. But I am afraid he was not a very professional spy. Not the sort you read about. He left it too late, you see. He had nothing left to sell. And in these circumstances the Russians are even harsher than we can be ourselves. I am afraid you will never hear of and from your husband again."

"Yes," she said. "Yes. Does John Cox know this?"

"*No one* knows this except us. No one must ever know this."

"I'll keep my secrets too, then," she said. "It won't be easy to live with."

He patted her hand and stood up. His hand was as cold as hers. "Goodbye, Mrs. French. Keep in touch."

He stepped into the night, peering for the car. It was a black night. Under a cloud base thousands of feet thick, hiding the moon and the stars from the dark side of the planet.

Patterson and the girl were sitting in the back seat.

"I'll drive," said Clough.

"OK."

"Where are we going?" asked Kyra.

"Don't worry," said Clough. "I told you, we are going to look after you now."

24

It took Karpov a lot of time and trouble to free himself from the British National Health Service. It was now 8:00 in the evening. In the Russian Embassy the central heating was always high; in winter, the heat brought the bluebottle flies into fruition. They buzzed noisily up and down the inner panes of the double glazing and presumably made a fat living from the embassy caviare, which was never cleared away until the morning after a reception.

Colonel Boris Orlov watched two flies chasing each other up and down a window. He pulled out his cigarette lighter. Behind him, he knew, Viktor Karpov was watching attentively and uncomfortably on the edge of his upright chair.

Karpov looked unhappy and ill. Orlov had had to smile at the unusual sight of his subordinate limping in, wearing a cheap, bulging suit which looked as if it had been dragged from a peg in an East End department store. Which it so recently had. He was aware that Viktor liked to ape his boss's expensive style and mannerisms even down to the platinum cigarette lighter. Hero worship from a man of such an age was irritating to him.

There was a brief hiss as the cigarette lighter stabbed two

inches of flame up the windowpane. The flame shrivelled the wings off one of the flies without killing it.

Orlov watched with interest as it fell onto its back on the sill and kicked its legs feebly in the air. He did the same to the other fly. He left them; they would die sometime in the night. He would check that the sluttish cleaner had swept them up. "And you say this man was not British Intelligence?" he asked Karpov. "Just because he knocked you about? Sometimes I feel like knocking you about myself, Karpov."

"I'm sure. I don't see why you are *insulting* me, Colonel," he whined. "If you let me handle this thing I am sure we get Professor French back. If you recall, I personally said at the time he couldn't simply have fallen into the sea."

"You said that in a feeble attempt to cover up the fact that you had made a monumental mess of the operation. I believe you suggested he was being *shadowed*—by a submarine!"

Karpov decided to let that go. "Anyway. This time we will get him. He's still desperate for the girl. And I have a contact point through *The Times* personal column."

"How nice. The British should make an interesting proposition. I expect they will ask for the entire KGB operational staff to queue up on Primrose Hill to meet him. Signed Michael French. You had no right even to talk to your butch boyfriend without referring it to me!" he bellowed.

"I was in a damned swimming bath. How could I talk to you?"

Orlov sat down and poured himself a vodka. Reluctantly, he offered Karpov the bottle. The man's eyes had been protruding with lust for it. "Thank you, Colonel. That's better."

"So once again you promised him the girl. And once again the usual slight problem."

"What is that, Colonel?"

Orlov hit the desk with both hands. "Because you lost the girl too, didn't you! You stupid Ukrainian pig! What do you propose to do about *that?* Advertise for her in your bloody *Times?*"

The phone rang. Orlov swept it up and barked, "Yes?" Then he said, "Indeed. Yes," and returned the phone. He considered Karpov for a few moments. "We have a visitor," he said. "Mr. Aloysius Clough. You still think your friends have nothing to do with the British Intelligence?"

"Clough? Here?" said Karpov. "I'd better go."

"Why?"

"But, Colonel. I am on *Operations.*" It was all right for Colonel Orlov to entertain visiting Secret Service chiefs in his office; they knew who he was and he knew who they were. But everyone else flew away.

"I don't think that matters anymore," said Orlov.

"What do you mean?"

"I mean you are going home next week anyway, Karpov. I meant to tell you. So it really won't matter if my friend Aloysius sees your beautiful face—does it?"

Karpov took it badly. He liked Britain. He was comfy here. He had a big fat Polish woman who cooked for him and kept his bed warm.

"Do come in, Mr. Clough," said Orlov as a silvery little man came in, two big attendants at each shoulder. "Let me introduce Viktor Karpov. He sells motor cars." The vodka bottle circulated again. "Now," said Orlov. "You first."

"We want Professor French back," said Clough. "No hard feelings. It was a good idea, but it went wrong."

"We all have our problems," said Orlov with a glance at Karpov.

"If you *don't* give him back," said Clough, "there will be unpleasantness. I can tell you. He hasn't anything for you. The ICARUS project is just a pile of wastepaper. We faked the whole programme just for your benefit. I can prove it to you."

"We know *that,*" said Orlov. "But our scientific friends have a naive confidence Michael French can unscramble it all

for us. Anyway, as you know, we don't have him. *You* do.
And if this is some curious new way to whet our appetites for
him, forget it."

"Of course you have him."

"Come on, Mr. Clough. Let's do business. Seriously. First
you have poor Karpov here beaten up by some thug who
wants that unfortunate girl for Professor French to play with.
Then you say you haven't got him. Why don't we just forget
the whole business? The girl is safely back in Russia."

"No she isn't," said Clough. "We've got her. And we are
ready to call the whole thing off and forget it. We'll give you
the girl. You give us French. Don't worry. We've finished
with him, too."

Orlov looked at him blankly, trying to look intelligent.

"All right," said Clough. "I'll give it all to you. That stuff
Michael has been putting in the computer the last few days.
You're right. He is going to make it work. Now you know
how to build a fusion reactor, and so do we. I suppose that's a
victory for the sharing of scientific information. But we want
him back. In one piece. If not, there's going to be so much
trouble it will make the Cold War look like a summer picnic.
Every damned one of you will be chased out of the country."

Orlov digested it carefully. Then he said, "You know,
Aloysius, ours is a peculiar job. I have always said we have a
lot in common. This time it is an interesting case indeed.
Both of us seem to have made what I believe you call a fuck
up. I'm afraid the truth is that we don't have Professor
French. And neither do you, it seems. We don't have the
benefit of his latest research. *Yet*. But he's coming along
nicely. We'll have him soon."

"If he's out there somewhere," said Clough, "it's worse
than I feared. He's getting himself geared up for coming out
of hiding. With an appalling story about the way he has been
framed. By both of us. He'll be backed up with a whole
documentation on the ICARUS project, which will entirely
match what we are now building, and won't match the phony
research he went off with. He will put this up to top scientists

the world over. We won't have a chance of discrediting him.
Then the sky will come down on our heads. Your lot will all
be sent home. Our lot will be sacked on the spot. The entire
mess will be in the headlines every day for a year and—"

"Yes," said Orlov. "You don't have to go on."

They sat in a huddle. A group of men busy with their
professional problems.

"And you've got the girl?"

Clough nodded.

"This is all Karpov's fault," said Orlov vacantly. "The girl
was his lunatic idea."

"It worked, though," said Clough. "You must admit that.
I can't see how you could have got him otherwise."

Karpov was touched. He beamed pathetic gratitude.

Orlov slapped the table again. "Aloysius, a toast!" He
filled the glasses. "To cooperation. The GRU and the British
Secret Service will for the first time cooperate in a single
important task."

"Really?"

"We are going to use all our resources to find our missing
professor, aren't we? Between us he should have no hope. As
poor Asimov would have said, 'Like the snowballs of Hell.'"

"I'll drink to that," said Clough. The operational diffi-
culties would be immense. But it was the only way.

"On one condition, obviously," said Orlov. "Whoever gets
him first, we get him in the end. So we both end up with the
ICARUS. I'm sure you agree. You wouldn't really want him
on your hands. In Russia he can have a quiet life."

Clough looked at him appreciatively.

"A very quiet life," said Orlov. "I promise you. And we
will take delivery of the girl immediately."

Clough nodded. It was much as he expected. That was
why he was keeping her ready and waiting in the car, despite
Patterson's protests. Normally, Clough liked to deliver his
goods in tiptop condition, freshly laundered. That had been
one of his hallmarks in the good old days. Right down to a
new set of underwear. Still, this one was a nothing, a ballet

dancer. There hadn't been time to wash her down. He picked up the phone and gave his orders.

"Fine," said Orlov, pulling up his chair. "Now, Viktor. Tell us all about your lovely adventures in the swimming bath. Then go put an advert in *The Times*."

25

"Where are we?" Kyra asked. It was a different car. It had a telephone in it. They had been sitting in a side street for ages. She was jumpy again. Patterson had tried to calm her by getting her to talk about her dancing. She was really a very beautiful kid. She talked nervously, kept coming back to Michael French. And asking about life in England. He filled in an hour giving her a crash course on everyday life in Britain. She was childishly excited. Wanted to know the price of clothes, food. She must have been kept under a tight rein, he decided. Probably they had just let her out a few minutes before Michael French had had his little rendezvous. When she told him, haltingly, the two of them had never made love, he was genuinely sorry for her.

Then the phone buzzed. He grabbed it. It was Clough again, speaking softly, decisively, urgently. When he was done Patterson felt his mouth was dry. "Are you sure?" he asked.

"Shut up, Patterson. Just do it. And don't tell her."

He put the phone down and turned around to the girl. Forcing a smile to his face. "You are travelling again. They're worried the Reds could be after you. You're going to fly to Edinburgh, Scotland. Just to settle you in."

She nodded. She had come to trust the young man. You had to trust someone. He started the car. They approached London Airport. She looked with interest as the bright lights and bustle swept by. Patterson seemed to have a magic way with the barriers. They just rolled straight through the obstacles and in no time at all they were on the runway itself, well away from the airport buildings.

"It is the airport?" she asked, suddenly fearful, remembering what Vladmila had told her of the time at Kennedy.

When the car stopped, four people, two men and two women, opened all the doors at once. Patterson didn't move. He just sat there and rested his head on the wheel. He'd seen the film of the earlier scene; he'd seen all he wanted about ballet dancers at airports.

Then she started screaming. Piteously. Struggling. It was of no use at all. The big stewardess hauled her out of the car like a grocery bag and carried her. When he looked up they were dragging her up the steps to the huge Aeroflot jet.

"You bastard, Clough," said Patterson. "You fucking little evil bastard." And where did he himself come in the list of bastards? he asked as he drove away from it. Pretty high up.

26

The personal message in *The Times* read: *Daphne. Forgive me. Ring 01 734 6170.*

Three Daphnes in a forgiving frame of mind rang the number in the next two days. Then Bridge.

His own call, like the others, was recorded from start to finish. It wasn't a conversation. It was information. It said: "Daphne. Lunch at Pomegranite Pimlico. One P.M. Wednesday." That was all. Today was Monday.

A lot of people were listening to the call. Everything had been set up efficiently. Bridge's voice was monitored by the GRU from King's Cross, by the Science Service in Victoria, and by D16 at Sentinel.

When it was done they chewed it over.

"Get down there now," said Theo Mardellis of D16, speaking on the three-way circuit, another of the arrangements. "That call came from Paris, we analyse. So let's get down before they get back. And we'll lunch there tomorrow. Just in case."

"He'll never walk into a trap like that," said Orlov.

Clough was listening too. What he would have liked to say to Theo Mardellis was that the call could have come from Paris simply because someone had told someone else in Paris to ring up and read a script. But the relationships on this business were difficult enough; he knew that after the recent mayhem in D16. Theo was a young man with big empty boots to fill.

In any case, the choice of Pimlico was clear enough identity. It took ten minutes to get the telephone number of the restaurant. It wasn't in the books. Restaurants come and go. So they had to go through New Numbers. The restaurant was on the corner of Tachbrook Street and the Vauxhall Bridge Road.

The restaurateur took the booking for lunch, for two, and turned back to the young blond man behind him with melting respect. "Yes," he said. "All right." At first, Louis Post, joint owner of the Pimlico Pomegranite, had thought his visitor this Monday morning had been some kind of criminal. He had read about protection rackets in Soho. The young man's story about belonging to the best-known firm of restaurant guides was suspect. Everyone knew that anyone announcing a visit from the inspectors of the guide was an impostor.

"I'm not an impostor. I am just bent," Bridge said, as if reading Post's mind, without smiling.

Louis hastened to take him into a corner well out of earshot. "You say they are coming here tomrorow at lunchtime?"

"And the day after."

The young man looked at him patiently. The sweat trickled easily off Louis' fat face. The restaurant meant a lot to him and his friend Guy, and to their relationship. The restaurant was not going too well. It was very new, but it should have been going better. "I think I ought to ring up your employers and let them know about this conversation," said Louis. Behind him he heard Laszlo, the new waiter, smash the sweets trolley into a table leg. In the nearly empty restaurant it sounded like a cannon firing.

"Fine," said Crispin Bridge. "You could. But then I would say you were the one who suggested the idea. That happens all the time. They'd believe me. You see, my job is to set up the arrangements. Believe me, Louis, I don't do this often. Only for restaurants that are deserving."

"Deserving of what?"

"A bit of help. A nudge in the right direction. It happens all the time, Louis. Or is it Guy?"

"Louis," said Louis quickly. He would like to keep Guy out of this. Guy was the creative one, the cook. Unfortunately not as good a cook as Louis, blinded with passion, had hoped. "OK," said Louis. "Thank you very much."

Bridge reached out for a roll and ate it thoughtfully.

"Would you like a drink?" said Louis.

"No. All right. Now you are doing what some of them do. You are thinking, 'The inspectors will come around tomorrow and we will put on the best food we have ever cooked in our lives.' So why do you need me?"

"I'm just listening to you," said Louis. The sweat began running again.

"Well, there are two reasons," said Bridge, crumbling the roll. "I expect you have just thought of one of them."

It took Louis a few seconds. He had had a bad day trying to fix the accounts. "You mean you would just go back to your office and say the inspectors needn't bother to call here, that you'd made a mistake."

Bridge nodded encouragingly.

Try as he could, Louis couldn't think of the second.

"OK," said Bridge. "I'll tell you. Beauty is in the eye of the beholder, isn't it, Louis? In cooking, especially, it is all a matter of taste. And, Louis, I know what these buggers like to eat, Just give me the kitchen for two days and I promise you I'll tickle their fancy straight into a two-star rating. They only ever order—well, never mind."

Louis was beginning to dissolve. He got up and snatched a bottle from the bar to steady himself. "And this will cost me?" he snarled.

"No."

Louis poured a drink with a shaking hand.

"You will go far," said Crispin. "I wouldn't dream of charging you. I know the kind of mess you are in. When you get a two-star rating you will go up like a rocket. They will beat a path to the door. Right? You will be in everybody else's guide. You will buy something bigger."

"Then you will start blackmailing me," said Louis.

Crispin Bridge bent over the table towards him. "Do I look like a blackmailer?"

Suddenly, looking at this gigantic man with a face chiselled out of rock and eyes as blue as mountain flowers, Louis said, "I don't know what blackmailers look like." He smiled. He could fancy Bridge.

"I am a businessman," said Bridge. "Believe me. I can tell you restaurants you wouldn't dream of in London that have their status from what I do. It's a hard world, Louis. You know that. If I came to unreasonable arrangements I wouldn't be in business. It's in both our interests. We'll sort something out."

Louis looked at him a long time. Then asked, "What do I have to do?"

"Just get rid of your chef for three days and hire me."

"I can't do that. Guy's my partner. He's the chef."

Bridge looked ironically around the empty restaurant. "Yes," he said.

"It would hurt his feelings."

"No," said Bridge. "That's just what it wouldn't do. Guy mustn't know, must he? Wouldn't that be nice? Let him think he got the two-star rating all on his own account."

Louis nodded. It made sense. It made sense to Bridge, too. He knew Louis would keep his trap shut about the scheme. He'd have to. Especially when the two-star rating never arrived. Because if he ever told Guy, Guy would throw a fit at not being allowed to throw off his duck à l'orange for the inspectors.

"It seems a good arrangement," said Louis.

"It is, believe me."

So it went. Guy was touched and pleased at his partner's solicitude in fixing him three days off to see his mummy.

Bridge moved into the kitchen Tuesday morning. Early. He wasn't popular, but he was very thorough.

Louis blenched as Bridge discarded the entire delivery of vegetables and told the greengrocer to try again, this time with *today's* crop. Then he collected all the menus and wrote out his own. "You want to forget all this crap," he said. "Look at it—guinea fowl, venison. You can't run a small restaurant by pulling stuff out of the freezer and sloshing sauce over it. Give them two dishes, and give it to them good."

"What are you going to do!"

"Steak and kidney pie," said Bridge.

Louis swallowed.

You couldn't tell if the two men who came Tuesday for lunch were enjoying their meal or not. But it was easy to see they were genuine inspectors. They kept glancing furtively around the room. They ate up their steak and kidney pie like good English boys. Louis began to breathe again.

Afterwards, he asked Bridge if he thought it had gone well.

"What were they talking about?" Bridge asked. Louis had done a lot of attentive hovering with the wine.

Louis grimaced. "Swapping stories. Rather gruesome. One of them was talking about electrically heated operating knives."

"Well, it's all meat," said Bridge.

"The knife slipped and punctured the patient's colon apparently. And he exploded. The gas—"

Bridge could imagine it. He'd seen worse.

"I mean, that's hardly a story for the dinner table, is it?" said Louis, with a flicker of suspicion.

* * *

The next day didn't go so well. Viktor Karpov limped in at ten to one, looking miserable. He sat sullenly, consuming vodka, until half past. When Louis approached him for the third time he glanced at his watch and said, "Yes. Bring me anything."

"Anything?"

"Whatever you've got. And quickly. And more vodka."

Louis was really upset. In the kitchen, he told Bridge, "A man like *that*. I'd ask him to leave. He's not eating. He's just feeding."

"Yes," said Bridge. "That's the test, you see. They like to know how you deal with different customers."

"I never thought of that," said Louis in admiration.

Neither had Bridge until that moment.

Thoughtfully, when Louis had skipped out of the kitchen, Bridge laced the Irish stew with a tablespoonful of Tabasco.

27

It looked as if French hadn't been working: the floor wasn't covered with paper as usual. It looked as if Michael had just been pacing the room. Which he had. Except for a dismal trip down the stairs to the New Cross High Street pub and back.

"You met him?" demanded Michael urgently. "How is she?"

Bridge stripped off his coat .The restaurant wouldn't get its two stars, but it had certainly been improved, and he was tired. "No," said Bridge. "Saw him, yes. Met him, no."

"Why not? I thought you fixed a time."

"Yes. I fixed a time."

"Then *what?*"

Bridge went to the fridge, pulled out a carton of grapefruit juice, and drank straight from it. "He was there," said Bridge. "Yesterday two British pixies were there. Checking the place out."

"I don't understand."

Bridge swallowed more juice. The sharp taste cleaned his mouth from the stain of the Pimlico Pomegranite's crummy kitchen. "It means," said Bridge, "that the British were there yesterday and the Russians were there today. It may mean they are just babysitting on each other as usual. But suppose it means they are *both* after you now, Michael! Anyway, I stayed out of sight. I was planning on catching up with Viktor after he left. But not if the British are following us all around."

"I expect they are."

Bridge looked at him curiously. The guy really didn't seem to mind. "Look," said Bridge. "Do you mind if I just explain something to you? You've got the police after you. You have the secret boys after you. You have the KGB after you. And the whole fucking lot are working on it *together*. Sometimes I wish we lived on the ground floor."

"Why?"

"Because when they find us and throw us through the window, we'd have a chance of bouncing."

Michael said with interest, "You frightened? I mean, if you're frightened, I'll go somewhere else."

Bridge crumpled the carton and threw it. "I like you, Michael. You're amazing. You know I've never told a client I'm frightened? Of *course* I'm frightened. They're dumb as planks but there's an awful lot of them. We are just you and me. The way you've fixed it, we've got nothing to sell. Yet.

Right? Until they build this damned machine and you blow it up we have nothing to sell. Nothing to keep us alive. How long does it take them to build it?"

"We built it already. Except for the lasers. A month?"

"Jesus. So what do we do for a month?"

"If we have to—if you can't talk to Viktor—we wait. Ring him up again and tell him he has to be alone."

"They'll find us," said Bridge. "That's what they're reckoning on."

Michael French picked up a white plastic shopping bag marked "Tesco's" and reached inside it. Bridge leant back in his chair and shook his head, then jerked up as the first bundle hit his lap. They were pound notes, singles. Old ones. Done up in elastic bands. Lots of bundles, one after the other. Michael kept throwing them until the bag was empty. It took quite a time.

"Everyone should have a good Building Society behind him," said Michael. "Cheer up."

28

Henderson was asleep when the phone rang. It was 1:00 A.M. Thursday morning. He hadn't got in until midnight, and a glance at Muriel showed she was asleep already, so he had dropped into the spare room. It had been a heavy evening on the Street with Foster's retirement party, first at the office, then down at the Bell, and Henderson knew he snored after an evening like that.

Funnily enough, just before he had dropped off he had been thinking about Michael French. He had been worried; French really *had* disappeared. Henderson had hoped old Wally hadn't put him into the hands of someone mad or bad—that guy in the pub looked capable of anything. Still, Henderson had tried. He had shaken up the SS and if they didn't want any more help, what could you do?

The phone went on ringing until he swam up into half-consciousness and grabbed it. The voice on the other end was breathy, fast, gabbling. Henderson had to stop it and make it begin again.

"Who?" he demanded for the third time. Then he sat up and sobered up in one movement. It was that young man called Patterson. Patterson had a lot to say. A very great deal to say, indeed.

"Tell us again," said Colonel Orlov. It was 2:00 A.M. Thursday morning.

Viktor Karpov sighed. They had been at it two hours. Karpov on one side of the metal desk, Orlov and Clough on the other. The bastards, he knew, were still enjoying themselves in a professional way. The Russian and the Briton each had his own style of interrogation. They made a good act together. Karpov felt a fleeting sympathy for any poor sod who could be the next victim of it.

"A man six foot tall, late twenties, blue eyes, corn-yellow hair. *Where* did he hit you?" asked Clough.

"Stand up and show us," said Orlov.

"Here and here. Then here."

"So he knew what he was doing. And he wasn't there to meet you in the restaurant?"

"I think I would have noticed," Karpov ventured sarcastically.

"Would you? Anyway, he's a professional. In Russia"—

Orlov turned politely to Clough—"we would be able to find such a distinctive person."

"That is because in any police state you have *so* many files on people, Colonel Orlov," said Clough, and turned back to Karpov.

"Tell me," he said. "When you first spoke to him. When the first meeting was arranged. Go through that again."

"He said," replied Karpov wearily, " 'That's fine. There's a swimming pool just near you.' "

"Wait a moment," said Clough. He began writing it down. " 'That's fine. There's a swimming pool just near you.' "

"No," said Karpov, remembering. "Not exactly."

Orlov opened his mouth; Clough hushed him.

"He said, 'That's . . . *handy*. I remember. I remember the word. It is a new one to me."

"Handy," said Orlov.

"Handy," said Clough. "Are you sure?"

"What does handy mean?" asked Viktor.

"Well," said Aloysius Clough. "It means 'Close at hand,' 'nearby,' 'convenient,' 'useful,' 'easy.' That sort of thing."

"Ah," said Orlov.

"Right," said Clough. "Thank you. I think that will do for the time being."

"As Clough reached the door, Orlov called to him, "Clough. If you find him, you *will* let us know. Of course."

"Of course," said Clough. He wiped his nose carefully and left.

29

"I was a friend of your husband's," said Henderson.

"Oh really," said Mary French. The door was only half open. "It's three in the morning," she said, amazed.

"I drove straight up."

"I'm not dressed."

"Mary," said Henderson. "Can I have a word with you? It's important."

She opened the door and he followed her in. She sat down at the kitchen table and folded her arms. He sat down at the other end of the table. She looked unfriendly.

"Actually," said Henderson, "I *am* a friend of your husband's. And I met you too one morning a few months back. I have to have your help. He is alive." He had wondered, all the way up here, how to say it, how she would react. He had been prepared for anything; he knew the marriage hadn't been good. But not prepared for her stony stare.

"Michael is dead," she said.

"No. He is in trouble. He is alive. You *know* he is, don't you?" he added, suddenly realising why she wasn't surprised.

"I don't want to talk to you," she said. "What's your name?"

"Mrs. French. We *have* met. My name's Jim Henderson. I'm a journalist."

"I want you to go. Now," said Mary. "If you don't, I will call the police."

"He could get killed. He has to know that. If you know where he is, you have to tell him he is in danger. He is still working on his fusion reactor. When he finishes, they're going to get him."

"I am not interested," she said.

"He's your husband. He's my friend. He's a good man."

"*Ha!*" she shouted. Her face was glistening with anger. She stood up.

"What did they tell you?" said Henderson, keeping his voice down. He knew there were kids. "Did they tell you he was a Russian agent? What did that little bastard Clough tell you? Look, Mrs. French. Your husband has been caught up in something he doesn't understand. This thing he was working on—there is a bunch of people run by a man called Clough. They're called the Science Service. They screwed up the work Michael was doing because they knew the Russians wanted to get hold of it. They've let the Russians go after him—blackmail, this Russian girl . . ."

"Oh yes," said Mary, clutching her hands together.

Again, he noticed her reaction. "You know about her?"

She looked blank again.

"A girl called Kyra?"

He saw her blink. "Christ," he said. "Believe me. Tell me what you know."

She sat down again. "Well, I'll tell you, Mr. Henderson. I am not interested. I am not interested in the whole thing. I have two children to look after. Michael never discussed his work with me. I don't *care* about you and your agents and your Russians and your problems. I don't know what Michael was into and he didn't tell me. Maybe he should have told me. But it's over. It's too late. I've got used to the idea. He's gone. He's dead."

"He's not dead. He could be, soon."

She just looked at him. A plump, motherly woman with red cheeks at a cottage table.

"That will be OK with you? Will it?" said Henderson. "You mean you've got used to the idea of him being dead, so—why not just do it and tidy it all up?"

"I told you to get *out.*"

"You could be an accessory to murder."

"I will ring the police."

"You may have screwed up your marriage between you, but that doesn't allow you to be a criminal."

She leant across the table. "They love each other," she said flatly. "This Kyra creature and him. Yes, I met her. And I saw *him*. That man Clough. They deserve each other. What do you think it's like for me, thinking of him in bed with that little whore?"

"It must have hurt your pride," said Henderson unwisely.

"You stupid male bastard," she said.

He couldn't help smiling, also unwisely. Then he said, "OK. The Russians got him into something with this girl. I've heard all about that. They know how to do that sort of thing. They pick someone—a pretty girl—and they get a man involved. I mean, come on. We're only human. He got infatuated with this woman. It wasn't really his *fault.*"

"Oh, poor little Michael," she said. "So he climbs into bed with a beautiful Red spy and I'm supposed to help him out? Stuff that, Mr. Henderson. A marriage contract is a contract like any other. He's not a child. He goes off and fucks someone else, that's the end of the contract. As *I* understand it. I suppose that shocks you. But you men are just great at running your damned world behind our backs and when you mess it up—*when* you mess it up, mind you, not before—then you come along and say 'sorry about this, old woman, but it was all a bit complicated and we got ourselves in a bit of a tangle on this one. *You'll understand.*'"

"You read a lot of books," said Henderson.

"What's that supposed to mean?"

"Well," said Henderson, relaxing into his anger, "That

stuff is straight women's lib crap, isn't it? Talking tough. It's a man's world. Shit, Mrs. French, that man was your husband. It's *not* a fucking contract. You are married to him and you have a relationship, not a contract. And you owe him some decency as a human being. He's in trouble."

"Then he should have told me, shouldn't he? All right? He could have said, 'Listen, darling wife, I think the Russians want me to go to bed with a beautiful Russian spy.'"

Henderson got up and pulled his coat on. "Yes," he said. "You're right. That would have done him a lot of good, wouldn't it?"

After ten minutes she phoned the Cambridge number Clough had left her. He wasn't there, but there was a London number immediately available. When she rang that, he wasn't there either, but there was a very friendly recorded message and a promise to ring callers back. In half an hour, Clough rang her back. As she talked, the clock hammered out 4:00 A.M.

"I'm so sorry," he said.

"Why?" she asked suspiciously.

"Because you have had so much trouble. I was afraid this would happen. They're bound to try this kind of thing, believe me."

"They?"

"This Henderson. I shouldn't be telling you this, but our Russian friends are well fixed up with British journalists."

"Damn all that. I'm just not interested."

"Of course not," said Clough quickly. "But I do want you to be left alone. So that everything can go ahead without any problems."

She was silent.

"Like the pension and so forth," said Clough. "Now, tell me exactly what was said. It will be a great help. I am very glad you rang me. It was very wise."

*　　*　　*

At 5:00 A.M. Patterson arrived at the Science Service office on Victoria Street. For once in his life, there was no parking problem. The kerbside yellow line was empty all the way to Westminster Cathedral. It was pissing with rain. Being dragged into the office at such an hour had to have some advantages. Patterson was scared shitless. Could Clough knew he'd spent last night in the office, doing the unforgiveable? Betraying the Science Service?

Clough was waiting for him in his pyjamas—big blue and white striped pyjamas four sizes too big for him. A comic sight. But Patterson was not looking for the funny side. His heart was hitting his ribs like a wet hammer, and not just because he had run up eighty stairs to the office. He'd done that before. What he hadn't done before was betray the organisation to a Fleet Street journalist. Behind his desk, Clough looked like a cartoonist's parody of a schoolboy: the pallid little head rising sharply from the wide collar. Pink and white, purple at the edges.

"I am very grateful to you," said Clough.

"What's up, sir?"

"No, but I *am* very grateful. How long have you been here, Patterson?"

"Six years."

"That's right. You're twenty-seven. Time goes so quickly. Patterson, have you ever wondered why all the young men in the SS—yes, I call it that too—come from just three Roman Catholic public schools? Or why we are here in the shadow of Westminster Cathedral?"

"Yes, sir." Patterson was careful, watchful. In the black night, the rain pounded against the windows.

"Well, it was *my* old school. Yours, I mean." Clough smiled. "We haven't talked about these things before." He had a clock ticking on the wall. Like Mary French, out of tune.

"No, sir." But he didn't need reminding. He knew Clough toddled off to Mass every morning at 6:00. He knew about "The Connection" as a phrase, but had never been able to figure out its roots.

"Well," said Clough. "It's about a different kind of loyalty."

Patterson looked at him and swallowed. He was a thin young man. His Adam's apple went up and down vigorously. He could feel sweat prickling on his scalp.

"I am sure you would have found things more normal in one of the more regular branches of the service. But then our job has never been normal."

Patterson smelt the musty air of the room. Clough's pyjamas, maybe. This room was always yellow and dark. At this time of the night more so than ever. Shadows crouched at the edge of Clough's desk light.

Clough looked at his empty desk. "When did they talk to you first? Fifth Form? Lower Sixth?"

Patterson remembered. It was Father Higgins. One summer's night, after Confession. A thin brown hand on his shoulder, suddenly. The dry voice saying, "Patterson, I want to talk about what you will do when you leave here. In private." The delicious smell of a conspiracy. Quite suddenly the whole world had changed.

Suddenly, for Patterson, the smell of a whole world outside the miseries of the Fifth. He had gone off with Father Higgins, that brown hand still on his shoulder, and had listened, soaking it up.

"Some of you young men," Father Higgins had said. He had lifted his hand. Patterson had watched it make an arc gesturing at the whole wide world. Actually there was a view of the back wall of the swimming pool. "You can do anything. Professions, business, trade." Even to Patterson, trembling, the categories had sounded archaic. "Or a vocation," Father Higgins had said. His hand went back, holding the youth's shoulder firmly.

OK. It's another of those, Patterson had thought. He had had one before. They always tried it. "I don't think I have a vocation, Father," he said.

"I'm sure you don't. Not in that way. But now I want to tell you something else. I want you to listen to me carefully. We have many traditions at Wastwater, Patterson. You know that. Now I want to tell you about something very special. Something young men from here like you have done for thirty years. Just a few of you. Did you ever notice on the Scholars Board the name of Aloysius Herbert Clough?"

Patterson now looked at Clough. He said, "What do you want me to do, sir?"

"*Loyalty*," said Clough. "We count on that."

"Yes, sir," said Patterson, eventually. He wondered where Vera was. The place was cold and empty as death.

"I *am* sorry to get you in," said Clough. "We seem to have got a few things wrong." He checked his watch. "A quarter to six," he pronounced.

Patterson checked his own. "No, sir. Five-fifteen."

"I want you to meet somebody, I mean. At a quarter to six. On Waterloo Bridge. The middle."

"Sir?"

"It's a woman," said Clough. "We seem to be plagued by Russian women at the moment, don't we, Patterson?"

"Yes, sir."

"You got the *other* one off OK?"

"Yes, sir."

"Well, they want to know anything she said. All right? They are working with us, Patterson. Does that surprise you?"

"Of course not, sir."

He parked on the north side of Waterloo Bridge by Somerset House and walked south. The roadway of the Bridge was empty. He stood in the middle for ten minutes, just watching. In all this time just a black London taxi and a juggernaut lorry sneaked through. Greenish-white, the lamps hardened the night air, lighting up the white stone arches of the most graceful of London's bridges. It was cold. It was *damned* cold. Feeling naked, Patterson walked a few yards towards the grey bulk of the National Theatre, then back. *What a bloody fool way of spending a life*, he thought, tied up to

a white slug like Aloysius Clough. He began shivering. No
time, this, to start reviewing your past life. Tomorrow he
would resign, like Benson. That was for sure.

When an L Registration Austin Princess stopped fifty
metres away and a woman got out, Patterson didn't even look
up.

It was going to be all right. His last assignment. Just see it
through, report back and throw the card on the table.

The Austin drove past him, smoothly, going south. He
heard it slow down. He smiled, waiting for the footsteps. He
leant over the stone parapet. Suddenly, below him, the bows
of a tugboat slid out, strangely silent, the engine muffled by
the bridge. Then, breasting the water away noisily into dirty
cream waves, four barges, riding fast on the ebb, their open
maws brimming with garbage for dumping far out on the
estuary flats.

Patterson turned his head back to the roadway, but the
woman was already at his side, dropping to a crouch beside
him. He began to straighten up, surprised. More so as she
gripped his left leg below the knee. He thought she was in
some trouble, that she was falling at his feet in desperation.
"What—" he began. But she was springing upright, raising
his leg, pivoting him on the balustrade. Patterson spread his
hands behind him, seeking the stone, but she had him up,
over, going over the edge. He began to scream, scrabbling in
the air behind him, still clutching, flailing, as the city turned
upside down and he dropped, rushing through the dark air,
eyes wide, still hearing the noise of the barges below him.
Few bridges on the Thames are lower than these elegant,
long-drawn-out arches. But it was enough.

It was surprise more than terror. All the way down it never
occurred to him he was going to die. All the way down to the
moment his skull hit the iron edge of the last barge and his
body disappeared into the trough of garbage, which moved
away like a wave, then back to embrace him.

As it happened, the boatman saw it. The tug pilot had
been looking back, getting his alignment right for Blackfriars

Bridge. He gasped, but kept on going. It wasn't his first suicide. Impossible to leave the bridge of the tug on this reach of the river and the current this fast. He stabbed for the siren. The five blasts for an emergency echoed far into the sleeping city, mournfully, like a brief requiem. From the Charing Cross pier, the river police tumbled into their launches.

Colonel Orlov was woken at 6:00 with the news by the GRU night officer. "Our friends really *are* cooperating with us," Orlov said. "You see? Now you can go to bed."

"With respect, Colonel. It was incredibly dangerous. Supposing she had failed?"

"Svetlana? Have you ever *seen* Svetlana?"

"She's a powerfully built woman, I agree."

"*And* the dearest friend of poor Lydia, who apparently fell into the River Severn. Believe me, Svetlana also jumped at the chance, as the British say. Now I must talk to our new colleague, Dr. Clough. I wonder what that young man did to upset him so much."

30

In the Army Records Office, Captain John Frost was viewing Clough with suspicion. The little man with the too-big overcoat and an irritating habit of picking his nose did not inspire Captain Frost with confidence. "I've never *heard* of the Science Service," he said.

"We don't advertise," said Clough. Then, with surprising crispness, "Let's get on with it, please. I have identified myself."

"All right. But where do we start?"

"I believe our man is what is known as a Minder. They're always ex-army."

"Bodyguards for Arab sheikhs, you mean? You're right. We did open a file on them. But your man won't be in it unless he's done a job for an Ay-rab. Blond hair you said?" They began to go through the pictures. "Probably dyed," said Captain Frost.

Clough looked at him with icy contempt. "I know he is still alive."

"Dyed his hair, I mean."

Clough flicked through the pictures: tough, uncompromising-looking men. "That would be unusual," said Clough. "The other way around, yes. But why draw attention to yourself?" He threw the papers back on the desk.

When the phone rang, Captain Frost picked it up. "It's for you," he said with irritation. Bloody cheek, giving anyone this number.

Clough nodded and took it. He said, "I see. Thank you, Vera. By the way, last night's recordings, have you . . . Good. Thank you, Vera." He gave the handset back to Captain Frost to replace; the captain gritted his teeth.

"Tell me," said Clough. "Just an outside chance. Is there anyone recently who has been investigated? Anyone who could fit the bill?"

"Blond? Thirtyish?" Captain Frost thought. Then he clicked his fingers. "*Yes,*" he said. "There *was*. That's absolutely right. I—" He stopped suddenly.

"Go on."

"Well. No. I can't. It was a secrets case."

Clough sighed. "Look," he said. "*Will* you ring that number? Will you just get it in your head there are no secrets you can't share with me?"

Captain Frost reddened. Then did as he was told. After which he coughed and brought his chair to attention. "Well, sir," he said. "It was the Salisbury Plain affair. When Commander King died. You know about that."

Clough nodded.

"We had to check into the background of one of King's people: Rigby was the name."

"I know about him, too."

Do you? thought Frost. It was more than he did. "Rigby was in the SAS until he got shot up by one of his own men in Northern Ireland. It was damn nearly a court-martial, because Rigby wasn't popular with his platoon. In the light of later events, we checked up on the man who put the bullet in him. If you wait a minute I'll get it. I remember *he* had blond hair."

"Thank you," said Clough.

Frost was away five minutes, then returned with a buff folder. "Not very hopeful," he said. "Seems to have led a quiet life ever since. Bit of long-distance lorry driving. Lives on top of a block of flats down Deptford. Not the sort of place the bent ones go for, sir. One thing you can be sure of: your ex-army crook always covers himself with home comforts. Roses round the door. Running pubs in the country."

Clough was looking at the photograph of a handsome young man. Bull necked. Chin up for the official army photographer. No smile either visible or imaginable. "Perhaps this one's clever," he said. "Tell me. Is Deptford near New Cross?"

"One and the same really. What's this guy done?" He knew Clough had found his man.

"I think he killed one of my staff," said Clough. "Last night. A young man, too. Of course I'll have to tell his mother it was suicide. Waterloo Bridge. I'll have to invent some story about him being in trouble with a girl." He seemed to rouse himself from a daydream. "I shouldn't have mentioned that," he said. "That was confidential. I would like our whole conversation to remain confidential."

"Yes, sir."

Clough got up. "Thank you very much for your help," he said.

"Excuse me, sir. You can't take the photograph."

"Yes I can, Captain. Thank you very much."

When he'd gone, Captain Frost opened a window.

31

"Do you mind if I make a suggestion?" said the new head of D16, Theo Mardellis.

Clough looked at him mildly. He had little time for today's young men. His hunch was that Mr. Mardellis wouldn't last long. Despite the clean sweep he had made of the Sentinel officer. Despite the tightly curled auburn hair clipped fortnightly in Jermyn St.

"If your professor and his Minder are sitting on the top of this block of flats, why don't you send four policemen round in a Panda car? I can't quite see why we are planning for a full-scale siege involving the Specials, D 16 and the GRU. It surely doesn't need twenty KGB pretending to wheel prams up and down either."

Clough sneezed and began wiping his nose again as if he were afraid it would fall off. "The Russians want to *be* there. They don't trust us, Mardellis. They think we might put Professor French in our pocket."

"Well, exactly," said Theo. "And I don't understand that either. I can see that you had to go to Orlov in order to locate French. But now you've found him, you hope, why on earth are you going through with the deal?"

"That wouldn't be honourable," said Clough.

"Oh, come *on*."

"What do *we* want French for?" asked Clough. "We've got his ICARUS work. What on earth would we do with him? He knows enough about the tricks we played on him to bring the roof down. If he gets to Russia he'll never be heard of again."

"That's what Orlov promised you. Supposing they produce the whole story as part of the May Day celebrations?"

"No one will believe a word of it. None of his scientific friends would lift a finger for him. Once he's in Russia he's finished his credibility. Anyway, the Russians won't produce him. They'll squeeze the pips out of him and then they will make him vanish."

"It *is* a high price," said David Kipling of M15.

"What is a high price?"

"Well you must wish you'd never started this, Alo. I mean, I can see the charm of exporting a scientist with his head full of phoney fusion plans. But now he's tumbled that one and got his sums right, it seems a shame he has to take his secrets with him."

"Of course he won't take them with him," said Clough irritably. "I'm not a fool, David."

David Kipling frowned. "You said you were going to give him to the Russians."

Clough nodded.

"But he's not taking the plans with him," said Kipling.

Clough nodded again.

"What are you going to *do* with him, Alo?"

"You organise the pickup," said Clough. "Tonight. And I'll fix the rest." He sneezed three times very quickly and stood up.

"*Gesundheit*," said Theo Mardellis without sincerity. "By

the way, I hear one of your people fell off a bridge last night. How come?"

"Tragic case," said Clough shortly. "Trouble over a woman, you know." He left.

When Clough had gone, David Kipling said, "That is definitely *enough*. When this lot's over I am going to the PM and the Home Secretary and I am going formally to request that horrible little man is closed down. He is the nastiest piece of work I have ever encountered. I'd no idea he was still actually *doing* anything until this came up. I thought he just brooded in that awful slum of his and sent his funny public schoolboys lecturing government scientists on security."

"He doesn't like nuclear scientists. Never did," said Theo Mardellis. "I agree with you, David. But I think you'll find it won't work. The PM wouldn't dare. They never do. They just hope and pray he'll die one day."

"But it's ridiculous, Theo. He's a freak show. God knows there are some curious corners of British Intelligence but— what do you mean, the PM wouldn't dare?"

"No one's told you then? Of course, you are rather new."

"About what?"

"About why Aloysius Clough is left alone."

"What did he do? Win us the war?"

Theo Mardellis hesitated. Then said, "Possibly."

"Explain."

"What do you remember about the Rudolf Hess case?"

"Deputy Fuehrer. Mad as a coot. Flew in on a crazy peace mission. Jumped out of his plane and was locked up until he died?"

"First and last statements correct. Nothing else. Hess wasn't mad when he got here. Not until we turned him over to Aloysius Clough to look after. It was the Science Service's first big project."

"Of course he was mad when he got here. He thought we were going to sign a peace deal with him."

"That is what we had led him to believe."

David Kipling looked at him in amazement. "You mean Hess was *invited?*"

"Of course he was invited, David. Why do you think three days went by before Churchill admitted he was here? If Goebbels hadn't lost his nerve and blown the whole story open no one would ever have known he was here. What happened ten days after Hess arrived? Germany invaded Russia. Which is exactly what we wanted them to do. Hitler really believed we were going to be sensible and pack it in, so he could go off and zap the Reds without distraction. At the Nuremberg trials Hess was complaining of loss of memory and believed the doctors were putting funnies in his food. Which was quite right, old son. Except it wasn't the doctors, of course." Mardellis looked thoughtfully at the ceiling. Then said: "Of course it took Clough five years to turn Hess's brains into porridge. I expect he's improved his techniques since then."

David Kipling felt sick. "What you're saying is that they're going to pick that poor guy up tonight and then scramble his head so he will be no use to the Russians when they get him."

Mardellis shrugged. "I agree. It's unpleasant. I wonder why Clough lives so long. Maybe they don't want him anywhere else. Come on, let's ring up the damned Russians and get it organised."

32

At 9:00 P.M. Crispin Bridge began looking at the blue telephone. He got up and looked out the window. Then he began rubbing the back of his neck. He had a prickling feeling there.

"What's wrong?" asked Michael.

Bridge took a good look. Down to the empty spaces twenty-two storeys below, across to the lights of Archer Tower. It was mid-March, but snow had fallen. A clear night now.

"Listen," said Michael. "I think I've found a way of speeding it up. I'd like to go and see a man called Sewell, in Cambridgeshire. If I'm right, he'd be running ICARUS now, and I think we could frighten him into—"

Bridge raised a hand to quiet him. Then he picked up the phone, keeping the bar down. When the headpiece was at his ear, he released the bar. He listened. He put the phone down. "Shit," he said.

"What's up?"

"They've put a tap on it. I think they've found us, Michael."

"We better go. Somewhere. We can afford to."

"Not until we know who's waiting for us." He unlocked a cupboard and pulled out a red phone, checked for a switch-in click, nodded and dialled. "Wally there?"

"Who?"

"OK. Get me John."

Even the barmaid knew whom he meant. "Hold on."

Bridge went back to biting his hangnail. He'd only once been molested up here. That had been easy. Two guys. He just left the door open for them and let them walk in. People seemed to think you were somehow vulnerable living up here. In fact the soundproofing was pretty good and if you left it until 3:00 A.M. to drag visitors down to the lift you had the place to yourself. But the prickling in his neck was telling him this time could be different.

"Wally isn't here," said a gravel voice. "Who is it?"

Bridge could hear the music in the pub. He wished he were there. "What about Nob?"

"No. Who *is* it?"

"Client. Waterside. No names, all right?"

"All right. What do you want?"

"I want three men. Down here by ten. Grand each."

"You *what?* You're not back on jobs, are you? Wally's retired."

"Three men. Look and tell. You know the place."

"O.K. I can get you three men."

"Shooters."

There was a pause. "All of them?"

"Wally could have done it."

"I can *do* it. I don't *like* it, that's all."

"Come on. They're not for using. Not for one grand. Don't argue, John. That's not the system."

"I know the system."

"Then *run* it. Or I'll get Wally out of retirement."

"We'll be there."

"Phone me. On the red number. But give me three flashes first. And, John—"

"Yes?"

"There's a new paint job on the road. Front wheels on top of it. Right?"

"Right."

"And you stay there till I or my friend get to you. Or forty-five minutes after the strike. Whichever is sooner."

"Who's the friend?"

"Jonathan. If he gets there first give me ten minutes. If you don't see me, take off. Look after him and charge it."

He slammed the phone down and switched off the light. Then he pulled the blackout curtains across the window and as he did so scanned the wasteland of the areas around the tower. Two new cars had parked at the junction of the service road to the estate, one behind the other. He secured the curtain and put on the light. "OK, Michael. We better get ready. Take your clothes off. Put these on."

He was hauling a whole stack of equipment from the big cupboard. He threw a plastic sack to Michael. "Do it," said Bridge.

But Michael was staring in sudden alarm at the nylon rope ladder lying snaked across the floor.

"What are you planning on, Michael?" said Bridge gently, zipping himself into a one-piece camouflage oversuit.

"What are *you* planning? We're not going . . . I couldn't do that, Crispin. No way am I going out of here except the usual way." The ladder was only twelve feet long, anyway.

"You won't go out the usual way," said Bridge. "If you go down in the lift it will be on a stretcher. With a couple of Specials at each end."

"I'm not a hero, Crispin. Heights paralyse me."

Bridge didn't stop to argue. He went on racing around the apartment, pulling stuff into the centre of the room, packing things into a rucksack. Michael watched in alarm as Bridge turned two screws at the back of the cupboard and the whole panel came away to reveal an illuminated display of rifles, telescopic sights, and things that looked like grenades. "Thirty years in Wormwood Scrubs will paralyse you," said Bridge.

"They couldn't do that."

"They'll think of something. Like killing that woman in the boat. My guess is they'll just throw you out the window anyway. I warned you they hadn't much use left for you."

"I'm not going out that window of my own free will."

Bridge paused, straightening up. "You're the client," he said.

"If they're coming," said Michael, "I'm sorry. I've landed you in it. If you've still got time to go, do it. Take all the money."

"Sure I can go," said the soldier, now confronting Michael. "I can walk out of here now and tell them you're here. You want me to do that?"

Michael looked at the black curtains and shuddered at the drop beyond. "It's just that I couldn't *do* it," he said.

"OK," said Bridge. "You've got one minute. What about that woman of yours, Michael? You want me to write her a letter in Lublianka Jail and tell you're sorry but you hadn't got the nerve?"

"Shut up."

"I'll do that for you, mate. Maybe she'll get it before they shoot her."

"Shut *up*."

"Well, that's how it goes, Michael. I don't blame you. I've never had an attack of the grand passion for a bird. But I've surely heard enough about yours these last weeks. Obviously it's just a load of moonshine. I always thought so."

"What do I have to do?"

"You've got ten seconds."

"What do I have to do?"

"You say yes or no. If you say yes then you do exactly what I tell you. Step by step. You ask no questions. You do it. Because if we do it then my life hangs on it too. You won't be the client anymore, you'll take orders. And if you don't carry them out I'll junk you. I mean that."

Michael saw the black drop again, the vertigo tugging at his bowels. Then he saw the pale face of the girl. He said, "Come on. We'll do it."

"Good. Get in those clothes."

Michael unwired the seal on the plastic bag. As it opened, a stench of ancient urine and vomit swam into the room. His mouth opened in a question. He shut it, began pulling out the gruesome garments.

"Authentic Deptford dosser gear," said Bridge. "When you're down there, you don't run, you walk. You walk very slowly and if you see anyone you start singing. Stagger from side to side in the road if you like. There's an A to Z on the shelf. Look up Scawen Road, corner of Grinstead Road. That's where you have to get to from here. There'll be a car waiting for us and you give them the name Jonathan if I'm not there. Right? And if the car isn't there don't hang about."

"Where would I go then? Dressed like this."

"Where you belong," grinned Bridge. "Straight down the New Cross Road and start throwing rocks through windows."

"You're joking. I'll get arrested."

"That's the idea. You don't want the police looking for you, do you? Just stay dumb. You won't get more than fourteen days. Give me time to work something out."

"They'll know I'm not drunk."

"You will be, son, by the time you get out of here," Bridge said, and put a half bottle of whiskey on the table. He looked around the room carefully. There was a big drum painted grey. He began stuffing the money in the rucksack. "OK," he said. "Now we wait. With luck we can put the whole thing away and go to bed."

He turned out the main light, took his new Japanese telescope to the window, and aligned its tripod on marks scratched in the lino floor, then, for the angle, against diamond-etched lines on the window glass. The telescope focussed down onto a distant network of frozen branches in a street a mile away. There was a streetlamp. Bridge turned a knob and dimmed the light input.

*   *   *

Wally's three boys were already cruising the estate. They had stopped off for a quick half at the Man o' War. They made it a very quick half indeed. At the suggestion of the landlord. By the time they parked the car in Scawen Road with its wheels on the splash of paint carefully maintained by Bridge they were very jumpy. Nob flashed the headlights three times.

"Now let's go," said John.

"He said wait."

"Not for one grand," said the big man in the front passenger seat. "No way. The place is *crawling*. Nob, come on. The guy's dead already. They're lying out there with fucking submachine guns. They're lying around in heaps. I saw them."

"Then go and phone him. See what he says."

John lumbered out of the car and went to the box. Nob turned off the sidelights. The car got colder. A mean, dry wind began to blow and shake the black branches above them.

Bridge answered the phone immediately.

"What in hell did you do, Waterside?" asked John nervously. "They're stacked out here. Guys on garage roofs. Trucks. And an *ambulance*. You hear that? Pub says it's an army exercise. You're not going to walk away from this one."

"You wait where you are. Like I said."

"When do we start counting the forty-five minutes?"

"When the fun starts."

"How do we know when that is?"

"You just watch. They covering every side?"

"Not unless they've got boats on the river. You learnt how to fly or something?"

"I'll see you," said Bridge. He hung up.

Back in the car, John said, "He wants us to wait."

"Then we wait," said Nob.

"He must be out of his mind," said John. "I know he's a clever one, but this is ridiculous."

"Johnny boy," said Nob quietly, "you ever seen what happens to people who let Crispin Bridge down on a contract? I don't like it either. But here we are and here we stay."

PART THREE

33

Like the Inigo Jones Tower, the "Big House" in Leningrad had been designed for multiple occupation. But more care had been taken to fit it into its own landscape. The vast prison compound did not obtrude on the iced-cake beauty of the city of the Tsars. Its exterior had been arranged in charming façades in a variety of architectural styles. They effectively disguised the immense thickness of the walls.

Ten huge iron doors closed behind Kyra Kruschev before the black limousine entered the prison courtyard. There was a lot of traffic, for the Big House was also the city's KGB headquarters. Through the car window she could see lines of men waiting in the cold for buses. The buses would take them to the municipal dumps, where they would sift refuse all day. All this was explained to Kyra by the "medical orderly" accompanying her. Strong young women also did such work, she was told.

She was led out of the car into the prison itself. Surely they couldn't just put her straight in a cell. Not in this dreadful place. She guessed the idea was simply to frighten her. A line of prisoners pressed back against the wall to let them pass. They looked at her without interest. A reek of herrings lay on the chill air. She looked up and saw the famous cages. These were actual cells, hanging like birdcages from the walls, it seemed, designed so that inmates could not see another human being through their bars. It wouldn't be the first time a ballet dancer had ended up in here, she knew. They'd put the indomitable Valery Panov into one of these cages, on a trumped-up charge of hooliganism. And taken care that his three other cellmates were amputees who nightly unscrewed arms or legs as a wordless warning of what the KGB could do to improve a dancer's prospects in the Kirov ballet.

The orderly thrust her along until they were out of the prison and into an equally dismal compound entitled Medical Block. They put her in a stone room with an iron cot. There were no explanations.

She lay on the bed three days. She became feverish. On the third day she opened her eyes and saw Viktor Karpov sitting on the single chair and watching her. "Tell me," said Karpov. "You didn't imagine we chose you for your dancing talents." He was in a vile temper. True to his word, Orlov had promptly packed him off to Leningrad.

For a moment the girl on the bed looked up at him, then she hunched into her coat and seemed to try to become smaller.

Karpov struck a match on the wall and blew cigarette smoke towards the bed. "I mean," said Viktor, "please don't imagine we spoiled your career. You would have had no career. You would be back in your stinking little town on the other side of the Urals. Look at me when I talk to you."

She drew her knees up to her chin and looked at him. Karpov smiled.

"You spoiled *my* career," he said pleasantly. "I pulled you out of that parade of horseflesh for one reason only. And you had the insolence to try to run away from us? What did you imagine you were going to do in England? Set up as a female Nureyev?"

She closed her eyes, remembering the day of the audition for the corps de ballet of the Kirov. The rapture of being chosen. The poisonous blandishments and veiled threats that came so soon after.

"How long have you been here?" said Karpov, looking around the chill room. Outside the high window, too high to see from, the half-frozen canals of Leningrad leaked a vile vapour. "Anyway. Tomorrow you can go. We'll send you back to your family. We will tell your father nothing, of course. I don't expect you will either. I must congratulate you. You are my very last assignment. You *ruined* me."

She began shivering.

"Oh, I forgot," said Viktor. "Your father is an alcoholic, isn't he? He used to knock you about? He thinks that a girl as beautiful as yourself didn't begin in his ugly testicles? Well, we all have our family problems. I wish I could arrange for a work permit for you to stay in Leningrad. But you know how difficult these things are. Stand up."

She didn't move.

"Stand up." He was sitting astride his chair, just the way he was at the audition.

Slowly she stood up.

"You know why we are sending you home?"

She shook her head.

"You want to know what happened to your beloved Englishman?"

She nodded.

"Take off your clothes first."

She gazed at him.

"You want to know what is happening to your beloved Englishman?"

Very slowly, not taking her eyes off his face, she undressed. He watched without expression. When she was standing naked in front of him, shivering, he lit another cigarette.

"Dance," he said.

She shook her head.

"Do you want to know what happened to your beloved Englishman?"

Someone was hammering at the door.

"Come in," said Karpov without turning round.

It was the so-called matron who ran the so-called medical unit. A squat, ugly woman in her late fifties. She came in and looked at the girl and then at Karpov.

Karpov glanced at her with a casual disdain. "I am impressing on Miss Kruschev that she has come to the end of the road. Once she was nothing and now she is nothing again."

With two short strides the matron advanced on Karpov; with a powerful backhanded swipe of her fist she knocked him clean off his chair onto the floor. *"You* are the nothing, Comrade Karpov," she said. "You get out of here and buy your amusement with your own money." She kicked him to the door and as he crawled to his knees shot him halfway across the corridor with a blow that would have won approval from the Dynamos' goalkeeper.

"Get dressed," she said to Kyra.

"What happened to Michael?"

"Just get dressed. There's been a change of plan. You are staying with us."

34

In London, at 11:00 P.M., the Specials, reassuringly dressed as uniformed police, began clearing the floor below. The routine was simple. Finger on the doorbell, then, when the door opened, another finger on the lips. "We believe there is an Irish terrorist upstairs. We want you to come with us, very quietly." No one needed asking twice.

They began on the twenty-second floor half an hour later. Here it wasn't so smooth. The Indian family at the end of the corridor began screaming. Bridge leapt like a cat to the door and pressed his ear against it. He could hear the soft burr of the other doorbells, the shuffling in the corridor. He had switched the main lights off again and pulled the curtains. There were buses down there now, taking people away.

He was getting the idea. He wasn't surprised at all when there was simultaneously a splash of breaking glass from below and a flood of white light into the apartment, etching every object into dramatic relief.

Michael felt his legs beginning to shake. It was what he was most afraid of, his legs giving way. Then he sniffed the air. "Christ," he said. "They're burning us out."

It was unmistakeable. An acrid smell of smoke. Outside the window, billowing in the searchlights' glare, the smoke was pouring up the walls of the block from below.

Bridge rushed to the window, clamping dark glasses to his face. He pushed the butt of a rifle through the glass and then crouched. He sighted carefully into the glaring disc of the searchlight. The gunshot and the extinguishing of the light came together.

"Time to go," said Bridge. "Come on, take a swig of that." He handed Michael the whisky bottle then turned and shot twice straight through the closed front door of the apartment then laid down the gun and picked up a screwdriver.

Michael had never seen a man move the way Bridge did. Bridge never hesitated between actions and seemed capable of doing six things at once, moving through his mysterious programme with balletic grace and total assurance. Michael watched as the window was released from its mounting and lifted into the room. The cold air and the smoke rushed in.

"Mask," said Bridge, who already had his on. He picked up the nylon ladder and draped it over his left arm. He went to the window; Michael saw him sway as he swung the ladder. out and up. It took three attempts. There was the clatter of the hooks catching above. Bridge pulled the other end of the ladder in and tested its hold.

"We're doing fine," he said. "Don't worry. The place isn't on fire. Yet. That's just smoke. Up you go. We're hanging off the gantry the window cleaners use. Just like walking upstairs. There's a gap between the rail and the parapet, but it's not too bad. Get up there and wait for me. Keep your body straight and don't look down. Come on. On the chair. I'll push you out. Wait for me when you get there, won't you?" He was actually grinning inside the mask, Michael could tell.

But Michael was paralysed, eyes staring. Bridge cursed and forced the whisky bottle at him, tearing his mask off, pouring the strong drink into his throat and over his clothes. *"Do it, you yellow bastard!"*

Michael took the ladder in his hands. Stood on the chair. Bridge put his feet on the right rungs then lifted him bodily up and fed him through the window. Michael yelled as he lost his grip, got it again and felt Bridge's muscles shake as he let the rope ladder slowly down.

Then he was swinging clear, in the pall of smoke. For a moment all his muscles locked. He was using all his strength just to hang on. The spasm was numbing the very grip he was trying to hold and his legs pushed in towards the building. The weight on his arms increased. His breath came in stifling sobs through the foul-smelling mask.

"Move!" yelled Bridge.

He got himself upright and lifted one foot. The ladder tilted. He got the next rung and moved a hand. Did it again. He knew he was never going to get there. He could feel the vertigo sucking at him. Was it earth or concrete twenty-two storeys below? He should have told Bridge the reason he couldn't stand heights. It was because he'd seen his friend Bristow die. Bristow's first parachute jump. They'd taken the family to see it. Fortunately the kids were too young to understand. The little black package falling out of the pretty little aeroplane on a sunny summer day. The gasps and the wails of horror from below as the parcel just kept on falling. The wails rising and rising in pitch as if they were trying to force the package back into the sky. But it just plummeted, endlessly, mysteriously, towards the pretty green field. And disappeared silently into the grass. Michael had been one of the people running towards the place. Though not as fast as Bristow's wife; she was running crazily, her arms stretched before her as if she were going to catch a ball. And he had seen the packet fall and then bounce, once, at terminal velocity. When they got there he was lying quite neatly in a small hole that someone had dug exactly to fit his body shape.

It was strange. They said you saw your own life going by, the minutes before you died. But he was seeing Bristow's.

Something had happened. He was at the top of the ladder. The hooks were over a square girder that was gleaming with frost and slippery when he touched it. The gap to the parapet was more than three feet. Much more. He began working it out automatically. Not because he was going to get across that gap but because there was nothing else to do before he fell off.

He supposed the idea was to pull yourself onto the girder and get your knees on it and then fall onto the parapet and get from your knees on to your feet. He was feeling childishly angry with Bridge. No one should be asked to do anything so unreasonable. He got one knee up; it slithered on the frost and he felt his bladder empty.

Suddenly anger took over completely. He fought his way onto the girder and hurled himself onto the parapet, tumbled and fell.

When he opened his eyes he was on his back and looking at the sky. A clear night sky full of stars. Suddenly, for the first time in his life, he knew that he was alive. Could feel his heart pumping obediently. And the grit of the roof sharp against the back of his hand. He looked at the stars; one day they would all be dead too, chunks of black diamond moving soundlessly in the black. After the agony of the death throes when all the hydrogen had been burnt in the core and the helium ash was ignited as the star collapsed in on it. He felt the death of the stars like his own and fainted.

Bridge kicked him awake. For some reason Bridge was kicking him across the roof, rolling him like a dog. Maybe it was because Bridge's hands were full. He was a grotesque shape, loaded down with equipment and silhouetted against a boiling mass of yellow flame that was pouring up the side of the building.

Michael got to his knees, still childishly glad to be alive. "I did it," he said.

"Yes. I shouldn't take it up as a profession. I thought you were going to spend the night there."

Michael blinked at the flames. "I thought you said they weren't burning us out."

"They weren't. I am. Don't worry. No one's going to miss the place. I'm on the rehousing list anyway."

Looking across the flat roof Michael saw a curious thing. The roof was bubbling up into blisters and the blisters were popping like crackers. Suddenly the thrill of standing on a solid surface wore off quite quickly.

At the junction of Scawen Road the argument had begun again.

"Let's just get home and order the flowers," said John. "He's not getting out of *there.*"

"Thirty more minutes," said Nob. They could hear the firebells racing in from Creek Road and South Street. "He said we'd know when it started, didn't he?"

"So?"

The tower block was like a square candle, with a plume of flame eddying in the wind. Nob looked at it with satisfaction. "Twenty-nine more minutes."

* * *

Bridge rolled the grey drum over to the building that housed the winding gear of the lift. "I can do it myself," he said. "But it's going to be quicker if you hand it to me. Don't drop it, will you? Or we'll be here for a cooked breakfast."

He climbed onto the gantry and shackled one end of a steel cable loop to the girder. Then he reached for the drum. Michael braced himself and held it over the edge to him. It was heavy. Only the pressure of his knees against the parapet kept him upright.

"Jesus, not like that," said Bridge. "Get down and hold it."

Michael crouched, tried again.

"Good."

He watched Bridge pass the steel loop through the hole in the middle of the drum, pull a wrench from his belt and tighten something with six powerful twists. Then he fixed the other end of the loop to a stanchion supporting the girder; the drum was hanging free, three feet away from the parapet. Michael peered over and saw, dizzying away into the darkness, a corner of the building where the lift shaft jutted out, like half a corridor standing on end.

"Hold this," said Bridge. He was standing on the gantry and passing him a wire that came out of the drum; the wire had a loop on the end. Then Bridge went back to fiddling with the drum. When he finished, he jumped back on the roof and said, "How much do you weigh, Michael?"

"Twelve stone."

"That makes twenty-five and a half. That's one and a half over the top. Let's hope they left a margin for error." He was hooking something that looked like a plastic shopping bag onto the end of the wire.

"We're going down there?"

"Arm in arm, Michael. That's an inertia reel. You know what that is?"

"Yes."

"OK. Sit on my lap."

Bridge put his legs through two holes in the shopping bag and fixed a belt round his waist.

"This is what the round-the-world-guys use when they have to climb the mast. It's tougher than it looks. Come on."

The flames from the other end of the roof were different now. They were blowing straight through the roof itself, like blowlamps. Obviously Bridge had used something pretty good to start a holocaust this fast, thought Michael.

"It's OK, Michael. No one's going to be looking from the river side."

Michael took one last glance at the view from this side of the tower. The River Thames was immediately below, taking its snake path through the dead land of the Surrey Docks. Though his eyes were scalded by the flames from the northern edge of the building, he could still pick out the dark path of the water far beneath.

Bridge braced his legs against the parapet from the outside. He was sitting in space, waiting. The scene was unreal enough to make it easier. Michael jumped into his arms and wrapped his own around Bridge's neck. Immediately they began to drop.

Michael could hear Bridge choking as they fell down the side of the building. They were going fast, starting to spin. Sometimes the wall hit the ragged clothes Michael was wearing and burnt through them to the skin. Bridge was cursing. Suddenly the drop stopped.

He was sitting on Bridge's lap. They were face to face, his arms clasped round Bridge's neck. He felt a surge of warmth.

"You know," said Bridge, "you stink. We made it, Michael. Now we just walk down the rest of the wall. We've ten minutes. Don't strangle me."

Michael looked down. "Why only ten minutes?"

"Because I'm blowing the lift shaft up in ten minutes."

Bridge began walking, pushing his legs just like a man walking backwards. Michael could do nothing but lie heavily on top of him. They were walking down a vertical surface and it suddenly seemed easy as going anywhere. Michael felt a huge admiration for this man who could arrange such things. Snug in the corner of the building, they were invisible.

"You worked all this out a long time ago," said Michael admiringly. "They're going to think we're dead up there."

"If you've got to go, you may as well do it properly," said Bridge.

He pushed again and they hit the ground.

Ten seconds later, before Bridge could climb out of the harness, the explosive blew above them and the wire went slack. Bridge pressed Michael to the wall as the blast rained debris around them. At the last moment the plastic shopping bag and the wire were whipped away out into the river; far above, the blast in the wheelhouse had thrown the inertia reel far into the Thames.

"Now *that*," said Bridge calmly, "wasn't right. Next time I'll make my own fuse."

35

In Whitehall this April day, the minister of energy and his personal private secretary confronted Derek Sewell and John Cox. At the end of the table, endlessly rubbing at a tiny stain on its polished surface, Aloysius Clough looked at none of them.

"I don't understand your reservations," said the minister.

"ICARUS is steaming ahead. You've taken the whole project on beautifully after your man French vanished. No news of him still, Clough?"

"No, sir," said Clough.

"Eloped with his mistress, didn't he? Anyway. I want you to go on television and tell us all about it. Not French, ICARUS."

"It's a security area," said Sewell.

"I know that. I'm not asking you to give away any secrets. I just want you to explain that Britain is leading the world in the field of fusion energy. That we have a patent on a limitless source of power. I want you to *do* it, Sewell."

"I think it's a good idea," said Cox quickly. He looked at Sewell, puzzled.

"Everything *is* going well, isn't it, Sewell?" said the minister anxiously.

"Of course. But why do you want this to happen?"

The minister breathed deeply. "Because, Dr. Sewell, next week's White Paper on the state of the North Sea oil fields is going to show that far from seeing us into the next century they are going to run dry in about two years flat. Which means that we are in one awful mess. That we have the imminent prospect of a balance of trade deficit running into the six thousand million pounds annually. It means that all the money will start pouring out of Britain again and the pound collapses. Unless we have the good news first. *You* are the good news. Energy from seawater! A triumph!"

"I—"

Clough coughed. "Minister. I think I understand Dr. Sewell's problem. Perhaps if he and I could have a little chat together when the meeting is over."

"The meeting *is* over," said the minister irritably. "I am very grateful to you, gentlemen, in advance." He strode out, the PPS scurrying behind.

After a moment Cox shrugged and followed suit. When he had gone, Clough asked, "What's wrong, Derek?"

Sewell broke a pencil. "I just have this feeling. I still feel he is out there somewhere. I have this thought of my face on

the television screen and Michael French watching me
from—wherever he is. And coming for me."

"Whatever other comforts they may have where Michael
went, television is not among them."

"You must tell me. What happened to him?"

"I must *not* tell you what happened to him."

"Then I'm not doing it."

Clough went back to rubbing the table. He sighed. "All
right. Three weeks ago the British Secret Service and the
GRU—and the KGB—surrounded the block of flats where
Michael French was living with an East End criminal. I'm
sure you read the story in the press. The Irish terrorists who
burned themselves to death?"

"That was French?" Sewell's eyes were greedy for good
news.

"That was French. A fanatic to the end."

"They found the bodies?" Sewell asked suspiciously.

"They were immediately under a roof covering composed
of twenty tons of asphalt. It burnt beautifully. I really think
you ought to be satisfied, Sewell, and get this thing ready for
the minister. They want it done by yesterday. When are you
running the first ICARUS warm-up?"

"Ten days. Eighty million degrees."

"I must be there. I do hope you'll reserve me a seat at the
ringside. Or would that be dangerous?"

"You know what they say. Fusion reactors don't blow up."

"Make that point tomorrow, won't you? That's the best
selling line. Now that the unions have come out against fast
reactors ICARUS is really the only egg left in the basket."

"You've taken a weight off my mind," said Sewell.

And indeed, as he walked through the first raw green of
spring in the park, Sewell did breathe so much more easily.
There were flowers. There were pigeons eyeing each other
with impartial springtime lust. The sun shone more brightly.

In the New Cross Hospital psychiatric wing, Dr. Gutteridge smiled but did not look up from his task as the door

opened and the next patient was shown in. He allowed the smile to spread its network of little laughter wrinkles all over his face and went on writing up the notes of the last visitor. It was necessary to do it at once because otherwise they tended to blur into a grey and generalised image of human misery at the end of the day.

"Do sit down. And how are you today?" He finished the notes and took the next folder, searching for the name. Then he remembered. This was the one without a name. He looked up. The man was sitting patiently in his armchair, watching him with his normal lack of interst. "Ah," said Dr. Gutteridge. "We're going to have another of our little chats, are we?"

Their little chats had been going on three weeks. Gutteridge talked and the mystery listened. It was damned foolery to send the man in here in the first place, A dosser who had been breaking windows in New Cross Broadway. Just because the magistrate had the stupid idea that the poor devil looked *intelligent*. Only social workers and writers of fiction still believed people looked intelligent. Back on the ward Dr. Gutteridge had an old guy who looked like Einstein and finished off every meal trying to eat his dinner plate.

"Well, we didn't get very far, did we?" said Dr. Gutteridge, looking through the blank pages. *"Patient admits to feelings of persecution,"* he read. "Anyway, I see you're leaving us tonight. Back on the road? Back to the bottle? We could help you, you know."

"I'd be grateful if you could do something for me," said Michael French.

Dr. Gutteridge raised his eyebrows. The man could talk in long sentences.

"Shall I tell you who I am?" said Michael.

Dr. Gutteridge nodded.

"I'm a nuclear scientist working on a very secret project called ICARUS. Now, the British and the Russian secret services are trying to kill me. What I want you to do is to ring up my doctor and tell him I am still alive and well. Ask him to come down and see you. As soon as he can. Then give him this letter." He held out a letter.

"I *see*," said Dr. Gutteridge. "You are a *nuclear scientist.* That must be a *very* interesting job."

"It has its moments. You will ring this doctor, won't you? Could you do that now?"

"If you like." Gutteridge was intrigued. He wrote the word *fantasy*. "What did you say the project was called? The secret project you were working on?"

"ICARUS."

"Do you know who Icarus was?"

"Of course," said Michael irritably. "Sometimes I think I am Icarus too. By the way, Dr. Orlov believes he is a colonel in the KGB."

Dr. Gutteridge nodded. "That's understandable," he said.

Michael showed him the telephone number, then took away the piece of paper it was written on.

Dr. Gutteridge dialled. "Is Dr. Orlov there? I have a patient of his. Michael French. The nuclear scientist. That's right." He moved the phone away from his ear and said, "They're going to find him." Michael nodded. Dr. Gutteridge flashed him a smile.

"It's *Professor* Michael French," said Michael.

Dr. Gutteridge nodded with conviction. "Oh, is that Dr. Orlov? Yes. Yes, that's right. No, I'm Dr. Gutteridge. Yes. Fortyish, brown hair, that's right. Yes. He's here. . . . No, I can't do that. He's going out. He's being released. This is the New Cross Hospital psychiatric wing. He has a letter for you. Would you like me to post it to you?"

"He comes here and gets it," said Michael.

"You *will* come here and get it? Oh fine. This evening? Well, I suppose so. Dr. Orlov, I have Mr.—Professor French with me here. I don't know if there is anything you ought to tell me?"

"Tell him," said Michael, "that I don't want to talk to anyone else. But if he doesn't get here tonight I will."

"He says you should be here tonight or he will talk to

someone else. No, I'm sorry, Dr. Orlov, I can't do what you just suggested. I understand from Mr.—Professor French you are a colonel in the KGB." Dr. Gutteridge regarded the phone in some surprise and then replaced it.

"He seems anxious to see you. Why don't you wait until he comes down? Is he a *private* doctor?"

"No. He's a KGB colonel. I told you."

"That must explain his ignorance of the workings of the British National Health Service," agreed Gutteridge. "What *sort* of nuclear scientist would you describe yourself as?" Sometimes the fantasists really worked these things out. "I mean," said Gutteridge, "do you make bombs? I hope you don't want to destroy the world."

"I turn seawater into energy," said Michael French.

"Really. That *must* be interesting."

"Or you could say I make sunlight. It's the same thing, you know. Thank you very much, Dr. Gutteridge. Do tell Dr. Orlov not to trust the British Secret Service. They double-crossed him, you see."

Dr. Gutteridge clicked his tongue. "It's a complicated world, isn't it? I hope your research goes very well, Professor. Are you sure you haven't a forwarding address for us?"

"The dossers go to Carrington House, don't they?" Michael said flatly and left the room.

The orderly took him back to his ward. It was visiting time. At the next bed Pop Andrews, eighty-two, was telling his son about the old days, again. Michael French began packing a small plastic bag with the dosser's clothes that had been efficiently laundered.

"We used to break the ice on the ponds in Blackheath," said Pop Andrews, staring from his sightless eyes. "You know that ice would last all summer in the ice cave in Diamond Terrace? That's where we put the fish, you see. There was a great fishing fleet from Greenwich in those days. Right out into the North Sea. We brought it all back live. Special holds with holes for the fish to swim about in. Then we'd be off under the hill, wouldn't we. Tunnels right up under Blackheath, son. No one knows where they are now. Underneath the Point. Great big cave. Took all the Greenwich tarts up there. You're a good boy. Good of you to come and see your dad again. What's it like in Australia then?"

"It's fine," said Crispin Bridge.

"Good of you to come back and see me. They don't, you know, most of them never care a shit. I'd have liked it out there, wouldn't I?"

"Did you do it?" Bridge asked French without looking at him.

"I did it. I think it scared them good."

"Hey. Son."

"Yeah, Pop?"

"You can't take me back with you, can you?"

"No, Pop. You'd fall over the kangaroos' tails."

The old man opened his mouth in a huge grin and drummed his fist on the bedcover. "You were always a one. Fancy ending up here though, eh? Loony bin, isn't it? They keep washing you, you know. All the fucking time. Taking your clothes off and washing you. Some of those nurses take *liberties*, too."

"You should be so lucky," said Bridge.

Pop drummed the bed again.

"Listen," said Bridge. "I've put a bottle of scotch in the locker. Don't drink it all at once." He stood up. "Ready?" he asked Michael.

"Sure. Was this a good idea, Cris?" He looked at Pop Andrews. Bridge looked at the old man, too. "I've got to go now, Pop."

The old man tipped his face to and fro, sensing the voice had moved. From his open eyes the water fell soundlessly. "Go on, then. You write to me. Not like the last twenty years."

"I'll write you. I'll write you rude postcards and the nurses can read them out."

"Come here."

Bridge came to the bed and took the old man's hand.

Pop Andrews didn't move his face but he raised his other hand and moved it over Bridge's cheek. "You write me," he said.

"Go well, Pop."

Michael French shook his head and walked out of the door. Bridge followed. "I'll bring the car," said Bridge.

They walked down the corridor. It was early evening. There was the smell of disinfectant and hot, sweet tea, the babble of television and the clank of food trolleys.

"What a fucking dump," said Bridge.

"Poor old Andrews," said Michael.

"Listen," said Bridge, stopping dead. "Poor old Andrews has been here fifteen years. He knows as well as I do I'm not his long lost son from Adelaide. Apart from thinking there's a bloody great snake under his bed he's as sane as you and me, and he's done us a bloody good turn these last three weeks."

"Where are you going?" asked the nurse, arms on her hips in front of them.

"Out of this pissing place," said Bridge.

"I know you're being discharged," said the nurse to Michael. "But don't just walk out of here like that. There are rules."

"What you want him to do, crawl?" said Bridge, and strode past her into the yard.

"He's getting the car," said Michael.

"Is he a friend of yours?"

"He's giving me a lift. Down the road."

"You're talking a lot suddenly, Mr. Nobody."

"I'm stopping now," said Michael.

She looked at him, then shrugged. Began to walk away. The quicker they cleared out the dossers the better.

"One thing," said Michael.

She stopped.

"Pop Andrews doesn't eat lettuce. He doesn't eat lettuce because he hasn't any teeth. He hasn't had any teeth for fifteen years and you've been giving him lettuce for fifteen

years. He's blind and he reaches into his bowl and he finds
lettuce. That's—"

"Mr. Nobody," said the nurse. "You handle your problems
and we'll handle ours."

Suddenly the glass doors of the hospital began to shake.
The sound of a huge engine labouring in reverse gear filled
the yard. Looking through the shuddering glass Michael saw
a juggernaut truck edging into the yard, the hiss of vacuum
brakes exploding like steam. Unbelieving, he went through
the doors, his small plastic holdall in his hand, and watched
Bridge climbing loosely down from a brand-new Volvo
Intercontinental. "*This* is the car?" said Michael.

"You said we had to get her out of Russia somehow," said
Bridge. "And like you said, it's good to have money in the
Building Society. Let's get out of here before Orlov arrives."

Michael went around the other side and began climbing in.
The yard was small. Bridge would have to reverse and then
edge forward.

"You ought to be careful," said Michael. "Dr. Gutteridge
has his Marina parked directly behind us."

Bridge adjusted the wing mirrors. "I'll remember that," he
said. He reversed so smoothly that there was hardly any
sound at all to say that the Marina was gently crushed into the
brick wall like a used can of Coke.

Colonel Orlov fell into Dr. Gutteridge's office. Driving
through the rush hour down the Old Kent Road had taken
time. "Is he still here?"

"No," said Dr. Gutteridge. "He left. As he was entitled
to. Perhaps *I* am fantasizing, but it suddenly occurred to me I
was doing a good turn."

"Well, you don't believe—"

"I'm sure you are not a colonel in the KGB. A private
doctor, though? Obviously the man *is* intelligent. I imagine—
forgive me if I'm wrong—he is someone who feels the need

to disappear. While perhaps his family doesn't want to let him. I have a special interest in amnesia. Do you work for his family, Dr. Orlov? Why does he identify you with the KGB, for example? We should take our patients' fantasies seriously, I feel. Now suppose—"

Orlov seriously wondered if he could just break this gibbering lunatic's neck. "Was there a letter?" he asked.

"There *is* a letter."

Orlov tore it open. It read: *The Deptford Infant, 7:40. Alone.*

"He believes he is a nuclear scientist," said Dr. Gutteridge.

"I know," said Orlov. "You are quite right, of course. I do work for his family. Please don't talk about this case."

"I don't chatter, Dr. Orlov. I wonder why he associated you with the KGB. Perhaps he has heard something about the dreadful things the Russian psychiatrists do to their political prisoners."

Orlov clenched his fists inside his pockets. "If he comes back," he said, "do be careful, won't you, Dr. Gutteridge? He has been known to attack people."

Dr. Gutteridge flashed his well-creased smile and watched Orlov stumble out. He was still smiling as he strolled into the yard to drive home to Beckenham. The smile faded only slowly as he saw the crumbled heap of new metal that had only three hours ago been his wife's pride and joy, and only lent him as a special favour.

"Your friend Sewell is going to be on the telly," said Jim Henderson. "Do those clothes fit?"

"Not bad," said Michael. "I'm grateful, Jim."

Jim Henderson looked round the small service apartment. "It's not much of a place. All I could find. How in hell did you get out of that building, Michael? I went down there next morning. As soon as Wally rang me. It was *still* burning. What were you doing in the nuthouse?"

"Lying low," said Michael. "Cris miscalculated there a bit. But we needed time to fix the next move."

Henderson shook his head. "The next move is mine. I'll just write it all down. Chapter and verse, and serve it them on a plate. They'll reinstate you. They'll do anything to keep it quiet. Do you want another drink, Mr. Bridge?"

Bridge checked his watch and shook his head. He was keeping an eye on the Volvo truck through the window. He liked nowhere that wasn't his own.

"No," said Michael. "We've worked it out. This time we make them an offer they can't refuse."

"Michael, you can't just wage a private war. You're not still hoping you're going to get that girl, are you? I just told you. They took her back to Leningrad. Patterson told me. Young guy who worked for Clough. He didn't live long."

Michael shrugged. "Then we'll get her back."

"Michael. You've got to understand this. This is just an obsession. It does look as if the girl was fond of you. And I see what you mean about your wife. I went to see her. No joy. But the last three weeks the Russians must have believed you were dead, right? You have to be realistic. I don't know what they've done about the girl, but there can't be a hope you'll see her again. I can understand how you fell. You've been on your own against this man Clough, and your colleagues have double-crossed you and your wife—"

"It's not really up to Michael anymore," said Bridge. "I met you before, didn't I?"

"Oh come on, Mr. Bridge. You were paid to do a job. You did it very well. Don't get this poor guy in any further."

"That's up to Michael," said Bridge. "These bastards burnt me out. They're going to pay for that. I've got to move. It's time I talked to Colonel Orlov. Thanks for the drink."

"He doesn't like journalists," said Henderson as they heard the truck surge alive below them. "What about money, Michael? You must be pretty thin on that."

"No, that's all right," said Michael. "We robbed the university computer."

"Jesus Christ," said Henderson. "You've changed, Michael. Do you want to see this thing about ICARUS on the telly? That's another thing. Apparently if we don't get ICARUS the country's going down the drain."

"Tired, darling?" said Mrs. Gutteridge. Dr. Gutteridge sprawled into the armchair and gazed unseeing at the television screen.

"Where's the car?" said Mrs. Gutteridge. "I didn't hear the car."

Dr. Gutteridge tipped his head sideways towards her but kept his eyes on the screen. It was a party political broadcast, but he looked interested. "The car," he said. "You won't believe it."

On the screen the minister of energy was mouthing ʼ ɩɪɪ ɪɡɪ ɪɪ ɪɪ.ɪɪʏ Thɪ.ɪɪ ɪɪɪ.ɪɪ. ɪɪ.ɪɪ.ɪɪ ɪɪ.ɪ.ɪɪɪɪɪɪɪ. You could tell he was a scientist because he had a white coat. The zoom lens swam in on him across huge fields and he was standing outside some kind of aeroplane hangar.

"What happened with the car?"

He leapt up to turn on the sound. Dr. Gutteridge gave his smile. "The car is ruined," he said.

From the screen Derek Sewell said, "The most important development in the energy field since man discovered coal."

"You haven't had an accident, have you? That's my car, Martin. I—"

"As you know, the oil-fired economy of the twentieth century is doomed to flicker out. Sooner, rather than later."

"What have you done to my car?"

"It was in the car park. I came out into the car park and I found the car was *crushed.* Just crushed. Believe me I was as appalled in a human—"

"But there is an alternative. And one in which Britain has taken the lead. The oldest and newest energy of all. The sun." Camera moves to sun.

"Martin. You have done *what?*"

"I went into the yard and I found the car had been smashed." He was watching the screen.

"By the process of nuclear fusion," said Derek Sewell. "In the ICARUS reactor we combine atoms of deuterium—that's heavy water—in order to—"

"I *told* you not to take that car into town. I *told* you."

"Shut up." He leant forward. "Did he say—Icarus?"

"I am not watching the television," said Mrs. Gutteridge. "I am talking about my *car.*"

"A lot of people. Professor Michael French. John Cox. Myself."

"*French,*" said Dr. Gutteridge.

"Are you listening to me?"

"No," he said thoughtfully.

36

Colonel Orlov entered the public bar of the Deptford Infant with understandable caution. He was beginning to have a healthy respect for Crispin Bridge's resources on his own ground. He wouldn't want Bridge introducing him as the man who had burnt down the Inigo Jones Tower, for example. Though in fact, in this pub, that would have got him free drinks all night. Two Irishmen were staring fixedly at a huge television screen whose picture was composed of pink and green abstract clouds. Occasionally one could see an image of a woman singing. Or possibly triplets standing very close behind each other. Certainly the Irishmen hadn't been watching Derek Sewell.

"A glass of real ale, mate," said Orlov casually. Like the rest, he'd had lessons from Asimov.

The licensee's eyes narrowed. "You what?" he said eventually.

Orlov told him again.

"You bleeding CAMRA or something?"

Orlov's confidence in his mastery of the vernacular took a dive. "I haven't a camera," he said.

Suddenly the light dawned on the barman. It was a bleeding foreigner, no member of the Campaign for Real Ale. He called behind him through a maze of bottles and mahogany and etched glass into the reaches of the other bar. "Crispin? Your poncy friend. Take him in the saloon where he belongs, will you?"

Bridge called him in. "In here, Boris."

Boris looked nervously around. "How do I get there?"

"Take a taxi," suggested the barman. "Or go through that door and in again."

"That says *Toilets*," said Boris shrewdly.

"Oh Jesus," said the barman. "Crispin. Get him out of here, will you? He's made the television go funny."

Crispin Bridge led him away. "What are you having then, Boris? I'm on Guinness."

"Would you mind not shouting my name? And how did this *peasant* know it anyway?"

"I think it's a *nice* name, Boris!" shouted Bridge.

"*Please*," said Boris.

Crispin brought him back a bottle of Guinness. "You're safe here, Boris," he said. "You're among friends. My friends."

Colonel Orlov hadn't done field work for a couple of years. When he had, it had been with professionals monitoring the hot air balloon escape from Germany. He didn't like the look of this man Bridge one little bit. He felt a grudging sympathy for the wretched Viktor. This one was obviously *un*professional. Even so, when he had dealt with the natives he had always found they responded kindly to a foreigner's natural interest in their folk customs.

"Guinness," said Colonel Orlov. "That is an interesting drink."

Crispin Bridge looked at him and sighed. Then he picked up the open bottle. "You're *right*, Boris. Did you know you can always tell the difference between a Guinness bottled in Ireland and one bottled over here?"

"No. How's that?"

"The ones bottled in Ireland always have the words 'Open other end' written on the bottom."

Boris looked down thoughtfully. But he wasn't thinking about the old joke, he was thinking of the half pint of Guinness Crispin Bridge had just poured into his lap.

"There you are," said Bridge. "This one must have been bottled in England. Stop fucking around, Boris. This is business time."

Orlov felt a huge rage boiling up in him in direct measure to the wetness soaking into his trousers.

"We're going to do a deal, Boris."

"That was unnecessary," said Orlov very quietly.

"So was everything else. You burnt my apartment, Boris. That's expensive. You want me to help you, you have to pay for that. For starters."

Orlov began to get interested again. "We'll pay for goods delivered," he said.

"Let me get you another drink."

"Vodka," said Orlov.

Bridge got it. "Now," he said. "You get the idea. I'm ready to do business with you. OK? This time. Just for once. We get it right."

"How did you get out of that building?"

"We weren't *in* that building. The British Secret Service were playing a trick on you again. So don't talk to them."

"That poisonous dwarf," said Orlov.

"Clough? Right."

"Who's got French now?"

"I have."

"You're doing business for him?"

"No, Boris. That's the new dimension. I keep telling you. This time we're *really* talking business. You can have the bugger. I just work for cash. He can't pay me. So you will."

Orlov looked thoughtful. "How much?"

"Thirty thousand dollars."

"Payable?"

"I've got a Leapman account."

Orlov looked at him with new respect. "Have you indeed?" He'd never met a Leapman account holder. The ultimate credit for the big operators. You paid your money into a Swiss bank and they notified the account holder it had arrived but they didn't pay out until both sides were satisfied the root of the business had been completed satisfactorily.

"What do I get for thirty thousand dollars?"

"You get a packet containing the full plans for ICARUS."

"I'm not interested in packets. The last time I bought secret plans they turned out to be blueprints for a sewage works. I think we'll forget it. After all, when your ICARUS starts running next week—we'll find a way of getting inside it. One day."

"I haven't finished. ICARUS isn't going to run next week. That's what makes Michael French worth buying. The stuff French fed into that computer is *real* sewage. Clough hasn't anything to sell you anyway. Have you got that in your thick skull?"

Even Orlov could see the irony of it. "So Professor French played the same trick on Clough that they played on him? What happens when they switch on?"

"I'm not too well up in all that. Something called scatter."

"Tritium radiation. Nasty."

"But they won't be switching on."

"Why not?"

"French isn't a mass murderer like you, Orlov. Before we move out, we'll tell them they're up a gum tree."

"I think I want to insist you let them go ahead and blow themselves up. With luck Clough will be there too."

"I don't care what you want, Boris. You'll be getting the real goods. And of course you'll be getting Michael French."

"He still wants to live in Russia? With this girl?"

"No, he doesn't want to live in Russia. He wants the girl. I hope she is in good working order."

"I telephoned Leningrad to make sure. Apparently they got her out of the clutches of Viktor just in time. Go on."

"Ten days from now: You hand over the girl. French hands over his plans. The girl and French get into my truck. We drive off. Ten miles up the road we stop. You'll be following in a taxi. It'll be a nice lonely place. I'll get out of the truck to look at a back wheel. Then it's up to you. You can take them away."

"So you would betray your friend? The perfidious English."

"I shouldn't joke if I were you. I said I work for money."

"There's only one little drawback," said Orlov. "About your lucid scenario. Where in the world is all this supposed to happen? I'm afraid my memory must be failing me. I can't seem to remember any frontier between East and West where one can hand over a Russian citizen and then quietly drive after them and take them and an English citizen back again. I mean, without starting a major international incident."

Bridge looked at him disparagingly. "Yes there is, Boris. It's called Turkey. To be precise, it's called Kusadasi. You know? Where the Black Sea cruise ships come in from Odessa and the party faithful are allowed out to buy rugs in the bazaars?"

"Kusadasi," said Orlov thoughtfully. "You are very thorough. Somehow I thought you were going to say that."

"You've been using it for years. There's no passport

control. The Reds walk off the boat in hordes and climb into their buses to go and see the ruins of Ephesus. From which some of them don't come back."

"How did you know this?"

"I drive trucks," said Bridge. "On the Middle East run. Like next week I'm taking a load of antiques to Iran. A whole lorry crammed with grandfather clocks and wardrobes and tables. You'd have to unpack the whole thing before you found Michael French. I drive to Volos in Greece and then on the new ferry to Kusadasi. Any more questions?"

"Date and time."

"Noon on 15 April."

"Your Leapman account number."

Bridge gave it to him.

"What kind of truck?"

Bridge led him outside and Orlov looked at the huge silver monster with respect. "You are through," he said.

"I nearly forgot," said Bridge. "The number of the taxi you'll be taking." Orlov wrote it down, too. "It's an American Chevrolet, vintage 1948, with a broken windscreen. The keys will be in it."

Orlov smiled. "Nothing less conspicuous?"

"In Kusadasi," said Bridge. "that is not conspicuous." He climbed into his cab and with a belch of blue smoke that nearly swept Orlov from his feet gunned down the Deptford Church Street.

Next morning the Volvo truck was heading north, Michael and Crispin sitting silent.

"He's really going to do it?" said Michael. "You must think I'm crazy to do all this for a girl I've never—"

"Anything with a woman in it is crazy."

"They're going to be pretty sore when they find out. I mean when they open the packet and try it. They're not going to play some trick on us, are they? I mean, I have this nightmare they give me Kyra and then—then they come after us again."

"Let me worry about that," said Bridge.

"You've spent a lot of money, Bridge. This antique deal for Iran."

"That *makes* me money. It's a contract. The Arabs love grandfather clocks. I'm loading up tomorrow. Down in Tilbury. You worry about Derek Sewell's nightmares."

"I'm just afraid I'm going to kill him."

"You're not the type."

"Who knows who is the type? I feel mad at him. I want to hurt him. I want him to go through the same agony I went through. You do that to a man's work. What he did. . . ."

"Where do we go now?"

They were coming into the flatlands of East Anglia. It was very early. A mist was still lying on the stoney fields. Larks, unheard through the din of the engine, were shrilling their threats at each other.

"Next left," said Michael. "He may not be there. But he always was a filthy little creature of habit."

They drove off the A1 towards the Old Warden airfield, then, on Michael's instructions, reversed into a narrow lane. Completely blocking the exit.

37

Derek Sewell left his country cottage at 7:40 as usual. Envy of Michael and Mary French's place had led him to buy himself an old beamed cottage in the hinterland of Cambridgeshire. He had few friends and found it strangely lonely, but the fashion on the ICARUS team was for rural dwellings and he wasn't going to be outdone. Anyway, on a morning like this, the mist dripping off the fresh green needles of the larch trees and the daffodils shining in the sunrise—it was very good. The broadcast had gone well. He had a hangover still from the amount of sherry that John Cox and Mary French had poured out to celebrate. Once again he wondered why Annie Cox had gone back to Canada. You could imagine that Mary French and John Cox were—anyway, Sewell didn't really care one way or another what people got up to.

Humming happily in the new release from anxiety about Michael French, he got into his car and drove out into the lane. Next week they'd run it to 80 million degrees. It would be a triumph. He tasted it already. The surge of acceleration as the frozen particles dropped into the laser beam, the—

There was a damned great truck parked at the end of the lane, blocking it completely. Sewell braked angrily and blew his horn. Bloody lorry drivers. Why couldn't they stay on the motorway to sleep at night? Kipping in *his* lane for the night. He hit the horn again. There was no sign of interest from the truck.

Cursing, Sewell swung his short legs out of the car and stood on the fresh smelling earth. Strutting slightly, he walked up the flank of the Volvo, looking for a name on the side. He would jolly well tell this driver's employers. Probably the man was fiddling the—

"Good morning, Derek," said Michael French, stepping out from in front of the lorry.

Sewell took in a huge, sucking draught of the fragrant air. His stomach shrivelled to a small ball and maybe his lungs had more space to fill. He had to lean against the vehicle. His upper lip was springing with sweat.

Michael French walked up to him. The Welshman began backing off. Not walking, just sliding his heels backwards, as if from the edge of a crater.

Very fast, Michael grabbed him by the shoulders and began shaking him. Huge jolting movements, back and forth, on and on, until Sewell's neck began clicking and he bit his tongue.

"That'll do, Michael," said the other man.

A dribble of blood crawled down Sewell's chin but he didn't dare lick it. The birds were singing as if it were a sunny day.

"You're going to do exactly what I tell you, Sewell," said Michael. "Otherwise I am going to kill you. You know that, don't you? Did you put that programme into the ICARUS?"

Sewell nodded.

"You better get it out again. You lined up the lasers the way I said?"

Sewell nodded.

"You've fixed to drop the pellets of deuterium the way I said?"

Sewell nodded.

"Then you bought an error," said Michael coldly. "I knew

you were too dumb to get it right yourself. You run ICARUS on that programme and you'll kill everyone within thirty feet. They'll have to spend ten years taking the pieces away and burying them. You'll live for about ten days, Sewell. Your hair will fall out the first day and your skin will start falling off the next. I don't want that to happen. Not even to you. You just tell Clough that you were so stupid you copied my input line by line. Tell him he hasn't got an ICARUS project. Why did you go along with this, Sewell?"

Sewell shook his head. All he could feel was animal relief that French wasn't going to kill him.

"Tell him, Sewell," said Michael.

Then Michael hit him. Not elegantly. But straight onto the nose. Sewell collapsed into a ball of pain and streaming blood. Dimly through the pain he heard the truck moving off. He looked up to search for the number on the registration plate, but his glasses had spun into the ditch.

"You're too emotional," said Bridge.

Michael French looked at a bruised fist, his first for some time. "I'm not emotional," he said, staring ahead. "I didn't want him to see the license plates. Well, maybe I am. I want him to know what I've gone through."

Bridge smiled. "Not bad," he said. He turned the truck onto the A1 again. "Your pal Henderson is right. You're turning into a tough guy. But of course I removed the number plates before we started."

"Colonel Boris Orlov," said Aloysius Clough. "I have the unpleasant feeling that you have not been entirely straight with me." Clough smiled palely as Vera brought him a cup of milky, very sweet coffee. Five sugars. He found a space for it on his desk, on top of the sticky rings made by twenty years of his favourite beverage, in between the files. Then he went on listening to the telephone.

Orlov, at the other end of the line, frowned. "I think that feeling is mutual," he said.

"Ah," said Clough. "So I was right. You *do* know that Michael French is still alive."

Orlov was silent.

"I'll tell you what gave me the idea that you knew that," said Clough chattily. "In my next office I have a very unhappy man. A Dr. Sewell. He has a broken nose. Now why should Michael French come back from the dead with a fanciful tale about the ICARUS blowing up if we run to his new programme? I thought to myself: that sounds like a man who has been making some arrangements for his future. Someone who feels confident he can push his colleague's nose in. I wonder what arrangements he has made with you, Boris? By the way, how long would it take to arrange the departure of your entire trade and commercial staff? In 1962 I think we gave you two days."

Orlov was silent. But thinking hard. "I'll tell you this," said Orlov finally. "Then leave me alone. I can promise you French was lying when he said his programme would destroy ICARUS."

"Of course. Dr. Sewell confirms that his own research exactly matches French's 'repair job.' I'm glad we all agree on something. Do you think two days would be enough to clear your people out? Of course they'll sack you back in Moscow if it comes to that, won't they?"

He let it sink in.

"Boris," said Clough. "This is very sad, you know. We would *like* you to have Michael French. We have no use for him. Now just tell me where you are going to pick him up. Not in Britain, presumably. But the trouble is that if we watch every airport and so on he's not going to get out of Britain. It was silly for him to go to see Sewell."

"You don't mind us having him?"

"We agreed that. *I* don't know how he got out of that building."

"You don't? If you are happy he can come over, why do you want to know the details?"

"I told you before. I want to see him before he goes. It's

the form. I want to make it quite plain to him that he has no chance of coming back. Ever. His wife is going to marry one of his colleagues. That sort of thing. You know how embarrassing it is when people start changing their minds and wanting to come back home."

And suddenly a very bright and special idea swam into Colonel Orlov's mind. "When are you running ICARUS?"

"Next Wednesday at noon."

Orlov decided to risk it. Because if Clough was threatening to pull the rug *now*, what frame of mind would he be in when he discovered French hadn't been lying about the appalling things that would happen when the reactor was switched on? "Next Wednesday at noon you can shake hands with Dr. French for the last time."

Clough sipped his coffee happily.

"You in person," said Orlov. "You alone. That's all. No weapons, no tricks."

"I am waiting," said Clough.

"You follow a 1948 Chevrolet taxi out of town. Until it stops. We'll pick up Michael French. It's arranged."

"What town?"

"The taxi will be on the waterfront. Don't make any move until we stop out in the country."

"What country?"

"Turkey, Mr. Clough. The town of Kusadasi. A very sensible rendezvous on neutral ground. Neither of us wants to upset the Turks, do we?"

Orlov put down the phone and mopped his forehead. He wondered how much force it would take to break Clough's neck and whether he would fit into the trunk of an old American taxi.

Sewell appeared, white faced, at the door of Clough's office. "Who were you talking to? Is it all right?"

Clough had almost forgotten Sewell. "Of course it's all right. I can assure you Michael French was lying. It would be strange if he wasn't, don't you think? Since you've always assured me his research only confirmed your own? Get back to Cardington and *do* it. I want that reactor run at noon next Wednesday and I want the good news in the papers the next day. Before the horror stories about North Sea oil break."

Sewell gulped and fled.

Alone, Clough went to his most secret cupboard of all. The one behind the grey picture of the Virgin Mary. From it he carefully took the pair of black gloves they had captured from the Bulgarian assassin squad two years ago. The Science Service had analysed the device and Clough had been pleased to see that the compounds he had used so long before on poor Rudolf Hess were still serving their function. Of course they had been much refined. It wouldn't take years this time. It wouldn't take even the five minutes Orlov had promised him. No more than a handshake and a gentle pressure of the thumb. Then, in the next two days, the slow crumbling of the cerebral synapses as the nerve fibres dissolved. He smiled as he tried the gloves on, carefully. Then he replaced them and went to fetch an atlas. He wondered how the resourceful Mr. Bridge proposed getting to his curious destination.

38

"This is for you," said the matron. She tipped a heap of clothes onto the cold damp bed.

"Thank you," said Kyra.

"I didn't buy them," said the woman.

"No. For stopping that man."

The matron buttoned her lips. She said, "A shit pig." She looked at the girl crouched on the bed. These boney young women from the trans-Ural. The sort the KGB went for. Maybe they liked the contrast. Not like a bit of solid Latvian hip and thigh. "Why don't you look at your clothes?"

The girl pressed her fair hair from her forehead. It was half blonde, half black now as the black dye was growing out.

On the bed were the best imitations of French summer clothes that GUM could devise for GRU. Even in her misery, her eyes focussed on them. "For me? I don't need those in Gorsk."

"You're not going back to Gorsk."

"Where then?" She looked up, fearful.

"You're going south to Odessa. It's nice there. The spring has started."

"Odessa?"

The matron folded her arms. The child *was* beautiful, there was no doubt. The matron bent at the hips and whispered: "I didn't tell you this, remember. That man you want. They're going to let you have him."

Kyra Kruschev stood up slowly. "He is alive?"

The matron huffed her shoulders. "So why don't you wash your face and get dressed?"

The girl stood looking at the high window, where the sky was brightening. "Michael," she said. "Michael."

39

"Now," said Bridge. He flicked his eyes round the dockside. The loaders were going back for some more. All over the concrete were the grandfather clocks and the chest-on-chests and the Welsh dressers. The open maw of the Volvo was a black crater. The scene looked like a surrealist landscape by Magritte.

Michael made his move.

"Plastic bags in the wardrobe," said Bridge. "Right? Full of food and water. When you've eaten them you can use them for the other things. Start chopping your way out as soon as we're over the water. I'll stop before we get to Paris."

The forklift truck came back across the sunlit waste of Tilbury dockside. "Where's your mate?" said the driver.

"He's gone home," said Bridge. "Start putting it in, will you?"

The forklift truck drove straight up the ramp into the cavern of the truck. "You want it packed solid?"

"Of course I want it packed solid. I don't want it falling around halfway over the Alps."

"Beats me why they want all this stuff. Fucking Ay-rabs."

Wedged inside the wardrobe at the far end, Michael French braced himself as the forklift truck roared up the ramp and delivered another huge Victorian wardrobe flush against the cubbyhole he was in. For reassurance, he reached for the short axe Bridge had provided. It was cruelly dark.

Out there, he imagined the sun was shining. Six days, Bridge had said.

"Come on," said Bridge, leaning out of the cab. "I've got a boat to catch."

The Customs and Excise man looked malevolently up at him. "You loaded when we weren't here."

"I can't be responsible for when you're resting your ass." He revved the engine.

"You got your papers?"

Bridge switched off the engine. "Of course I've got my papers. You want to unpack the whole fucking truck? Or not?"

"I could."

"Well you do that. It's only on the return trip I fill it up with Pakis."

"I have a responsibility to see you have your export papers in order."

"Right on," said Bridge. He started handing them out. "France. Belgium. Germany. Austria. Yugoslavia. Greece. Turkey."

"Tell me about Turkey," said the Customs man. "You ever been there?"

"I've been there."

"How much Turkish currency have you got then?"

"Three hundred dollars' worth."

"You know you can't cash that in?"

Bridge started the engine again with a flourish. "I know *all* about it. I know that no TIR driver is let into Turkey without three hundred dollars' local currency and I know I'll never see it again. Now get out of the fucking way, I've a boat to catch."

40

"**D**o it," said Derek Sewell.

In the cavern of the old airship hangar John Cox narrowed his eyes on Sewell. It was only 11:00 in the morning but he could imagine Sewell had been drinking. "Why?" said Cox.

"Because I say so. Who's running this thing?"

"That's a very interesting question," said Cox. "But a little late in the day. Why do you want everything moved back?"

Sewell looked behind him; there was the huge hulk of the ICARUS reactor. It hadn't changed much since Michael disappeared. Except for the twelve laser guns. The lasers brooded over the doughnut-shaped heart of ICARUS, floating in their baths of oil.

"You can't suddenly say something like this," explained Cox. "Will someone get some light on this place?" Above him, as in a film set, the lights outshone the spring morning. Outside the hangar it was bright, but they needed light inside here.

Cox looked carefully at Sewell. The Welshman's face was maybe just puffy from the broken nose. Cox wasn't happy about it. You shouldn't be running a fusion reactor if you were the kind of guy who walked into lampposts.

"I mean," said Cox. "Next Wednesday. You're not thinking anything could go wrong, are you?"

"All I want is for the consoles to be moved back. Thirty
metres. That's just half a day's rewiring."

"Thirty metres? *Why?* There's no radiation problem. Is
there, Sewell?"

"Of course not," said Sewell. He smiled without much
humour. "Anyway, John, you and I will still have a grand-
stand view."

John Cox looked thoughtfully at the ICARUS. "Yes," he
said. "You and I are going to be sitting right on top of it,
aren't we?"

41

The huge silver lorry hurtled eastwards. They were in
Austria. The sun was rising ahead of them on the second day.
The world was warming up. Bridge had driven for eighteen
hours. Michael French lowered the cab window and let in the
fresh mountain air, sharp with the scent of new grass and tree
sap from the high pastures.

Michael inspected the blisters on the palms of his hands. It
had been hard work chopping through all that woodwork to
emerge, dazzled, from the womb of the Volvo into the layby
in Belgium.

But the journey since then, riding high in the cab, filled him with elation.

"Talk," said Bridge. "Keep me awake. What are you thinking about? That bird, I suppose."

"When I was a kid," said Michael, "and got my first bicycle, I'd go out on a spring morning like this. You remember that sort of feeling? As if you would get over the next hill and the sun would shine forever. Do you know, I have this extraordinary feeling, now, that for the first time in my life I'm going *home.*"

"When did you start this ICARUS thing, Mike?"

"Look at that!" said Michael.

They crested the hill and the huge golden globe stared level at them through the mist rising from a lake.

"That sun really does something for you, doesn't it?" said Bridge. "You should try inland Turkey on a hot day."

"Well, if you like, ICARUS was exactly that. You could say I was trying to get the sun down to earth, in a fusion reactor. I lived in a cold house as a kid. Cold every way. I wonder if that had anything to do with it?"

"A lot of people could be wishing you'd left the sun where it belongs. Up there. You plan on trying again?"

"You know what? I've got superstitious. When you think about the tricks people like Clough or Orlov got up to. Maybe the human race just deserves to burn up all the oil and the coal and then get off the stage. What would governments that employ men like Clough and Orlov do with unlimited energy?"

"Something evil. So you're giving it up when you get out of this?"

"I reckon. You don't believe in my destination do you, Cris?"

"The bird? I'll take you where you want to go. I hope she's the sun and the moon and the stars. Miracles happen."

"Where's home for you?"

Bridge patted the wheel. "Here. I'm just the driver, Mike. I've done this road twenty times. Turkey, Iran, Pakistan twice. I know every thieving inch of it. The guys who will help you along the way. And the ones who will take your wheels away in the night. Travelling's good enough."

"You're a good driver, Cris. I've always needed something at the end of the road."

Bridge smiled. "Stop worrying about her. You'll get what you're looking for. Everyone does."

The truck cruised down the flank of the hill into the levels of mist in the valley, like a huge silver fish plunging back into water. Bridge jabbed the lights.

"That's a philosophical point of view," said Michael. "Everyone? What about the Cloughs and the Orlovs? Do they get what they want?"

"Especially them," said Bridge. "The other rule is: everyone gets what they deserve. At this moment, everyone's going exactly where they need to go."

"Cris. What did you hit up with the Russians? There's something you haven't told me."

The truck lifted out of the next valley with a surge of power. "I've got my own scores to settle," said Cris. "OK? You won't be getting any more trouble. When we get there, you just do exactly what I tell you. Like on the roof, only quicker. It'll be OK. I don't want Orlov not getting where he wants to."

The truck rejoined the motorway and pressed on towards the Yugoslav border. Above them, a hawk, gleaming godlike in the morning sunlight, tipped its head to watch the gleam of silver sliding away towards the rim of the world.

Colonel Boris Orlov raised his binoculars and scanned the dockside of Kusadasi. It was 11:00 A.M. The white flanks of the Russian cruise liner, straight from Odessa, dropped cleanly into the blue Aegean. Orlov had a good view. He studied the jumble of fishing boats and the bright awnings of the open air restaurants that crowded to the water's edge. There was no sign of a Volvo truck.

The captain of the *Larissa* coughed. "Ten in the morning, Comrade Colonel, usually."

Orlov knew he was talking about the passengers. The grey little Party operatives on the pensioners' outing from Odessa. And their huge wives in flowered dresses. They must be getting impatient for their trip. Orlov searched the view again. "They can wait," he said.

From a distance the muezzins' call to the faithful sounded. In Kusadasi it was a question of putting a scratched gramophone record on the turntable. The Faithful took little notice.

Orlov wondered where Clough was. He could see the battered taxi Bridge had promised him. It was parked at the water's edge. A family of stray kittens tumbled carelessly under its wheels.

Viktor Karpov dug an elbow in Orlov's ribs. "There," he said.

The binoculars swam southwards. Coming down the hill road, ghosting past the cluster of shish kebab stalls at the entrance to the castle causeway, came the silver truck.

"Get the girl," said Orlov.

He didn't let the truck from his view. He sniffed the air with a feeling of triumph. Maybe this was going to work. With a bit of luck, Clough wouldn't make it. He could hardly complain if he missed the appointment. He turned to the captain. "Let them out. The passengers."

A row of buses was waiting sullenly in the shade of the dockside palm trees, ready to take the pensioners to Ephesus. The *Larissa*'s captain ran down the deck.

The Volvo Intercontinental eased its way across the dockside. Bridge was tired now. Really tired. They had been on the boat twenty-four hours from Piraeus, which should have been a rest. But the ancient wine-dark sea of Greek mythology had been unusually bloody minded. Short but vicious waves like jolting cliffs had shaken the Volvo loose from its deck anchors. The crossing had been a new route. Bridge never ceased to be appalled by the seasick proneness of the Greek race. For a maritime nation it made no sense.

He drove across the dockside and parked in front of the old taxi directly above the small fishing boats. A rabble of children left their job of untangling fishing nets and clustered around. Bridge swung out of the cab. Maybe or maybe not he exchanged the smallest nod with a huge middle-aged Turk lounging against the almond seller's barrow.

The Turk lifted another pinch of skinned almonds into his huge mouth and glanced towards the taxi. "Someone got in," he said, to no one in particular.

Bridge walked towards the back of the truck and looked at the old American taxi, its chequered yellow and black band the cleanest thing about it. Through the broken windscreen he saw only the leaking upholstery. He wasn't going any closer. He wouldn't put it past Orlov to do a messy shooting job. Even here.

On the bridge of the *Larissa*, Orlov watched. The pensioners were filing down the gangplank and towards the open waterfront. Viktor came back. The girl walked behind him. Blinking in the surprise of the Aegean spring after two days and nights in the cabin.

"Wait," said Orlov.

Viktor stared malevolently at the Volvo and the strolling figure of Bridge. "I don't like it," he said. "I can't see French. I don't think we should do this sort of thing in Turkey."

"That's why we are *doing* it in Turkey," said Orlov. He pointed at the long line of pensioners strolling straight onto the dockside through a wide open gate. A Turkish customs official waved them on, counting heads.

"Now we go," said Orlov. "Kyra, my dear. You see that almond seller's barrow? You go ahead and wait by that. We will be behind you."

She began to walk. For so long, she had been a doll. It was the only way she still retained their faith in her. The ballet training had been useful. Now as she walked to the West, she began to walk like a woman again. She would surprise even Michael.

On the quayside Bridge walked back round the truck and came up to the Turk. He gave the Turk an envelope. The taxi owner weighed it. He seemed surprised. "Mr. Cris," he said. "I don't need to know. But what's *he* doing down there?" He nodded to his right, towards the water. A small passenger boat was flying its Greek flag defiantly over the rim of the dockside. In the prow stood a silent young Greek, handsome as a god. The Turk and the Greek stared impassively at each other.

"You don't need to know," said Bridge. "If you don't like the Greeks that's your problem."

The Turk weighed the package again. "Am I going to see my taxi again? I fixed it like you said."

Bridge clapped him on the shoulder. He was really very tired. "You know something, Ecevit? You're like your premier. You don't know when you're on to a good thing. You *need* a new taxi."

Bridge turned around and winked at the young Greek. Despite the hatred between Greeks and Turks, this far end of the Aegean had to make allowances. Asia and Europe were just three miles apart across the blue sea. The Turks let the little Greek boats from Samos in, to take the tourists on day trips, even if the Greek Aegean islands were crawling with soldiers and the Turkish skies filled with NATO planes and the two countries were on the edge of war.

"They're coming," said Bridge. He reached up and slapped the door of the Volvo. Michael French slid across into the driver's seat and then down onto the quayside. Bridge watched the ship's passengers unloading. He recognised Viktor and Boris. The girl between them, as they walked away from the white cruise ship, must be *her*. Too far away to see more than that she was young and slim.

"Kyra," said French. He gazed at her with tears in his eyes.

"You just concentrate on remembering what you have to do," said Bridge.

Outside the gate the trio stopped. Behind Bridge the Turk slit open his envelope with a knife and counted his greasy notes rapidly. Then he put the notes away and kept the knife easily in his hand. He didn't know what Mr. Cris was doing at all, but since the day he'd crewed for Bridge through Cappadocia and Bridge had saved his life from the bandits, he knew he owed him a turn. Even if there were pig Greek boats involved.

Orlov put his hand behind the girl's elbow and pushed her forward. "Walk out." Uncertainly, she stepped ahead. Past an old grey taxi and the kittens now fighting over a fishhead. Towards the glass box on wheels where the almonds rested ιιι ᴜ ΙιᴇΙ ιι Ιᴜᴗ

"Start walking," said Bridge to Michael French. Bridge was leaning against the front wheel, cleaning his fingernails with a short knife.

On his boat, the Greek started his diesel and a foul cloud of blue smoke drifted onto the quay. The Turk wrinkled his nose in disgust, watching the two men behind the girl.

Kyra Kruschev and Michael French approached each other. He could see she was frightened, wide-eyed. Suddenly, like a hammer to the skull, the thought, *She's a stranger, I don't know her at all.* He was looking at the girl in a clumsy flowered dress, whose hair was half black and half blonde. "Mi-kay-el," she said. He raised his hands as if someone were throwing him, gently, a ball of light. She had stopped walking, was searching to see him, moving her head sideways as if dazzled. Then she raised her own hands towards him. They were five metres apart. It was a dancer's gesture, the way she lifted her small hands.

They walked to each other and he took both her hands in his and held them at a distance. "Listen," he said. "It will be all right. But this is what we have to do."

Behind her, Orlov came forward. Behind Michael, Bridge straightened up from the truck and took a packet from his hip pocket. He held the big brown envelope in front of him a moment, just to show Orlov, then put it under his blue denim jacket and strolled past Orlov without stopping. The Russian took the packet and went to look at the taxi.

Bridge strolled to the old taxi and opened the front passenger's door. He left it open and walked back to Michael and the girl. *"Now,"* he said.

Michael pulled the girl towards the truck. The kittens scattered in alarm. Bridge had opened the door and Michael pushed the girl up into the truck and jumped in after.

"Come on," said Viktor.

But Orlov was watching them climb in. "No hurry," he said. "After all, we don't want Professor French to know we are about to chase after him and take him back. He might give our friend Bridge a rough ride. What a pity poor Mr. Clough couldn't make it."

"They could be doing another trick," said Viktor. "I don't like it."

The Volvo shuddered in a burst of power and began to move off at surprising speed for so big a vehicle. But then, Bridge had arranged some modifications for this particular occasion.

"Get in," said Orlov, who then pushed Viktor across the front seat and reached for the ignition. The Chevvy lurched into life. Orlov shouted in triumph, "There you are, doubting Viktor! I knew we could count on Bridge. If he was trying to escape us he wouldn't let us start the car. Mr. Bridge is a good business proposition. He'd sell his grandmother."

Viktor watched the Volvo move away down the quayside. "Hurry," he said.

In the back seat Aloysius Clough said, "I should if I were you, Colonel Orlov."

Orlov stalled the car and swung around. "What are you doing here?"

"That was our arrangement."

"Our arrangement was you should follow us."

"I *am* following you," said Clough calmly. "Closely. Believe me, I am as anxious as you are that Professor Yeremenko gets his goods." He sneezed. The pollen of the Turkish spring was bad for his hay fever. "Get after him." Clough kicked aside the rug he had been lying under for thirty minutes on the floor. Then picked up his small attaché case and took a pair of gloves from it. He put them on. Orlov shook his head and stamped the accelerator. At which moment the damned almond seller moved his trolley straight ahead of him and the Chevvy smashed straight into it, the trolly exploding in a cascade of glass and nuts and ice.

The Turk began shouting. Orlov suddenly went very calm and tried to discover where the reverse gear was.

The Turk began trying to get into the car. Orlov locked the door and went on looking for the reverse gear and when the Turk put his fingers through the window Orlov took a bunch of them and broke them, found the reverse gear and damned nearly sent the Chevvy into the dock. The rest of the town began running their way. With his hand back on the horn, Orlov hit the accelerator again. The car sagged on its rear suspension as it surged into the chase of the truck, which had just vanished uphill from the waterfront in a shriek of burning rubber.

42

"I'm ready," said Derek Sewell.

"It's supposed to be twelve noon," said Cox.

Sewell said: "What do you want, Cox? A countdown? Ten, nine, eight, seven, six?"

Cox looked at him. "I see the press has assembled. How did *they* know?"

"I expect that evil little bastard Clough told them," said Sewell.

"Oh. I thought he was your friend."

"No," said Sewell.

Outside the old airship hangar the press cars waited at the security perimeter. The young Australian, Keegan, had been sent to keep them at bay. He resented the chore. Jim Henderson was standing, arms folded, in a ploughed field with a cameraman and a good view of the gaunt black hangar.

"Now," said Sewell.

"OK," said Cox. "We're all ready."

They had moved the consoles back, as Sewell had insisted. The generators were already humming, creating an invisible web of magnetism that would pinch the sun-hot plasma stream into a tight band, its 100-million-degree heat safely separate from the walls of the Torus.

The frozen pellets of heavy hydrogen were already firing through the focal point of the lasers, at the rate of one hundred a second. Now it was just a question of starting the lasers. And seeing what happened when the programme Michael French had fed into the computer unrolled.

Sewell walked across the hangar and climbed onto his perch above the grey flanks of the Torus.

Cox glanced back at the reassuring figure of Mary French. He smiled with more conviction than he felt. As far as Mary French was concerned he was beginning to appreciate Michael's problems in that direction, despite the undoubted warmth of a young middle-aged woman's sexuality, when released. Cox could also see, at a safe distance, the bottle-green dress of Hilary Reynolds, who was tending the console of the lithium blanket which would soak up the radiation from ICARUS. She gazed back frostily.

"Go on then," said John Cox. "Do it!"

Derek Sewell calmly reached out and switched the ICARUS on.

43

"I don't believe it," said Colonel Boris Orlov. He tried to press the accelerator through the Chevvy's floor. They had finally escaped the tangled streets of Kusadasi. There had been a bad few moments in the meat market and some more bad moments at a street corner which was slicked with wetness. The Turks seemed to spend their spare time washing the street just for the hell of it, Orlov had noticed. He knew the town from two previous changeovers and he knew where Bridge had to be going. "Why is he in such a hurry?" said Orlov.

They had climbed the cliff road, gone past the last resort suburb and were nearly at Ephesus already. On the right they could see the huge amphitheatre of the ancient city. The Volvo truck was accelerating away from them, as if trying to escape.

Orlov cursed. "He doesn't propose to run away from us, does he? He's given us a full tank of petrol."

"Why don't you catch him up," said Clough.

"Because I am going as fast as I can. What's the bastard up to?"

Viktor Karpov stared gloomily at the distant and retreating image of the silver truck. "I've met Mr. Bridge. I know what he's like."

"So have I," said Orlov irritably. Then he stood on the brakes.

The turning to Ephesus had arrived. A deserted motel crouched on the junction. It was flat here, for in the past Ephesus was a sea town, and the land was still brackish.

"This is the place," said Orlov. "I don't like it. Hasn't he stopped?"

Ahead, across a huge plain, the Volvo halted. Then it manoeuvred to turn about.

"He's coming back," said Orlov calmly, gazing through his binoculars.

It was a very empty place. The spring wind from the heart of Anatolia swept past them, rattling the tatters of the makeshift plastic tents left by last year's migrant harvesters.

"I think we should get out of here," said Viktor.

"It's the rendezvous," said Orlov. "Where he hands our scientist over. He's coming *back*, Viktor. I knew he would." Orlov watched the far end of the valley and the truck reversing in the noonday sun, beginning to come back. He switched off the ignition.

"I don't like it," said Viktor.

"Come on, Viktor. I promised you, you can screw the girl all the way back to Odessa."

"I don't think they are in the truck," said Viktor.

Orlov laughed out loud. "We saw them get *in* the truck," he said.

"Maybe they got out the other side."

Orlov sighed in impatience. "If you *noticed*, Viktor, there was nothing on the other side except the big blue sea."

"Exactly," said Viktor. "And a boat with a Greek flag."

Orlov's hands froze onto the wheel. He frowned, looked down the road and saw the huge *camion* coming straight towards them in the middle of the road. "Why the *hell* didn't you say that before?"

"I think we should get back to the town," said Clough calmly.

Cursing, Orlov twisted the ignition key and began scrambling through the gears.

44

Derek Sewell watched the needles revolve on the dials. He could feel the sweat running down his forehead. There was little noise. Just the tremor of the Torus and the scratch of the tracers recording what was happening. Fifty million degrees. They were still in known country; already hotter than the sun, but that was now familiar. It would happen very quickly, as soon as the lasers were switched. Then there would be a new world. One way or another. Sewell watched the needles swing steadily up and put his hand on the very simple black plastic button in readiness. He knew that when he did it, really ran ICARUS for real, there'd be no sound, no drama.

"Now," said John Cox alongside him.

Sewell hesitated. If he pushed the button it would happen. If Michael French had been lying it would be OK. But if Michael French wasn't lying then there wouldn't be anything at all. Ever again. Not that anything would explode or make a noise. Nothing so crude. Just a silent flood of subatomic particles coursing through his bone marrow. Scrambling the basic neurological instructions of the body, so that it began to fall apart. At the core. Just a white-coated doctor bending over the bed saying, "We're going to make it as comfortable as we can."

Michael French had put it crudely. If Sewell knew any field better than French, it was the area of radioactive tritium assault. It was much worse than Michael's threats about your hair falling out. It was the bleeding from the gut that happened to frighten Sewell. It took time.

"I said *now!*" shouted John Cox.

Sewell looked at Cox and made a promise to himself. Then, with his entire left palm, he pressed the button and fired the twelve lasers into life.

45

The Chevrolet taxi lurched into a 180-degree turn and began chasing back to the security of the town. Orlov tipped his rearview mirror to see the pursuer better, but it was star-crazed and showed only fragments of the silver truck barrelling down the road after them. Orlov licked his dry lips and tried to concentrate on driving.

"He is gaining on us," said Clough calmly, twisting his scrawny neck around to see through the blue back window.

Orlov hunched his shoulders and drove.

"Faster," said Viktor. He too had risked looking back. He had seen the great chrome square of the Volvo radiator; it seemed closer.

"I promise you," said Orlov. "I know what is going on. Bridge and I did a deal. He has French and the girl and—" Suddenly his neck snapped back as a huge force hit the back of the car.

Orlov's mouth dropped open. The ram from behind had knocked the car into a skid. He corrected it a few centimetres from the ditch and aimed the taxi back down the middle of the road.

The Volvo hit him again.

Orlov got the idea; Bridge was going to kill them. It was the noise that was surprising. Each time the Volvo smashed into his rear it jolted his brains inside his skull as if a kid were hammering a tin of biscuits. Orlov couldn't understand it. The road began lifting now, back to the cliffs above Kusadasi. He hoped he could outpace a heavy truck on the hill. He gripped the wheel and drove like hell. The Chevvy surged up the hill. A rear bumper came loose and spun over the cliff edge as Bridge worked on the taxi. Again and again, nudging and pushing.

Orlov saw the rim of the hill; beyond it the sun was at its height. It was bright, too bright. He scowled at the sun and then forced his eyes onto the right-hand edge of the road, where it vanished into the drop to the Aegean. About five hundred feet below.

"He is going to pass us," said Aloysius Clough calmly.

Orlov looked to his left; the road was narrowing. Hideously, the huge wall of the Volvo was drawing alongside as they came down the hill. Orlov drove like a madman for ten seconds, then changed his mind and tried to stop. The truck seemed to nudge the Chevvy, quite gently.

Orlov opened his mouth rather wide and went on turning the steering wheel this way and that, more out of habit than anything else, because they were flying, first the right way up, then the wrong way—down. No one said anything because there was really nothing to say. Orlov wondered if it would hurt when the car hit the rocks. It didn't.

It is much more uncommon than the movies would have us believe for cars to explode in balls of yellow flame after going over the edge of a cliff. In an interesting, if expensive, experiment the Germans demonstrated this conclusively with the help of one hundred Mercedes. But the old Chevvy was the exception to prove the rule. If he had had the time to think about it it might have occurred to Orlov why Bridge had thoughtfully provided a full tank of petrol. It was a spectacular event and visible far out to sea. Naturally, Bridge reported it fully to the Turkish police, because it didn't pay to put a foot wrong with them. The police agreed that the Russians are, as a race, lousy drivers and they chased the cruise ship smartly out of port with a warning that the next time visiting Russians jumped into empty taxis and drove off despite the owner's courageous attempt to stop them there would be a major international incident. They were just a little bit cross with Bridge for taking the wrong road out of town, since long-distance lorry drivers had to keep to a very well defined route, but they had to agree that, once he had discovered his mistake, he had turned around and come back as fast as he could. They shook hands on it and Bridge pointed the Volvo eastwards towards the sands of Arabia, the fat wallets of the oil sheiks and their insatiable appetites for Victorian grandfather clocks.

The little Greek pleasure boat chugged slowly away from Asia Minor. Samos, the first of three thousand Greek islands, rose greenly across the black water. The boat moved out of Turkish territorial waters as fast as it could because its navigator knew the Turks would be watching very carefully to make sure he did so. The ancient enmity between Turk and Greek was at flash point again, this time because of a complex and intricate debate about who owned the offshore oil. The day was pleasantly warm. Michael and Kyra stood at the prow and watched the first of the Eastern Sporades approach. There are those who say this green and fertile island group is the most beautiful of all the islands of Greece, but there are people to advance that claim for every Aegean island. Certainly, Kyra believed she had been taken straight to heaven. Only the pain from a bruised shoulder, collected in the tumble out of the waterside door of the truck straight into the boat moored alongside, reminded her she was still flesh and blood. "Where do we go?" she asked the Greek.

"He doesn't speak English. He's taking us where Bridge wants him to take us."

"Breej?"

"The other Englishman."

"You don't think they'll follow us again?"

"If I know Bridge, I doubt it. He didn't tell me. He had his own scores to settle."

"Scaws?"

"I'll have to teach you the language."

She looked up at him and smiled. They were strangers; they both knew that. But they knew it didn't matter. This time there *would* be time, all the time in the world.

"How do we live?" she asked.

Michael laughed aloud. "I have money. Bridge and I seemed to be very good at getting money. I took up a life of crime for you."

"They won't catch us?"

Michael looked at the island of Samos, and beyond it, another island and very distantly, still another.

"I think we have probably come to the best place in the world to vanish." He turned back to the young man, who grinned encouragingly. Michael pointed. "Samos?" he said.

The Greek shook his head and pointed away to the horizon. An island that lay on the sea like a green bone was just visible.

"Is good," said the Greek. "My mother, my father, my uncle, my aunt, my children. Good. Very peace. We show you. Friend of Mr. Cris. Good man."

Michael nodded. He said to Kyra, "I think he's taking us home." He called to the Greek, "What's the name of the island? Name?"

The man pointed to it. "Is Ikaria. Icarus. Yes?"

Michael looked at him in astonishment. *"Icarus?"*

"Icarus live there." The young man tried to see a way to explain. "Icarus?" he said. Then he took his hands off the tiller and raised them like a bird's wings.

"Yes, I know," said Michael.

"What is wrong?" said the girl. "You crying again? You stupid Mi-kay-el."

"We *are* going home," said Michael French.

Postscript

Extract from the Blue Guide to Greece, p. 634

IKARIA, a green, well-watered island with many scattered hamlets among the orchards and vineyards, is noted for its honey as well as for its radioactive hot springs. With Fournoi it forms an eparchy (9000 inhab.) of the nome of Samos. The name, perhaps deriving from the Phoenician "ikor" in reference to an abundance of fish, attracted to itself a legendary past in which Ikaros and Daedalus figure prominently.

Extract from the Sunday Times, April 16. Copyright Times Newspapers and Nature Services. Byline: Jim Henderson.

ICARUS FLIES

In a controlled "first-run" on the Cardington Torus yesterday, Britain took a giant lead in the long search for an alternative energy source for the human race—a quest made

doubly significant by this week's gloomy news about our
dwindling off shore oil position.

Nuclear fusion, the process that powers the sun, combines
atoms of hydrogen at immense speeds. As a result, high
temperatures are yielded. Unlike any other energy source the
fuel is limitless, for all practical purposes. "We are literally
making sunshine out of seawater," said a triumphant Dr.
Derek Sewell outside the huge hangar that once housed
Britain's airships.

Details of the reactor are classified, but Dr. Sewell
yesterday paid tribute to its creator, Professor Michael
French, whose disappearance this summer was the subject of
a police enquiry which is now closed.

"I want to pay tribute to Professor French," stated Dr.
Sewell. "This was his programme absolutely." Dr. Sewell
discounted reports that the ICARUS reactor had been dogged
by problems and that yesterday's first-run was in any way
hazardous. "We knew that Professor French was just too
damned good a scientist to get it wrong." From October Dr.
Sewell will be Cavendish Professor of Nuclear Fusion, a chair
originally destined for the late Professor French.